Praise g

Each year, the Britis ... Day – also called Remembrance Day – on 11 November by laying wreaths of poppies at war monuments and memorials across the country. I met Caroline Chu and Clive Harvey two years ago, when I first attended the ceremony.

At the time we met, Chu and Harvey were collaborating on a novel to bring the story of the CLC to a broader readership. This November, I met the two again just before Remembrance Day, and they handed me a proof copy. 'We finally finished it!' they told me proudly. 'We hope the fiction inspired by true stories can resonate with more people.'

Xing Yi – *China Daily* Europe correspondent

* * *

DR FRANCES WOOD

'A very clever and moving account of the dangers and horrors faced by the CLC in the battlefields and factories of Europe during WWI.

The denouement is very cleverly achieved, an emotional fiction that doesn't stretch history too far!'

(Dr Frances Wood received a Special Book Award of China in 2023, the highest foreign-related publishing honour in China's national honour framework, organised by the National Press and Publication Administration.)

* * *

NOUVELLES D'EUROPE 欧洲时报

'*For Whom The Temple Waits* is an important reflection on a part of Western History that is broadly forgotten – the contribution of Chinese workers to the war effort through the Chinese Labour Corps. It is admirable to pursue this goal, and I hope this book can help inform more people about the important history of the Chinese Labour Corps in WWI.'

Liangyi Yu – *Nouvelles d'Europe* 欧洲时报

(Established in 1983, Nouvelles d'Europe 欧洲时报 is the most influential Chinese news organisation in continental Europe and the UK)

SING TAO DAILY (星島日報)

For Whom The Temple Waits is written against the backdrop of World War One, arguably the most brutal war in history, and commemorates the Chinese labourers who endured extreme hardship and sacrifice in Europe. More than 140,000 Chinese labourers provided vital logistical support to the Allied forces, working at the front lines and in workshops digging trenches, building roads and railways, manufacturing weapons, transporting supplies, carrying the wounded, burying the dead, and clearing landmines—often in dangerous conditions and at the cost of their lives. Despite their tireless, loyal, and selfless dedication, their immense contributions were neither widely recognised by the victorious nations nor remembered in the years that followed.

One of the book's most prominent features is its accurate and reasonable account of the background to the recruitment of Chinese labourers. While France initially conceived the plan, the main implementer was Liang Shiyi of China's Beiyang government, with Britain and France acting primarily as employers and beneficiaries. The book clarifies common misunderstandings, showing that Britain ultimately recruited around 100,000 labourers, far more than France, and that recruitment took place not only in Shandong but also in Hong Kong—an aspect rarely discussed elsewhere. In doing so, the book corrects long-standing misconceptions found in many Western accounts.

Rather than treating the labourers as a single collective, the book focuses on individual stories, following two protagonists recruited in Shandong and Hong Kong. Through their physical and psychological journeys, it offers a humanistic portrayal of Chinese labourers' lives in both China and Europe. A distinctive highlight is its exploration of cross-cultural relationships between Chinese labourers and French women, a largely overlooked aspect of this history. Written in a concise, unadorned style yet rich in drama and emotion, the book restores the true face of this forgotten history and serves as a valuable and accessible introduction for readers unfamiliar with the Chinese labourers of World War One.

Alego Poon, Chief Editor (洛文)

ANNA BRANACH-KALLAS
Professor at Nicolaus Copernicus University in Toruń
President of the International Council for Canadian Studies

For Whom the Temple Waits is a historical novel that pays tribute to the Chinese labourers who worked for the French and British armies during the First World War. It provides information on China's unsuccessful attempts to dispatch soldiers to the Western Front, and their negotiations with the French and the British, which resulted in 140, 000 Chinese 'coolies' being sent to Europe. On the example of two protagonists, Ming and Yun, it explores the dramatic war experience of the Chinese, the former manipulated to join the French contingent, the latter press-ganged into the Chinese Labour Corps. The personal tragedies of these young men, separated from their families, uncertain about the meaning of their contracts and traumatized by their ordeal in France, form the core of the book. Harvey and Chu depict the dramatic transportation of the Chinese men to Europe, Ming's ship taking a diverted route around the African coast to avoid German U-Boats, Yun transported by rail as 'unwanted cargo' across Canada. The plot follows the different destinies of the two men, Ming working in a French munitions factory, Yun at the Tank Corps' Central Workshop at Erin. The reader thus learns that the professional and intimate experience of the Chinese labourers in France was far from homogeneous.

The novel exposes the amnesia surrounding the role of Chinese volunteers in the First World War, yet, it suggests at the same time that 'if it had not been for their contribution, the ultimate course of WWI may well have unfolded rather differently indeed'.

For Whom the Temple Waits illustrates other interesting aspects of early twentieth-century history. Fleeing anti-Jewish violence in the east of Poland, Alice's family migrates to Northern France in the first decade of the twentieth century, the father becoming employed as a miner in the French Pas-de-Calais after the 1906 Courrières disaster, Europe's worst mining accident. While depicting the liberation of French women who took men's jobs during the war, the book also shows how they felt threatened by the Chinese non-combatants employed in the same factories. If the Chinese workers feel initially 'unsettled' and 'intimidated' by female company, for the

French munitionettes, their arrival creates an atmosphere of 'suspicion and bemusement'. Labour's work stoppage proves an efficient weapon for both women and the Chinese men, discriminated against in various ways by the authorities. The overlap of the history of women and Chinese workers in France is one of the most interesting aspects of the plot, but Harvey and Chu refer to the repercussions of the first global conflict in China and Japan as well. Although describing many tragic facets of the First World War and the 'contemptible colonial hubris' of the imperial armies, the book is very accessible and contains tender scenes, as well as humorous episodes. Importantly, like Clive Harvey's earlier novel, *Yang's War: A Forgotten Chinese Hero of World War One* (Menin House 2017), *For Whom the Temple Waits* includes photographs from W. J. Hawkings' Photography Collection, courtesy of his grandson, John De Lucy. Together with the photographs of Sino-French families in the final section, they add to the authenticity of this engaging narrative.

FOR WHOM THE TEMPLE WAITS

FOR WHOM THE TEMPLE WAITS

CLIVE HARVEY
& CAROLINE CHU

MENIN HOUSE

Menin House is an imprint of
Tommies Guides Military Booksellers & Publishers

Gemini House
136–140 Old Shoreham Road
Brighton
BN3 7BD

www.tommiesguides.co.uk

First published in Great Britain by
Menin House 2026

A catalogue record for this book is available
from the British Library

All B&W photographic images by kind permission of John De Lucy
unless otherwise stated.

Front cover image with thanks to Monika Ekiert and David Chour.

ISBN 978-1-0683111-2-3

Cover design by Menin House
Typesetting by Vivian Head @ Bookscribe

Printed and bound in Great Britain

CONTENTS

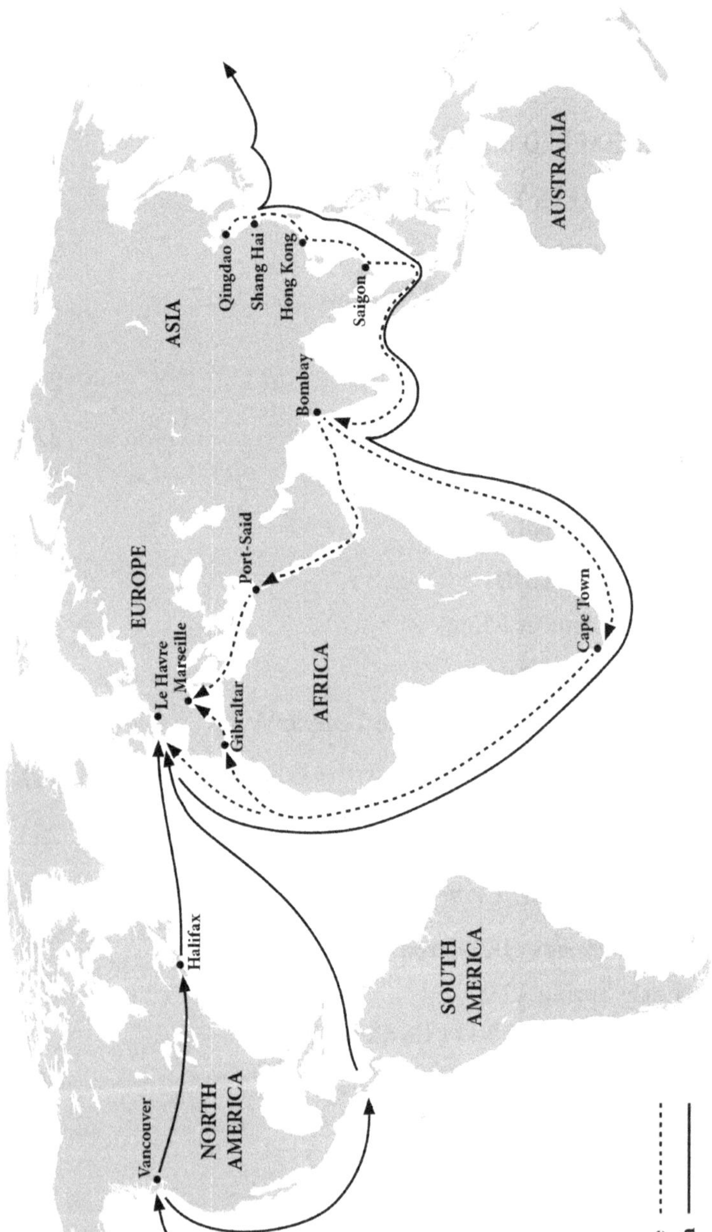

CLC ROUTE MAP FOR BRITAIN AND FRANCE

AUTHORS INTRODUCTION
The Story

This story is both about the unthinkable human transportation over 8,000km, with at least 140,000 working men leaving China to reach the shores of France and its battlefields, and also the history of the First World War and its horrors.

The lives of women and men were put to the ultimate test. Some were destroyed, others saved. Courage and hope were inspired or crushed, loves were strengthened by the onslaught, others thwarted, but overriding it all was that irrepressible instinct to survive in the face of impossible odds. This historic novel traces the separate lives and trajectories of two young Chinese men, Yun and Ming, and shows us how the destiny of each of them rests on that of a young woman, Alice, a beautiful Polish Jewish immigrant. Through this telling trilogy of lives, the true rigours of the war, the treatment reserved for its participants are clearly exposed, as are the brutal events that came to engulf the main belligerents in this conflict.

For the first time, women played a dominant role in the lives of workers and in the State's essential industries. Not only did they seamlessly fill the shoes of absent men in agriculture, in industry, weapon production and manufacturing, but in doing so, they unwittingly sparked the most dynamic social and cultural change in history and of modern humanity.

During these long years of unprecedented upheaval, women became aware of their own emancipation. They become real decision-makers, the pillars of the family unit, reorganisers in a man's world; influencing the unfolding of events, being able to change the course of history in the blink of an eye. As so many men's lives were lost, women became widows, families were forced to migrate in search of work and security, mothers had to raise their children alone.

PROLOGUE

A Trilogy of Lives – 1906

YUN: Yantai, China, circa 1906 – Shandong Province

A small language class, run by a missionary

Had it not been for his mother, Yun knew his hunger for languages would have withered away. He adored her, as much for her love as for her foresight and steely resolve. It was she who saw to it that his father had to release him from his duties at the family business, to attend classes. She, who covered Yun's tracks so that his father would hardly notice when he had slipped away.

Now an impressive looking sixteen-year-old, tall for his age, he was also head and shoulders above the rest of the class in both English and French. He may not have excelled in his other studies, throughout his school life, but he thrived on his exceptional hunger to communicate with others. He so wanted to extend that enthusiasm towards peoples from other parts of the world.

In any case, Yun had witnessed, for himself, the alternatives to a full existence, in the stunted wheat and potato fields surrounding his Yantai township. He so feared a life wholly reliant on the unforgiving earth for survival, and the abject poverty of some of the farming families he had seen.

The missionary teaching Yun's class was full of praise for

him. He was her star pupil, and Yun was so focused that he couldn't care about the resentment the others in the class may have felt. So, when it came to the end of their summer term, and each pupil was asked to confirm their plans for the holiday, in both English and French, YUN took the class by storm:

'I shall be back to my cousins, in the countryside, where my uncle teaches me how to nurse injured birds back to health...' His fluency was remarkable, and once he had concluded his account, the missionary could not resist prompting a round of applause from the others. Nor could she resist expressing her radiant joy, 'May the Lord be praised!' She smiled, admiringly.

MING: Elsewhere in China, circa 1906

Guangdong Province – a village near Hong Kong

Ming had never known accomplishment. He had also never been burdened by the demands of ambition.

Small, for his age, slight in build, he was less suited than most for a life in agriculture, but that was all he knew. Destined to spend his youth helping his father, and learning the ways of the land from him, he had learned to tolerate the unforgiving earth. That didn't stop him resenting the exhaustion it caused him, the aching through his body, and, unremittingly, for testing his will to face another day of hard graft.

A teenager, a reluctant apprentice to adulthood, more was expected of him, but he had little more to give. Breaking up the arid soil in a line of working men exposed his shortcomings horribly. His father, performing to his fellow workers, would tut and shake his head, disconsolately, towards them on seeing his son struggling. Yet Ming, through it all, knew that he was loved. His kind face and his determination endeared him to many.

His reward for sticking to it, for never giving up, came when his parents realised he should soon be suitably betrothed to the only girlfriend he had ever had. It couldn't have been a better match, and Ming was too unassuming to ever hope to find anyone vaguely comparable.

Ming's parents may have been poor, at times on the brink of bare subsistence, but what they lacked in resources, they more than shone with their support for their son. It hadn't been lost on them how smitten Ming had become with such a pretty, local girl, or how affectionately she seemed to view Ming. The young couple may have believed they had eloped covertly, but there were few secrets in Ming's tiny community, nor many in hers. Their charming love, despite the couple's sweet diffidence, seemed truly to blossom.

Also born into farming stock, Ming's young wife-to-be had her own mother's resilience and was fiercely loyal. Whenever Ming might flounder, as he was sometimes prone to do, she would be there to spur him on. Ming's parents had seen these qualities in her, and in her family, and if marriage, and then children, were to follow, they were wise enough to know that tenacity would be crucial if the two of them were to survive. Life was tough.

Never feeling that he had earned his luck, doubting that he was worthy, he quickly became a hopeless romantic:

'As long as there's work for me, my darling, I shall make you proud, I truly will. We shall never go short, I swear.' Ming adored his future wife, and she loved him, but she quickly learned not to rely too heavily on his well-meant promises.

ALICE – Born Maria Alicja – Bialystok – POLAND
(Then W. Russian Empire) – June 1906

The explosion wasn't all that close this time, but enough to rattle the frame of their dining room window sending a plant toppling from the sill, then smashing on the floor.

Maria Alicja, known as Alice, rushed to get the dustpan to clear up the mess. An only child, the apple of her mother's eye, she was, exceptionally, allowed to leave the table on this mission, but her father was ordered to stay put when he went to rise:

'We will not let those thugs disrupt our meal. Next, they will destroy our lives!'

The resolution in her voice, her fierce stare, were all Alice's father needed to remain seated. A traditional Jewish meal came with its attendant rules and Alice's mother was sticking to them, even though her husband was a reluctant participant. Not adorning a Koppel, Catholic from birth, he may have tutted, shown signs of irritation, but he invariably did as he was told. His wife was the glue for family unity, the one who had every reason to hide away, but didn't.

A pogrom may have erupted in Bialystok, but Alice's family were not as vulnerable as others. Protected by their Catholic family name, disguised by their Catholicism in public, they may well have had good reason to feel safe, but Alice's mother fretted, felt the signs of danger in her bones.

Though the candle-flames from the menorah flickered from further tremors during the rest of their meal, she conducted the remaining rituals as best she could. Alice, though young, sensed her mother's growing uneasiness, and it worried her deeply. Her mother stayed calm:

'Many families are leaving you know,' her husband scoffed. 'Of course, the thought of anyone uprooting themselves, when they are not visibly compelled to go, is extremely disturbing for everyone.' To this he nodded. 'But they have decided they dare not wait until things get worse.' Alice grimaced as she hung on every word her mother uttered, and she felt her anguish.

Bialystok may have been blessed with a predominately Jewish population, but that didn't reassure Alice's mother one bit. The word was that the move towards extreme discrimination was growing in intensity, and only those perceptive and brave enough to leave might survive.

The meal over, and whilst Alice's mother stared at the kitchen wall as she washed up, she could not hold back her tears. She sang through her distress to disguise her breaking heart.

1 HISTORIC BACKDROP

The Prelude to War

Late 1914 – Tsingtao, China

The British Navy had earned its imperious world status; they were the mightiest sea force in existence, yet they were destined to play second fiddle here to Imperial Japan. There was nothing they could do about it, not here and now. The two were bound by 'marriage', courtesy of their 1902 Treaty, so Japan risked taking liberties like this with Britain, with relative impunity, if it used guile and common sense. The British Navy was too engrossed elsewhere, by half, and this was a long-awaited quarry for Japan.

The Japanese Seaplane Carrier, *Wakamiya*, lay patiently at anchor beyond detection. It was far from resting idle. Anything but. It was there, ready to launch its inaugural reconnaissance foray in search of Japan's first real prize in WWI. This was why they had thrown their lot in with The Allies, and they had not hesitated. Let China protest as much as they wished, let Britain mistrust them as deeply as they saw fit, Japan would seize Tsingtao from Germany's precious grasp and there was absolutely nothing anyone could do to stop them. However, wisely, they needed to take a 'recce' first.

This was to be all about Japanese opportunism, and Japan had chosen its time for action to perfection. Flight Lt. H

O'Hara, ('H' as he was known), hadn't run away from the safety of his family home in Tokyo to play boyhood war games. He had fled in search of real action, and he didn't care how long it might take to find it. With the first truly global war barely underway in Europe, the thought that a local confrontation, somehow linked to WWI, may yet come his way, filled H with excitement. He couldn't wait. But for now, his brief was clear; he was sworn to secrecy. A true home-grown warrior, he would take his silence to the grave.

Light years distant from where the real action was, H was content to seek engagement in his own backyard. Not yet a fully trained fighter pilot, H was already a respected young airman in the Provisional Air Corps. Reconnaissance it might be, but H knew, all too well, this first venture into the unknown was as risky as it could get. If he was spotted, and close enough to get hit, he might be shot down like a hapless pigeon.

At times like this, poised on the threshold of a life and death enterprise, H's steadfast mindset was bound to weaken, just for a moment. He succumbed to those reflective tugs of memory, thoughts of how he got here, and it stirred him up. He had been close to his father and influenced heavily by his patriotism. It was he who had spurred H on to break away from their country home to learn all about Japan's prowess, the historic courage of their people throughout history, their principles and traditions. H might never have pushed himself hard enough to gain entry to university in Tokyo had it not been for his father, but little did his father realise the influence university would have on his son, less still where it would ultimately lead him. H smiled as he recalled it all now.

It was such a stimulating place to be for a young aspiring man. At the heart of Tokyo, the hub of Japanese life and culture, speculation was on every student's lips how yet further opportunities against China may soon come their way. Caught up in the whirlwind, pumped up with bravado, wanting so badly to make his father proud, H concluded his destiny was not behind a desk after all, but in the air! He wasn't going to be some stuffy academic, debating politics with all and sundry, finding vent through books and propaganda, he was going to be a pilot for Japan and nothing less would do, nothing would stop him. So here he was.

H could have screamed with joy, but his cool head held him back. The adrenaline rush was irresistible. He had long accepted he would have to bide his time for real action, but the danger he now faced was thrill enough. He had wondered if he was being offered-up as expendable 'fodder', but H was blessed with enough arrogance to feel certain that he wasn't. This was a key mission, needing a confident pilot they could trust, so that was sufficient reassurance. H had been brought up, and trained this way too, to believe in himself.

This was a spy mission, after all. Destined to be the first reconnaissance flight in action by Japan in WWI. He knew he should be very proud, and it was fine to feel a little scared too. He welled up to think he was about to offer his young life, on the line, for his beloved country, and the plane he was to fly was no shabby craft.

Yes, the Maurice Farman MF7 Seaplane ('MF'), had unsuccessfully attacked a German ship with bombs, but H was confident, it would not fail him on his mission. The MF was a sight to behold. A two-seater biplane, the MF was designed to take a pilot and navigator in tow, so it wasn't designed to test a pilot's stamina for solo campaigns. H was fortunate, and he knew there was a good reason for his selection; he had trained in these French-built beauties since 1912. They had joked about these creations back then. Fabric covered, wooden framed, every aspiring pilot sneered at the chances of these holding together at all! Yet 'wings of the rising sun' was how they later came to be named, and the task now facing H was going to make the doubters repent. His comrade joining him felt exactly the same way.

Winched safely onto the lapping waters of the sea, from here there was no turning back. The *Wakamiya* was of no use to him now. With his map strapped to one knee, pad and pencil to the other, H was well and truly ready. He prepared to open the throttle. This was the tricky bit. If anything were to go wrong, it would be now. His trusted sea-floats would ensure his safe return-landing on the surrounding waters at his mission's end, but they must serve him well here first. All H needed now was to build up enough propulsion on those floats to lift him up from the sea. The signal was given, the deck flags were waved, and H opened the throttle.

Just for a moment, as a freak gust rocked him to one side, he doubted he would avoid plunging seaward, but he needn't have wavered. In seconds, his trusty MF seemed to catch a rising swell of air and up he launched. H heard a little squeal of pleasure from his mate behind him, above the engine roar in his head. It took his breath away too, and in moments his tingling skin confirmed why he would never wish to do anything else in his life, but fly. H grinned with pleasure.

‘All the better for just being alive,’ he yelled but knew his fellow observer hadn’t a chance of hearing him.

It was a perfect day. Crystal clear visibility. Ideal for observing, but ideal too for being observed! This H knew only too well, but he had been trained to counter this danger. For now, and only for the coastal approach, he had to gain maximum altitude. Too high to usefully observe, out of sight from below, and too high to take a shot at. Up and up he took the plane, until his ears popped and his eyes streamed. H couldn’t tell if it was the increasing altitude or the caustic smell of burning oil that had caused his lungs to sting. The MF felt as light as a seagull, tossed around by unpredictable gusts, it made him feel in tune with the natural world. Once he had levelled off, he was better placed to drop his shoulders and crane his neck to take in his surroundings.

‘Now I know where it gets its name,’ H mumbled, in awe, as the sun lit up The Yellow Sea like a vast ochre lake. The water below him was rivalled only, for its yellowness, by The Yellow River itself. He could see the impressive waterway in the distance, oozing out its milky richness, like a child surrendering into its mother’s bosom.

Then a cloud, of all things, caught him napping. Just for a moment. H had been so focused on the sea below him, that he suddenly found himself gasping as the chill inside a dense, billowing cloud, arrested his breathing. His mate behind him seemed to survive, well enough to drop a cryptic note over his shoulder, which read, in bold letters: ‘Are you trying to smother me out of a job?’ H welcomed his humour, and the reminder he wasn’t flying alone.

Then, as his trusted craft lanced its way out the other side, the sudden reappearance of sunlight blinded his vision. The unfettered view returned, crystal clear, paying testimony to the purity of the atmosphere that only pilots get to witness. But he had other, more pressing, observations to consider, and as the once distant coastline drew ever closer, H knew that his hour of reckoning was fast approaching. Then, for the second time, a pang of terror struck.

It was as the MF engine strained to maintain its altitude that H felt his fear the most. Then his torment dissolved as a further note, a more serious one this time, found its way onto his lap. He was directed to study the sea swell below. It was littered with mines, clear as day. Even at altitude, he could see them as unmistakable bobbing dots. His observation training had done him proud; 'So those Germans have been busy!' he concluded, frowning. H knew this didn't mean the enemy were expecting trouble. Far from it. The German fleet were almost entirely on active service far afield, so the mines were just a parting gift to intruders that might attempt to creep their way, covertly, into the harbour unnoticed. Yet this was the first observation of substance by H and his mate, and the fleet would need to navigate past these perils.

They were now almost directly over the harbour defences. If they were going to get shot down, now would be the moment, yet nothing happened. H was dumbfounded. He didn't need another note from behind, what appeared was as clear as day. The harbour was flanked by a collar of hills on either side. They presented natural fortifications. Worse still, each was peppered with gun bases, neatly dug in, yet H just believed, in his gut, that he either hadn't been seen, or not a soul below cared a jot about them at all. They would have known about it had this not been so.

Perhaps they were high enough to avoid detection? Perhaps they had been seen but were beyond striking distance, or deemed of no threat as a harmless single craft? But there was more to it. As H took a turn to repeat the exercise, now feeling cockier by the minute, worrying ever less that the dull drone of his MF might blow their cover, what he saw sent him into involuntary fits of laughter. 'My God,' he exclaimed, but not expecting his mate to hear him, 'look at those arrogant blighters, they've all got their backs to their guns and they're knocking back grub and booze!'

There was no doubt about it. Gaining confidence by the minute, H had dropped down to a daringly low altitude to check his findings out for certain. Sure enough, now feeling they were almost close enough to touch, H could see the lot of them, clear as day. He could now feel the mad laughter of his mate vibrating through the frame of his seat.

Well beyond the defence redoubts, the main danger had passed. It was time to spy on Tsingtao itself, and H couldn't wait. He had been briefed, that although this had long been a traditional Chinese fishing village, he must be prepared for something entirely different now. A complete transformation. They had not exaggerated, but he remained on full alert for the troops he might witness, and he hoped they too would have their guard down. It was just as he had hoped, a repeat performance. There must have been some form of celebration going on. A German festival of some kind. This was the only logical explanation for the crowds of German troops milling around down below. Most appeared to be drinking booze or gathering in groups for posed photographs. Neither he, nor his flying mate, could possibly have known, that they were observing these Germans on the occurrence of the 10th anniversary of their prized brewery, 'Germania-Brauerei' and would have had little else but revelry on their minds.

He was so impressed with the bold Bavarian-style buildings lining the city streets. He hadn't ever been to Germany, but this was how he had imagined it might look. It all reeked of wealth, of splendour, but right now his overriding observation was that these troops were nothing to be feared. He exchanged notes with his mate. They both concluded; perhaps this was just a momentary lapse, luckily for them. Even so, after a rough headcount, they observed no more than a few thousand troops. This best guess total was precisely what the Japanese Naval Command would have hoped might be the case, essential data from this daring aerial venture. They had seen enough. Their mission was accomplished. H turned about, regained maximum altitude, and headed back to the sanctuary of the *Wakamiya*. There would be more spying raids, H was well aware of that, and with more than one MF seaplane next time around. But H had concluded the first, and the most important reconnaissance, and he was proud.

The Siege of Tsingtao – 'Pearl Harbour' style

Then came the first use of air power in warfare, and Japan alone could claim this dubious honour. What could not later be denied, was that this action, by Japan, heralded the uprooting of Germany from its Far East holdings, and it would hurt them more than they would ever admit to anybody.

Germany had made the city an enticing target for acquisition. Having themselves wasted little time evicting its poor Chinese inhabitants, under gunpoint, Germany had left themselves free to tear down their traditional homes, then systematically lay out their new Bavarian street-plans to perfection. Rulers since 1898, they had poured in manpower and resources, including a new locomotive works and a major rail line, destined for crucial wartime transportation. Yet what Germany had not prepared themselves for, was the first air–sea battle in aviation history.

The Imperial Japanese Naval Air Service was in complete control. Thanks to Lt. O'Hara, and the brave reconnaissance pilots that followed, the fleet was well aware of the mines, and that they might still lose a ship or two in the impending excitement. They had factored this in. What they had not quite bargained for was the astounding resilience of the retained German Defence Force. Hopelessly outnumbered though Germany clearly was (H had been right about that), the Germans' recent revelries had proved ephemeral. A fleeting party, a momentary blip in concentration. In typical style, the men were promptly back on duty, had seen the gathering ships, accepted the threat, and were ready to give it all they had; and they had guts aplenty.

How could they not have been aware of what was coming. Under Vice-Admiral Katō, the Japanese fleet had successfully blockaded the coast, laid total siege to it. With the German Navy absent, and The British Navy a much-reduced presence, meekly there to pander to its own suspicions about its ally, Japan was conspicuously in charge. Britain had already been bullied into subservience by a friendly-fire incident by Japan, at sea. Since then, all British personnel were under strict orders to don traditional Japanese raincoats whenever on deck, to avoid a repeat performance! Ever-mindful to follow due-procedure with Britain, their distrustful ally looking on, Japan issued the German command their ultimatum to hand Tsingtao over to them. A token process, and one they knew would be rejected. The predicted reply handed to Japan their moment; war was officially declared on the 23 August 1914.

With their superior numbers, and factoring in their loses from mines and Germany's established defences, the 20,000 strong Japanese (18th) Infantry, took to their boats and made for the shore. They were fully equipped, as their reconnaissance and air fleet planes had been with pre-ordered aircraft parts from their French factories. This would tell in the end, but when would Japan prevail? How long could proud Imperial Germany hold out?

As the siege reached its climax, the city was bombarded in a concentrated onslaught, from both sea and land, for seven solid days. The ordnance panoply was spectacular, but the German garrison was well fortified, H and his followers had established that. What had not been quite so clear to them were the lines of German-constructed, long established, trenches. It took the might of Japan's fearful 11-inch Howitzers to force a German retreat, but they simply withdrew back to the redoubts with the reserve trench networks and gun batteries, meticulously established around the city. All that followed was that the Japanese moved their own trench positions ever forward. With overwhelming Japanese troops deployed, 140 artillery pieces in support, they could press forward with grim determination. Their ferocious and sustained bombing raids, uniquely both day and night, proved a template for future conflicts.

Whilst the German resistance held good for some two months, a testament to their spirit, the inevitable outcome of Japan's relentless onslaught, to be entitled 'softening-up', was the exhaustion of Germany's ammunition. They had put up a stiff and sustained fight, they had been valiant, but the resilient German military finally folded; their white flag was reluctantly raised. Their first military humiliation.

Yet not an entire humiliation, not through Germany's eyes; their own history refers to… 'Our sole Wolf in the air?' As it happens, in the face of Japan's utter command of the skies over Tsingtao, Germany did muster two planes to face their invaders. The first crashed almost immediately, but the second did not. Flown by one Lieutenant Gunther Plüschow, this single surviving plane went on to leave its indelible mark on the records of this siege.

Gunther became quite a legend in German circles, and helped their propaganda claim that their territorial loss hadn't been the full story. They had gained a hero, who would go on to achieve ever-greater things for the Homeland. In his seaplane, *Heinkel HD24*, Gunther managed to shoot down an opposing Japanese plane with his pistol. This proved to be the first recorded aerial victory in aviation history, just the start of Gunther's fighting prowess. He went on to carry out further nuisance attacks on the enemy, until Germany's position became unsustainable.

Having started out on reconnaissance, much as his counterpart, H, had done earlier on, Gunther had accumulated enough aerial records and official despatches, to be of great value to Germany. But how would he deliver these? The saga that followed is a long and remarkable one. Suffice it to say, that he escaped the enemy's clutches at Tsingtao (on the 6 November) to fly a further 160 miles, only to survive a crash into a rice paddy, then head off from there towards home on foot!

Yet, of course, this German tale aside, there was no doubt who the true victors were.

The transformation from a German-Bavarian city and its environs into a distinctly Japanese conquest, was as swift as it was ruthlessly actioned. What a glorious spectacle ensued for the victorious Japanese. Their Imperial Cavalry led the parade through the streets, headed by General Kamio Mitsuomi. The buildings on either side were lavishly decked out with their proclaiming banners. Then, in their wake, the British Cavalry followed. They might well have wished they had not bothered with their symbolic appearance. The German troops, now Japan's prized prisoners of war, stared on at the Japanese leading the show past them. As for their British counterparts, these German captives had other plans in mind. They spat in disgust at the British, or turned their backs as they passed.

As for the, now empty, prized German brewery, the Germania-Brauerei, this was not to remain abandoned for long. Inside, pictures of German leaders, proudly clutching overflowing beer steins, were left broken or hanging lopsided from their frames. A transformation was on its way. With damaged furniture replaced, the disruption from a hasty evacuation put straight, the uncompromising ordeal of imposing the emblems of the new Japanese owners on this thriving industry began.

Now full of uniformed, Japanese workers, the ceremony of removing the old labels from thousands of bottles got underway, as did the relabelling of every bottle in existence with Japan's 'Dai-Nippon' Brewery replacement insignia.

Germany had not only surrendered its prized territory to Japan, it had also lost its treasured brewery to them too.

Meanwhile, elsewhere in the Far East, life for the colonial powers bumbled on in luxuriant domination, as though no troubles existed at all, let alone any spilling through their homelands. How grotesque the contrast, and how reminiscent of that astute imagery by the artist, Bruegel, observing how life goes blissfully on whilst darker times unfold elsewhere.

Shanghai – 1914 – Colonial Heartland

'Get a move on, clumsy oaf!'

For an overweight, arrogant Brit, and one usually too short of breath to yell at all, Sir Peregrine Percy could launch a formidable tirade. Booming though he sounded to his regular, long-suffering, rickshaw runner, this was just his normal bark of rebuke. The poor man was doing the best he could, bearing in mind the excess weight he was paid to carry, but apparently, as always, it wasn't good enough.

Probably the richest city in all Asia, Shanghai was a flourishing metropolis, and it had fostered a burgeoning expat community of some 20,000, well-heeled souls. This, ironically, pretty much matched the number of pulled rickshaws in Shanghai, so there was always enough work to go round. This man was content enough. He had managed, somehow, to own his own cart, and it was a handsome thing to behold. Sir Peregrine would not have dared be seen in it had that not been so. As with all Shanghai rickshaws, this one was painted bright yellow, adorned with a white upholstered double seat, which suited the girth of its current occupant.

A peasant by origin, this rickshaw runner knew all too well, but he was a well-liked and respected worker. If he let slip the occasional expletive, as he had just done in reaction to his passenger's rant, then so be it. Restricted to his own dialect, Sir P was none the wiser, although he might guess, if he chose to, what was said. These runners were used to colonial-style bullying. It was a way of life, and they all needed rich foreigners.

Viewed by the Chinese, 'The International Settlement' in Shanghai had succumbed to its inevitable foreignisation. All the indigenous people moaned about the transformation, but never dreamed of reacting visibly to it. Work meant everything to them, and most aspired to a better life. Each of them, with any sense, kept well away from trouble. As this runner went pacing past a group of municipal policemen, he knew he must put on a show. Alongside the one-mile bund of the Huangpu River, the great waterfront, this was not the moment for slouching. He upped his speed and kept his head high, just noticing one officer gesture a respectful salute towards Sir P.

Unless you were British, French or American, you were here to exist and to mind your own business. There were rich pickings if you played the game, and this rickshaw puller knew every trick in the book. His kind had long learned to accept the cosmopolitan population that now held sway. Locals had long forgotten Shanghai was part of China.

The rickshaw runner may have wondered, for a moment perhaps, why such grand trees had been chosen to line some avenues. He would not have been surprised that the French had introduced these, ironically, London Planes, and that French interests had been competing, successfully, with their mighty colonial rivals. It was all simply non-Chinese wealth to him. He just calmly, secretly, dreamed that his homeland would, one day, expel these intruders, every single one of them, but only once their wealth had been dutifully passed-on to the souls who had been enslaved for so long at their behest.

With the police guards now well behind them, the runner slowed his pace to regain his breath. Able now to glance around, he looked up towards the smart, framed windows, of a prominent building he was passing. This was one of the best traditional tea shops in Shanghai, and he admired it greatly. There, in full view above him, sat two daintily dressed British women, and both were now looking down, nonchalantly, towards him. He hoped it was his smart rickshaw that had caught their eye, but then, most likely, the sight of Sir P sprawled across his twin seats, had most likely captured their attention. They resumed sipping tea, without averting their eyes, leaving the runner to imagine from their subtly moving mouths what they were saying to one another. Perhaps – 'How quaint', one had said, and 'Yes, a charming view of the working class we have from up here' the other.

The problem was Sir P had glanced up too as the rickshaw slowed; he had followed the puller's line of sight. He barked again, this time with enough volume to make sure the two ladies would admire his commanding tones.

To the rebuked worker this transient scene will have appeared as a vignette, a perfect satirical cartoon. It would somehow precisely epitomise the skewed world his city had grown into, the vast gulf now dividing excess from the deprived, the respected from the scorned. This served also as a sad reminder of China's pitiful weaknesses, Republic though it now was. How hopeless life could feel for men like this runner, and for poor struggling folk. Yet he nurtured a deep belief in himself and his family. He just sensed some overseeing power close by, watching.

2 ALICE

Part 1

Alice's mother had made her mind up. There was no way now that she would falter. Not that she didn't suffer doubts. She most certainly did, but the way ahead for her was clear, and this overrode everything. Her mind was, doggedly, focused on their future and not on their past.

Uprooting themselves from their home was no small undertaking. Leaving behind all those familiarities, the trappings of their established lives, their family and friends, was to be the greatest challenge of their lives. Now she had to dig deep, deeper than ever before, and Alice's mother knew she could fight off those demons, nagging in her head, taunting her for her recklessness. Her innate tenacity, her inherited wisdom, would gift her a cool head.

She had convinced her husband that this wasn't an irrational 'dash for the border', for it really wasn't. They weren't refugees, not in the true sense, but migrants by choice, and the truth was they had been struggling for a while. As hard as she looked, there were only diminishing prospects for them in Poland, and the word reaching her was that industries in Northern France were suffering dramatic shortages of skilled labour. Opportunities were opening up.

So, even as a surreptitious Jewish mother, steadfastly

sporting their Catholic credentials, she feared squandering a life-changing opportunity more than blowing her cover in the process.

Alice, in her nubile naivety, had come to cultivate an excitement about leaving. In her fantasy, this was a holiday; they were going abroad for the first time in her life and she would bolster her parents' spirits. She didn't have to try that hard with her father. He knew, from the outset, that it was pointless to resist his wife's resolve in the state of mind she was in. He chose to trust her instincts, believe in her judgement, that his prospects were best served by relocating, starting afresh. He had never seen his wife so driven with purpose.

She had not left a stone unturned. Once they had concluded their attendance at the City Consulate to register their family's change of name, to Leclerc, there was nothing left to hold them back. With their documentation in order, the family set off across Germany, towards France, with all the belongings that they owned in the world.

Part 2

Courrières – a small town in Northern France – 1906

France may have been blessed with some of the most impressive landscapes in Europe, but this region was an exception. Known, locally, as 'The Black Country', Courrières sat right at the heart of this region's mining territory, and it was an important national asset. A vast expanse, dramatically interrupted by towering slag heaps and accumulations of open-air mining waste, this area might only be of interest to an artist or an historian. Corrupted by its destiny, this land was condemned to serve one purpose, and one alone – the extraction of coal.

As for the inhabitants, they had, affectionately, become known as 'The Black Faces'. If the sight of ugly wooden and brick structures to live and work in, had not been enough, their means of delivery to the work face was by primitive steel cages more suited to animal transportation.

In the distance, up on a pallid, grey ridge, a soot-covered youngster stood, for a moment, staring motionlessly across the town. His name was Marcel, and this was his home from birth, yet none of this mattered one jot.

He could not have grasped that his life here was a mere 'dot' of an existence, the same for all the children toiling alongside him, born to bolster the industrial prowess of yet another, brutal, colonial power.

There had been a landslide. It was a near calamity. The erupting siren always added to the terror, especially for the employed youngsters. Unversed in the unwritten rules of mining, the children jettisoned their tools, in an instant, leaving them to sink into the mud. Their panic cost them dear. Marcel was amongst the frantic rush of children scampering home in tears on learning their pay had been docked. Their parents were as much distressed for the loss of income as they were to see the suffering pervade their children's strained faces. A pitiful sight, but for the owners this was just a blip in proceedings, an irritation. The workforce was ordered back to their workstations in no time. Once again, the cage cables creaked with the returning miners, and the conveyors groaned back into action deep down below.

Then disaster really struck. A catastrophic explosion erupted deep within a mineshaft. Shock waves ripped through the earth, the sirens cranked into action, and within minutes it was mayhem. Some 1,099 perished – 'Europe's worst in history'. Only thirteen survivors were miraculously rescued alive because they had sustained themselves by feeding on the bark of the mine crossbeams, and then the rotting remains of a dead mining pony.

Part 3

Courrières – circa 1910

'*Salut Alice, ma Chérie*,' yelled an old man, from across the Rue Principale, 'give me that lovely smile.'

Maria Alicja never dared to correct anyone, calling her Alice, but inside, she was proud as punch of her Polish origins. She was Alice to everyone, and even though her subtle Polish accent gave the game away, her striking good looks forgave her everything. She was a pretty, vibrant, young teenage girl, and she had the world at her feet.

She bounced along the street with her two, fully-laden bags, one hanging from each arm. She broke into a skip to make better progress. She was already late. Then that unmistakably French smell of freshly baked croissant, slightly burnt, overwhelmed her, and she swung into Madame Blois's shop. She was salivating as she joined the short queue. Madame Blois greeted her immediately. Alice blushed, but smiled back, impishly.

'*Salut ma beauté, mon bijou*,' she exclaimed, prompting the shoppers to turn their heads. Alice giggled, replied politely, only to prompt a retort about her accent, and how *charmant* it was… and intriguing. Madame Blois asked how her parents were. Alice assured her they were well, but that she always worried about her father working in the mine. Whenever he was late home, she and her mother feared bad news. Her remarks struck an immediate chord:

'*Je sais, mon Alice chérie*, we all understand, and with those poor injured survivors in view here, each day, we can never forget. But things are much safer now, really, and we must be happy for that.' A lady in the line ahead of Alice nodded, then began her own diatribe, which made Alice even later for getting home.

It was no wonder the mine disaster in the town was a daily topic. It was only a few years ago, March 1906, that this worst mining tragedy in Europe's history had struck this little town, Courrières. With over a thousand dead, it had made the world's press, and rightly so. It had highlighted the industry's dangers so many exposed themselves to on a daily basis. It also exposed the despicable absence of modern safety measures, all a grim warning to the wealthy mine owners. Strikes had since ripped through the business, exploited by the press.

Once methane ignites from a miner's naked flame ('firedamp'), the outcome is inevitable. Coal dust explosions will sweep through the long corridors and shafts in an instant, the more so here, at Courrières. A particularly complex structure, there were several pitheads on multiple levels, and all linked by underground galleries. This was the perfect design for a rapid explosion to cause maximum carnage, and it duly obliged, with a vengeance. The expensive new Davy Lamps were not yet in commission here, to limit the risk of explosions. There was a lack of trained mine rescuers in France too, all of which added to the already toxic ingredients for an inevitable tragedy.

Yet this ghastly episode, in the otherwise unremarkable history of this town, briefly transported this seismic event into a symbol of hope. It brought to the surface a primal, festering desire to overcome deep-rooted antagonisms. As ever, the headline story quickly pushed aside any human philosophical narrative. Once the press learned that thirteen survivors, later coined 'Les Rescapés', had been found some twenty days after the disaster struck, the papers were over it like a rash. It was swiftly front-page news throughout Europe. Predictably, however, it was only once the gory account emerged that this group survived purely on the remains of a, long-dead, mine pony, that this delayed news took both the public, and The State, by storm.

With Georges Clemenceau visiting the region at least twice, 'Légion d'honneur' for the oldest, and 'Médaille d'or du Courage' for the young, were inevitably issued. Courrières was now firmly on the map, if only for this tragedy. For Alice and her family, the incident at least satisfied local curiosity as to why a foreign, Polish family, had arrived here at all. There were vital vacancies to fill. This, in turn, made Alice even more determined to seize the opportunity to integrate fully into a French way of life.

Alice had tried to cut her losses by running the last few hundred yards with her heavy bags. She pushed open their front door, with her rear, to be greeted with a reprimand from her agitated mother. Why on earth had she taken so long? They always spoke in Polish at home: 'I suppose you got waylaid with the usual chitter-chatter, but you really must be firm with people, and keep an eye on the time.' Alice apologised, but made light of it, proudly lifting her bulging carrier bags onto the kitchen table. She let out a conspicuous grunt to make clear her efforts, and to excuse her lateness. As an only child, she was quick to craft a favourable life for herself. Stern though her mother could be, her parents were, in truth, putty in her hands.

'Where's Papa, mother?' pleaded Alice. 'Is he late home again?' Her concern always melted her mother's crossness.

Her father had been on an early shift and was due home to eat with them, after a thorough wash. Her mother changed the subject.

'I do love the way you use typically French phrases Alice, when you talk to me in Polish, it's so funny,' she chuckled, not meaning to mock her.

'Oh, I just can't win mother. I get teased in the town for my Polish accent, and now I get ribbed here for my French!'

The truth was, Alice was already fluent in French, way better than her parents, and her subtle Polish tones charmed the pants off the locals. This, along with her irresistible good looks, were serving her well. She was growing into a woman to be reckoned with, her mother could see that in her every day. No wonder then, she tirelessly instilled in her as much wisdom as she could.

Moments later her father arrived. He struggled towards the stove, his face black with coal dust. Alice rushed over to him but he gestured for her to keep her distance until he had washed himself properly. Exhausted, he wasn't talking.

'You do worry us darling,' Alice's mother broke the tension. 'Whenever you're late back from your shift, we fear the worst.' He just looked up from the wash basin, his head still dripping with grime, then shrugged and went upstairs.

Alice looked upset. Her mother reassured her that conditions in the mine, since they arrived, were a 'world apart' from those that had precipitated the 1906 disaster. Everyone had accepted that, so they should too. This didn't stop Alice from fretting, but she took heart from her mother's natural strength, her tenacity, and the way she could turn things around when everything appeared so bleak. She reminded Alice to always look on the bright side:

'Remember, my darling, everything happens for a reason. Yes, the disaster was a dreadful thing for this town, and we will never be allowed to forget that. We must also remember, it was because men suddenly lost their lives here that we were able to find work, and our home, or we would still be struggling with our hard previous existence in Poland, forever fearing the next pogrom in our town.'

Alice could but look back at her mother with love and admiration. How she prayed she might become a little like her.

Part 4

Northern France. A village – circa 1915

The bedside alarm rang harshly. It shattered the calmness in an instant.

General Alan Thompson desperately groped towards the clock to silence it, for fear of waking his lover.

They had just met, yet it had proved to be an immediately passionate affair. Alice was some beauty. With her fragrance still lingering in the damp air of the room, he remembered every detail from the night before. How sweet her lips had tasted, how fabulously soft her youthful skin. He had wished the passion of their lovemaking could linger in his mind forever, but their time was running out.

Although the General had been intrigued by her subtle foreign accent, he hadn't ventured to question her about it. It was enough that he had found such a seductive woman to make love to in this ghastly war and, for that, he was eternally grateful. He was also feeling more than a little pleased with himself.

The clock had clattered to the floor and he had cursed his clumsiness under his breath. Alice was wide awake but chose to disguise it, just for a precious, further moment. She wanted to steal this parting chance to admire her new lover's muscular, shirtless physique as he struggled to locate his clothes in the dim light.

Still feigning sleep, Alice looked on as the General assembled his military gear. A chanced fragment of light slipped through the curtains of the half-open window. He spotted her looking but attempted not to show it. She sensed it rather turned him on that she might be admiring what she saw. He had reason enough to be vain. A tall and powerful, red-headed, British General, he was surely everything a young, attractive, French woman, on her own, would wish for. At least that was his perception, but as it happens, he was right.

Yet, for Alice, there was more, much more, to her perceived infatuation for this man. Had she not been an immigrant by origin, nor come from a people and a family who had known truly harsh times, she might have been more vulnerable to those basic instincts that beset most young women of her age. No, beneath it all, a more complex chemistry was at play deep within Alice, such that an arrogant British Officer could neither suspect nor fathom. It was all about survival for Alice, survival and security, if such might somehow be won from this passionate liaison. It was a gamble, a reckless one perhaps, but what had she to lose? Buoyed up by her own sexuality (for this General was some catch), she was content, for now, to play the long game and see how fate might unfold. Brimming with confidence, deluded by fantasy perhaps, she performed like a cat playing with an entrapped mouse in her clutches:

'Monsieur General,' she mumbled, barely audibly, 'my secret lover from La Grande-Bretagne,' she added seductively, but he did not react, pretending not to hear. 'When will you visit me again *mon chéri*?' she added, audibly this time. Her irresistible accent, her femininity, might have enticed him back into her arms, but he was now fully kitted out, and in regimental mode, and as much as he grimaced with the agony of it, his duty was the greater force.

He finally responded to Alice, in his rudimentary French,

that he was now, officially at least, on duty 'so to speak', and he must return to his tank depot at Erin '*tout de suite*'. She chose not to tease him, not at this moment, for his English accent and poor command of French. She knew that she had taunted him enough about all that last evening.

'That sounds important,' she echoed his serious tone, now turning in her bed towards him, not attempting to stop the loose white bed sheet from sliding down and exposing her breast. 'More important than me, *chéri*?'

Now that he was leaving, she feared he may not return, but Alice was strong and she had faith in her sexuality. Still struggling, in the poor light, with some final adjustments to his uniform, he cursed how his unit was still 'bloody short of men and equipment', and that it was 'all down to me to sort it out and to win this ruddy war', but now in guttural English, in full flow, Alice had no clue what he was ranting about. So, she just smiled, and asked that he took care.

Alice sat up in her bed, pulled back the curtain to watch her lover leave. He marched away towards his jeep, every inch a British General. She rose, hoped he might glance back and see her naked, have second thoughts, but he did not.

3 CHINA – TENTATIVE MOVES TOWARDS WWI

'The weak pleading with the strong'

Dubbed the 'Chinese Machiavelli', Liang stood out as the only influential political player who could possibly navigate a way forward for China. They desperately needed to take part in this war, join the major players, just as their old nemesis, Japan, had already so opportunistically actioned. Confident that the Allies would ultimately be victorious, China hoped at least to leverage this for the return of territory previously stolen from them. Shandong Province would be their main prize, from the spoils of war, and Liang had his sights firmly set upon this. Joining was the only avenue for leverage. With his experience, his undoubted credentials, both in industry and in government, he was ready to do everything that he could. He proved a truly remarkable historic figure.

There had been devastating setbacks, but Liang had learned from them. Within weeks of the outbreak of WWI, Britain's Minister, John Jordan, had rebuffed Liang's proposal to supply Britain with Chinese troops. Britain's arrogance had become insufferable. Still convinced that the war would be a short affair, that its supply of its own colonial manpower would outlast demand, why would it need to resort to Chinese support? Already allied to Japan, its principal partner in the region, Britain was not looking to provoke any antagonisms. The campaign at Tsingtao had reminded them of Japan's opportunistic capabilities, yet that same event had spurred Liang into new initiatives.

Liang quickly realised he was banging his head against the wall offering troops to Britain, or France for that matter, so he cunningly changed tack. He proposed a worker/soldier compromise, but a further rejection followed. This certainly tested Liang's resilience, but not his resolve. He just had to accept Britain's established view that Japan was at the helm for them in East Asia, and the British Trade Unions were the unavoidable hostile force obstructing change.

Liang was up against it, particularly with his President Yuan, feeling the weight of national weakness on his shoulders. With their recent history of losses from the Sino–Japanese defeats, and the throttling Boxer Indemnity, Liang knew he would have to rethink his strategy yet again. His President was only likely to endorse his plans once he could show that all the major players were either on side, or sufficiently appeased, so as not to be of any threat to China.

Liang was not one for giving up. With Britain, for now, remaining the harder nut to crack, he turned back to France.

France Finally Capitulates

With Britain ever-rejecting China's approaches, Liang sensed that France remained way more open to persuasion. The French Ministry of War had, after all, considered China's involvement for them before, but the notion had been dropped. Liang moved in to pick up the pieces. China was sinking under the weight of foreign acquisitions of its lands, and the unbending threat of Japan's insatiable greed.

He had to do something, and swiftly, and that 'something' had to prevail.

Liang cut an impressive figure on the French political stage. They liked him. A strong-set, fine looking man with his manicured, drooping moustache, his image seemed one that the French would likely take to. He certainly commanded attention. France had, for some while, feared for the depletion of its own colonial manpower. It had pressed Senegal, Algeria, Morocco, Vietnam and the like, as far as they felt they dared, and with a commitment of some 180,000 men already secured, France had little appetite for bullying for more. Liang's relentless diplomacy finally paid off.

Liang set up a private recruitment organisation called The Huimin Company. It was an ingenious move. With one stroke, any charges by Germany, or Japan, that China was violating its neutrality, could be rebuffed, and any protestations by the Unions outwitted. Appearing all the world as a legitimate, commercial agency for finding work for Chinese labour abroad, who could possibly launch a sustainable protest? A covert device for supporting France in its war campaign, the scheme had been too masterfully presented to be successfully challenged. It was destined to succeed on all fronts.

To the public gaze, there was nothing suspicious about it, at least not on the face of it. Now in full view, China could feel confident, at long last, that their beleaguered workforce might yet find employment if they responded to the call.

For France they saw this as a godsend, a reprieve. French political tension had reached its peak, with the news flooding in about carnage on their soil, getting worse by the day. Their homeland was under siege, and with no end in sight. The papers were full of gloom. French workers had begun to gather on the streets in threatening groups. Newspapers were racing off the shelves, growing numbers of idle men could be seen pouring over the headlines on street corners and outside shop fronts. Unsustainable losses were being reported, graphic details being printed, there to view in black and white. The Authorities had thus come under intolerable pressure to do something meaningful to alleviate the situation, and the Chinese solution seemed the obvious one to embrace.

'*Merde, c'est la merde*,' one man barked out, losing it, as he stamped his half-smoked Gauloise into the gutter of a Paris street.

The French Military had enlisted the services of Alexandre R. Conty to carry out the research needed to justify their decision. He proved to be only the fact-finder. It was the appointment of one Georges Truptil who was destined to deliver the final master stroke. A retired French Army man, but now heralded as 'an agricultural engineer', Truptil was appointed to run the recruitment show. This he did in some style. Appearing as neither a war minister, nor a political appointee, Truptil's apparent commercial credentials seemed perfect in a labour market dominated by Chinese agricultural workers. 'The Truptil Mission' was born.

Though it was decided The Huimin Company HQ would be based in Peking, the organisation depended for its success on its multiple outlets. Whilst Britain would never have considered Hong Kong for such an enterprise, Truptil thought otherwise. Promulgating their slogans in print would not be enough. So it was, that Hong Kong, among various other centres, was set up with well-briefed campaign teams to recruit workers for French industries. This however, did not protect it from the growing unrest now festering, even endemic, in some regions. It was a race against time.

As fast as the recruitment propaganda could be launched, posters were being torn down and replaced. The ever-growing numbers of protesters were slowly waking up to the reality of the horrors of war that these Chinese recruits would soon face. Agitators were fighting to be heard. Those desperate for work, sadly mostly illiterate, were gradually being swayed by the rumoured promise of good, reliable wages, a short and trouble-free voyage, fully paid for, and the verbally reiterated assurance of a safe working location.

So, who would prevail in the end? The substituted slogans, by the agitating gangs, were clear enough to those who saw them, but still only to those who could read:

招募苦力华人，以供战之驱使

'Coolies are being recruited to be employed on the front in the war', 'Ignore the Liars'.

4 MING – GUANGDONG PROVINCE

A rural village near Hong Kong, late 1916

Unlike the Allied-run ports of Shandong Province, not a soul out here, among the tough regions surrounding Hong Kong, would neither know nor care that a war had been raging for the last two years thousands of miles away. They had their own challenges to face and survive. To hell with any distant squabbles. In any case, Ming was rooted to his locality, to his local existence. He had never felt he was mature enough to be a family man. He couldn't even remember growing up, so he wasn't sure that he ever had! He certainly had his hands full now.

A twenty-four-year-old conscientious agricultural worker, Ming had never known anything else. Every day it had become an increasing struggle to find anything other than the most menial work. His main impediment had been that he never found himself at the front of any queue when it came to looking for work. Whenever jobs were being offered, they were vastly oversubscribed, and the gangers would always sift through the waiting-hopefuls for the fittest, burliest looking men. Ming was too slight, too nice to bully favour, too reserved to garner the nerve to win preferential treatment. Yet he was skilful and courageous, with an endearing face and manner, but these qualities only gave him half a chance if he could just get to show his worth to someone that mattered.

Ming had tried, every day, to make the best of the attributes that he had, but he still acted as, and appeared like, a young lad. That didn't hold him in good stead for earning meaningful pay. His best card, and one that had helped him the most throughout his adult life, had been his local roots. Ming had never moved away from the region where he was born, and grew up, so here he was known as a 'goodun'.

When Ming's wife fell pregnant again, he truly felt the weight of responsibility on his shoulders. So now his dear wife's precious pay would soon be in peril too, then what? Things had never been this dire since they got married. There had been better times, but very few. If it hadn't been for his wife's resilient spiritual strength, Ming might have crumbled long ago. She was his anchor, and his first love.

She had hoped for at least a flicker of joy from Ming when she announced her pregnancy, but he could never feign his feelings. Not with her. He had felt depressed for so long, that the only passion he seemed able to muster was anger, borne from frustration. He thought himself a failure, no matter how often his dear wife would shout him down for it. He so wanted to provide well for his family but found he could not.

'It's no good sinking into that mood again,' she would moan, 'that won't get you any work, not from anyone that matters.' Yet she too was fighting against despair, but also her diminishing health, she just didn't show it. Her maternal strength had let her sense a deeper purpose from her pregnancy. She ached for another child, yet feared down to her toes for the extra mouth to feed. As ever, it was her mettle that helped drive her husband on, her inner strength that prevailed.

'If they won't offer you proper work around here anymore, you'll just have to look further afield my darling.' She had never ventured to suggest anything as wayward as this before. She knew how rooted Ming was to where they lived, and it disturbed him to hear this from her. Was she going mad? How could she even think that he could travel any distance and leave his family exposed? Yet there was a steeliness in her voice this time, an urgent tone, and it spooked Ming to witness it from her. His mind yelled inside his head, as loudly as a scream, 'I don't belong anywhere else, I would shrivel up and die away from home,' but he only knew the conviction of silence.

Ming knew his wife was right. She was always so wise, but he was a 'home boy', through and through, and he had learned to feel safe, secure in his environment, even if, right now, nothing seemed solid to him at all. Even the thought of being anywhere else might make him throw up with fear. If 'further afield' meant leaving the countryside, well that was out of the question. He had found farm work tough, impossibly so at times, but he loved his rural life. He could disappear, bury himself in his thoughts close to the naked brown earth. It was all that he knew. But his wife was on his case now, more than ever, and she wasn't letting go. It was her new demeanour, the angst in her voice, that troubled him. It made him feel vulnerable. Every time she brought the subject up, he would shrug, make an empty gesture with his hands, walk away, but he knew she was right and he was weakening to her persistence by the day.

As Ming arrived in Hong Kong his heart missed a beat; he had bitten the bullet, confronted his fear, yet he felt utterly overwhelmed. This was another world to him. He had been to Hong Kong, the city, before, but that was a very long time ago and it had grown beyond measure. It had been with his father, when he was a boy, so he would have seen the metropolis as a fun place, loved the chaos, but not now. The utter madness, the mayhem, the suddenness of everything, threw him into a whirl and he hated it. He didn't know where to start, at least not until the direction he had taken took him brushing past an endless row of small shopkeepers. This seemed more benign, an eddy, away from the force of the current that mightn't harry him so. Ming was really rather taken by these small stalls. Curiously, they reminded him of home. The way they had been thrown together, like makeshift farm sheds, spare lengths of timber covered over by flapping canvas, fraying from the repetition of reassembly. Perhaps there was some hope for him here, yet he quickly realised he would need to take the initiative if anything were to happen at all. Where he lived, you just knew where to queue for work, and when to do it. From there it was just a question of persistence, and a dollop of good fortune on the day. He wasn't streetwise, nowhere near, totally ill-equipped for what he faced here. He felt like a fish out of water and he was losing his nerve.

All that Ming could hear, lodged in the back of his head, were his wife's words, coaxing him, over and over again, to show his worth and find well-paid work to improve their lot. He owed it to her to try, not to give up. He adored her too much to let her down without a fight. 'I won't let you down my darling, not if my life depended on it,' he muttered bravely.

Ming walked for miles, still taking to the street extremities wherever the small shops were. The brash signs, the adverts, were dazzling. The sudden appearance of a youth, dashing across him from nowhere, nearly sent him sprawling. The odd eruption of a yelling shopkeeper shuddered in his chest and made him gasp. Yet Ming could not think where else he might venture. He paused, for a second, to catch his breath. He leaned against the frame of a sign to shelter him from the passing crowds. He thought of them as 'street tangle', a menace to avoid tripping over. He was watching the pacing rickshaw pullers struggle past him. He certainly didn't want to be one of them. Then, out of the blue, he became aware of a tugging sensation, somewhere around his feet. He ignored it, until that same feeling yanked at him again, more forcibly this time, so he looked down. To Ming's horror, what had drawn his attention was the struggling grip of a beggar's hand on his trouser ends. It was a man in the gutter beneath him, and when Ming realised his predicament, he gasped in horror, 'Ughh!' The man had no legs and he was pulling his way along, attracting attention in whatever way he could to secure loose cash. Ming could neither reach for any coins, nor stay where he was to try, for a second longer. He threw the beggar's gripping hand aside, then ran for it, just to get away as quickly as he could.

Poor Ming was just too callow for city life, and he was really feeling it now. He soon stopped running and recovered his composure. He felt terrible that he hadn't given the poor devil some coins, but he had taken him by surprise and he wasn't going back. He was running out of time and, feeling the pressure of it, he decided to bite the bullet. He began approaching some of the small stores to ask for work. It took every ounce of courage he had. His problem was that he was too meek, too reserved in his manner for city types. Most rejected him out of hand, others just pretended not to understand him, and he didn't persist.

Losing any mojo he might ever have had, Ming was barely hanging on, when he spotted an elderly stallholder struggling with some boxes. He seemed alone and certainly in need of help, so Ming ventured towards him. Purely out of desperation, Ming had foolishly, in that moment, built up a surge of optimism that here, miraculously, was his chance. His pace became brisk, he even knew exactly what he was about to say, and he was certain he would be successful. Here was a man who desperately wanted paid help, he was certain. Then, from nowhere, a youth appeared and immediately started giving the old man a hand:

'Hey, father, I told you to wait until I got back, and now look at you. Leave this lot to me, you'll do yourself a mischief!'

That was it for Ming, the last straw. As he sloped away, feeling desolate, he found a bench to slump onto and broke down:

'What on earth am I doing here?' he wailed. "But I can't go home with nothing, I just can't,' he sunk his head into his hands.

A gathering group of people across the way, caught his attention. He had ignored them at first, but the group became a crowd, and the relative calm of the spot Ming had chosen, was fast becoming a public assembly. He sat up, propped oddly, as if resisting being noticed as an onlooker. Temporary hoardings were going up, posters were being glued to them, which he couldn't read, but individual speakers were taking their turn with animated announcements. This happened to be a freshly set up, official recruitment centre for working abroad.

Ming's illiteracy made it pointless to wander over to take a look, but what was being said had certainly resonated with him. 'Real wages for downtrodden workers', 'Chance of a lifetime, free travel to a country near China' … the announcements kept coming and Ming was entranced. He rose and strode towards the gathering which was, by now, quite a bustling throng. This time, through sheer fortune for being on the spot, Ming found himself first in a line of workers wanting to know more. With the propaganda being chanted out, Ming became mesmerised, as though a ray of warmth had struck his face and dried his tears.

'Come to sign up young fella?' enquired the seated official, now facing him, who didn't seem old enough himself to use that term. 'I can tell you've got ambition, no need to suffer on peanuts anymore, eh!' Ming tried to ask intelligent questions, but he was so taken in by this apparent opportunity for salvation, that he just nodded his way through the process. He hadn't really understood much of what was being offered, and the thought of travelling by sea anywhere, for any purpose, filled him with trepidation. He had never left Hong Kong, for any reason, and he certainly hadn't ever been on board a ship. Needless to say, very little, if anything, was said about a war going on. If anyone had asked, it was said not to be relevant to the work being offered anyway. Reference to Europe, let alone France, meant nothing to these individuals, desperate for jobs.

Most of the applicants were either illiterate workers, or close to it, so the process of commitment was cleverly managed. These men were fodder in their hands. Full details of the men were written down by the officials themselves, confirmation of the men's agreement to serve was confirmed by their mark. A copy of the document was supplied to take away with them. 'Congratulations young fella, the path to wealth lies ahead of you.'

As he left the city for home, Ming was in a turbulent state. He wandered back through the streets in a total mental fog. He couldn't remember how he got home, but he managed it somehow, and all with the preoccupying anxiousness in his mind as to what his wife's reaction to his news would be. As he entered the house, he rushed to find her. He hadn't expected to be emotional about it, but he really should have. He was in utter torment. As they met, he threw his arms tightly around her and wailed like a baby. He stammered his explanation to her through his tears. They stayed glued to each other.

'Don't weep my dear husband,' she somehow found the breath to at least whisper to him. 'Feel proud,' she added, now shaking, 'you must go to that "France" for us, and earn all the money that you can, and we will be fine, just fine. It's for the best.'

Neither released their grip on each other, but she sustained the greater outward countenance. Still holding him tightly, she felt the pressure on her tummy, and real fear in her heart. Unbeknown to him, her tears ran freely on his shoulder.

French Recruitment of Chinese labour – Farewell Ming

Ming had settled down during the weeks since his return from Hong Kong. He was resigned to his fate, yet he had convinced himself, and what had pacified him, was the delusion that the 'moment of truth', his 'call up' demand from The French Authorities, would never come to pass at all.

What had also helped him, was the odd run of work that had come his way since he was back. Perhaps, he thought, even prayed, that this alone would sway his wife on side, and that he could yet get released from his French contract. His wife may have reacted with joy for the money now coming in, but these spells of good fortune had all happened before, and she knew all too well, 'luxuries are fleeting', so she tempered Ming's transient optimism as best she could.

As with any pending event, one as life-changing as this, where no date had been specified, the entire prospect of actually leaving China for work, had quickly melted away from his consciousness. For Ming, it had become a 'possibility' rather than a 'probability', and that suited his state of mind down to the ground.

Yet, what had ultimately recalibrated Ming's mindset, his fragile confidence, was the strengthening contagion among his fellow workers that the prospect of recruitment, to work abroad, might be a road paved with gold. The relentless 'air waves' announcing unmissable prospects, the opportunity of a lifetime, had begun to resonate and take hold. The word amongst the men was to forget about this new, unexpected, boost in local work opportunities. They had all long-suffered harrowing times, toiling on the land, and as time passed, Ming found himself caught up in the fervour of it all. For the first time in his working life he had felt, been touched by, that boost of self-esteem that makes life feel worth living. He had sought out, and secured, a prized opportunity, after all, and he had bravely done so, on his own, in the daunting streets of Hong Kong. Now, even in rural areas, French propaganda had reached out far and wide, but only just ahead of the growing subversive messaging taking hold.

So, when the moment arrived, Ming's newfound enthusiasm for his recruitment by the French was to be well and truly tested. His date was set. The notice had arrived. He must now prepare to leave. All that he could hope for, as he felt a surge of doubt rip through his veins, was that the 'voyage of a lifetime', would prove not to be a lie, but his salvation.

The protesters in the city, and now in some rural areas, were beginning to make an impact. Social unease was palpable. The word had got out; the official line about the recruitment of labour was no less than treachery, but would the draw towards a promised land win through?

Unbeknown, even to the agitators, Germany had added their weight to this seditious movement, behind the scenes. They had good cause to worry. They had complained bitterly to China that the drive to recruit labour was a violation of Chinese neutrality, but in their weakened state, Germany had been rebuffed. Covertly, Germany sponsored counter-publications, in a last-ditch attempt to foil the recruitment momentum. The conflation of these strategies had nourished the energies of the street protests, and concerns were growing that the 'Truptil Mission' might flounder. It was becoming clear that there was good reason now for France to fear that their efforts in China might hit the buffers. The counter-slogans, the leaflet drops, crafted propaganda, were now reaping rewards. The messaging was powerful:

'You will suffer the worst atrocities… you will be buried

away from your homeland…' but how would illiterate farm workers get to learn what was being cautioned, be made aware of the true horrors of the war that they were soon destined to witness? Already on their way to the docks, by now utterly indoctrinated by the prospect of salvation for their families, many had signed, and ever more were due.

Ming set off with his wife by his side. To pacify him, she agreed their route would avoid the hubbub of towns and the city. She had lived with the impact of Hong Kong on Ming, his demeanour, so she didn't want a repeat performance. It might take them a good deal longer, but closeting Ming, in his present state, was a priority. This played, cruelly, into the hands of fate. The recruitment centre was away from the city in any event, at Laichikok. Now the reality of Ming's enrolment had well and truly sunk in, Ming was fragile and his wife was worried. This was surely 'stage fright', nothing more? She had to believe this, having witnessed a real transformation in her husband. It may have been beefed up bravado, encouraged into him at work, but there was a real new spring in Ming's step, and she had to do all that she could to prevent this change from melting away. As the, no longer distant, prospect of leaving China really took hold of Ming, she knew she would need her inner grit.

She held and stroked his hand the whole way, focused on the passing scenery, did all she could to distract him. Ming's wife did catch some of the propaganda now erupting near to the docks, but not enough to fully grasp the messaging, though she strained her gaze, searchingly, in their direction. She felt some doubt, but kept her silence, even though this was the first time she had heard such words as: 'war zone' and 'munitions factories' mentioned.

As they arrived, they were cunningly separated. Somehow, they hadn't immediately worked out what was actually happening, yet this was to be their final parting. The way the recruits were 'plucked' away, averting predictable high dramas and extended desperate 'goodbyes', was a masterclass in human management. Ming knew his fate was sealed. He may, finally, feel mentally prepared to board ship, but not for what was to happen next.

Once the line of would-be recruits had filed through the main centre – the 'welcoming façade' – they found themselves in a large, secure compound. He hadn't the first notion of what a 'war' might actually be, or the reality of it. What Ming was experiencing now was how he had imagined it was like to be called up for some battle for his homeland! Brutal, undignified medical checks were carried out, which included curious eye checks. Ming had no clue what these were for, but as his turn came for this procedure, the prodding and shoving ceased for a moment, as an officer, with a contraption on a stand, asked everyone to freeze!

They were posing for photographs, but Ming had no idea what was going on, nor why the process was so painfully slow. Irritating as this might be, it soon proved insignificant compared to the agitation the medicals that followed imposed. With his eyes stinging from the drops for trachoma, he then had to strip naked alongside several other recruits,

They found themselves in a large, secure compound

to then be scrubbed in open baths. It so reminded him of the chaotic dipping of farm animals in rural Guangdong, but what those creatures did not have to endure was head-shaving, close to baldness!

By now Ming had been well and truly softened up for anything they might throw at him, but when he saw his precious braid, his queue, fall to the floor behind him, he had a fit. Rural men like Ming, had long defied the national directive to remove their hair plaits as something from their scorned past. It was a symbol to Ming, a traditional motif, and he had worn it with pride. They restrained and cautioned him. After that, giving his thumbprint, and having an aluminium ID dog tag secured by a necklace around his neck, seemed tame.

How ironic, Ming considered, after the indignity of the medicals, that the recruits were handed a bundle of fresh uniforms, smart hats and new shoes to wear for boarding ship! None of these bemused recruits fathomed they were being 'tarted up' to deceive. The only thing on Ming's mind right now, was getting to wave to his dear wife from the deck, so he began staring intently, desperately trying to spot her. As it happens, she was close to the front of a large gathering, but the officer-photographer was in her way. As she craned around him, feeling very agitated, she could see a line of odd, smartly kitted-out men, filtering away from her and up onto deck. With only their backs to her, she had to assume Ming must surely be amongst them, but felt appeased by their appearance. She could no longer hold it back. Her chin dropped to her chest. She wept bitterly.

None of these bemused recruits fathomed they were being 'tarted up' to deceive

As the last of them vanished within, and with no further men boarding, she guessed she had missed Ming.

She stood there, welling up. As the ship sounded its horn, slowly pulling away, she froze where she stood. She sensed something in her tummy, pressed it gently with her hand. Still looking on, she agonised – had she been right to encourage him to go? She wondered too, as her tears fell, if she would ever see him again.

5 STABLES – NORTHERN FRANCE

She knew it wouldn't be easy from now on. She was feeling the burden of it all too heavily. At least here, in this soft rural landscape, Alice sensed a detachment from the war, though it raged perilously close by. For now, in the moment at least, she embraced the calmness.

The horses in her care seemed curiously placid. That swift spell of heavy rain, a deluge, had gusted by as promptly as it had arrived. The weather had been capricious for days. She so loved the thrill of heavy rainfall, watching the plump droplets bounce off the horses' backs like translucent pebbles. These fabulous creatures, with their taut impervious hides, could repel any tempest. Now, in triumph, their sweat sent vapour rising like steam into the stillness. It was cleansing, cathartic, she breathed it in, she shared in their strength, their stately defiance.

Tending horses had become a job made in heaven for Alice, except for the pay. It wasn't really pay at all, in fact. Apart from a nominal subsistence, the job had come with accommodation, and that alone was a prize to guard jealously. It had enabled her to continue her independence from home after her relationship with her elusive British General had come to nothing after all.

She always had her parents to run to if she really had to,

and that security was to be cherished above all else.

Then, that distinct whirring sound of war reached her ears, and corrupted the moment. She may have heard those fearful engines of enemy planes, or the ordnance of some other ghastly weapon, she couldn't tell. She just turned her back on it all, treated it all with contempt, resumed grooming and exercising the long-suffering horses she had neglected whilst she had placed her duties on hold.

Then, just as she had dismissed all sounds of war as a myth, a rude invasion of her peace of mind, a biplane blundered into the sky from nowhere, sending the horse she was tending rearing in alarm:

'Damn you!' she cursed in Polish. 'That's exactly what I didn't need right now, scoundrel warmonger.' As the plane vanished just as abruptly as it had arrived, Alice regained control and calmed her horse.

Dusk was approaching, and the last fragments of cloud had been ushered away. The stables would soon plunge into darkness but she wanted to hang on, linger in the gloom, for just a while longer.

She wondered if her mother had felt the same way as she did at this stage in her life. She might ask her. Feeling the effort nagging at her spine, she sloped away to lean against the stable door frame. With some light still lingering, and totally on her own, she lifted her smock to cradle her tummy with both hands. It gave her tremendous comfort to support her bulge securely, clutch it with purpose. Only a woman might fathom her thoughts right now, she mused, and perhaps only her dear mother. An inexplicable yearning rose up inside her, consuming her utterly, and the effect on her was profound.

In an instant everything seemed connected, it all made sense. If she had been sinking into some dark, suffocating place, she certainly wasn't right now. There was something primal about the way she now felt. She needed to capture all these sensations, commit them to memory, she sensed it in her bones. She suspected she might need these in reserve, on tap, ready to summon up, sometime quite soon.

6 MING'S ORDEAL FOR FRANCE
Part 1

'Tout en Mer'

If only he could have seen his wife, caught a glimpse of her, spied her final wave of recognition, it would have given him heart. It wasn't to be. Now Ming had to nurse his mental wounds. It wasn't as if he hadn't tried. He had been harried along with the others, boarding ship, all spruced up for show. Desperate as Ming was to catch sight of his wife, he had been too distracted, too overwhelmed, to get a proper chance. He had been clinging for dear life to his belongings, all that he had, as they progressed on board. He had lost his bearings and his brain had turned to fog.

It plagued him. All that invaded his head, now that his chance had gone, was the persistent sloshing of the ocean against the side of the ship, rocking it, and the hungry protests of complaining gulls. Ming could not have predicted that this benign backcloth, this music of the sea, was soon to corrupt to more threatening rumbles and swell to an overwhelming force. At its mercy, trapped within, it would torment him, become his nemesis.

The sterilisation process, the infamous 'sausage factory', at the docks, had completely knocked the stuffing out of Ming. He hadn't suffered alone, but Ming wasn't made of stern enough stuff, certainly not mentally. The initiation, preparing him for the voyage, and then losing sight of his beloved wife, had all been too much. Yet, in a way, the enrolment procedure had done Ming a favour. He'd been bruised by it, at first, felt the full impact of losing his precious queue, the indignation of being stripped and scrubbed, but it had left him feeling immune from any further psychological damage. At least back there, behind him, within the depot, some banter had been exchanged along the way. Something to lighten the load, but there was none of that relief here. Subdued into silence, he reflected on the utter dejection everyone was suffering. For Ming, his wounded state had gone way beyond the reach of any medicine, way beyond healing words. He wasn't sinking from the symptoms of an illness; his were the inflictions of total despair. An unreachable helplessness.

As Ming and his cohorts found themselves being filed, ever deeper, down into the bowels of the ship, a wave of anxious sweat rose from their backs. Each breathed in the rancidity of the other, made the more disconcerting by the grunts and groans from the men as they felt the sharpness of the steel steps press through their soft shoes. Away from the balm of fresh sea air on their faces, they had entered a suffocating world. An altogether more testing place. Securely incarcerated, they would soon get to know, and to dread, the brutal mood of the ocean and the wanton will of the sea.

Had Ming allowed it, succumbed, as he so nearly did, a surge of claustrophobia would have engulfed him. Had he not been conscious of a ticking time-bomb within the men around him, he might well have lost control. Somehow it helped him resist a common foe, draw some resolve from the resilience of his comrades. Any mental outburst would, more than likely, trigger others, and in the confinement of the ship's hull, the outcome would have been mayhem. Ming shut everything out, all but the ship's shuddering, the monotonous drone of its labouring turbines, the rocking of its bulk on the impatient sea.

As he continued his ever-descending journey down into the hull, how Ming now cursed that his native existence had denied him even a shred of seafaring experience. Such was the lot of the poor. Secure, perhaps, within the confines of their farms, their closeted agricultural existences, they were now horribly exposed in the world beyond. Unable to tap into the pacifying reservoir of familiarity, Ming was left with whatever innate strength he had. He prayed he had enough in store, sufficient in reserve to save him. His doubts now hung darkly over him. He could now, for the first time, sense the callous irony in how smartly they had all been 'packaged-up' for transport, in clear sight, as they boarded in China.

From some mutterings from one Chinese man, close by, Ming nodded to acknowledge him. It was this individual's surprising optimism that struck him. This man expected the 'imperious French' to look after them well, treat them like human beings, just as he had been led to believe they had done with all their 'Colonials', whatever their place of origin. Ming drew comfort from his hopeful attitude, not knowing if he was delusional or not, but then another butted in more caustically:

'Fine, sounds great, pity we're not "Colonials" then!' Ming decided to cling to the wings of hope, but he was far from certain.

The cruel truth was that The Ministry of The Colonies was, in reality, in overall charge of these Chinese Workers, even though China, of course, wasn't a colony at all. The conditions they were now having to endure were unthinkable.

As Ming's group ultimately reached the base of the hull, at least that jarring sound of the ship's steel panels, creaking and straining on the upper decks, finally faded. They stalled, where they stood, for just a second, discovering what now seemed destined to be their quarters. Could this really be where they were all to be lodged until their destination? Surely not? Ming thought he may have arrived in hell, if they were to be stuck here for an indeterminate number of weeks. Ming was at least able to salvage a crumb of comfort from being among the first to be allocated their spaces. Tucked away in one of the far corners, with at least one side structure to stare at, to prop himself up against, Ming almost raced forward to stake his claim, fearing his chance might vanish. Releasing his heavy bag from his back, he slung it down like a prospector claiming his territory. With only one body rooted down beside him, he purposefully caught his eye, briefly, and detected a glimmer of some humanity. Thank goodness. He took in a deep breath, eager to suck in some relative freshness, the succour of oxygen. Others, not so fortunate, were now arriving in droves, cheek by jowl, on either side of them, with all the row-ends now occupied. One late arrival seemed to peer over towards Ming, looking acquisitively at his superior spot. He scowled, dumped his belongings, disconsolately. His dark, saturnine, face grimaced with menace. He spat towards the floor.

Ming nursed his sore feet. The flimsy slippers they had been issued with offered no protection for treading the ship's unforgiving metal walkways. He hated them. Resented the discomfort. In the dull light, a maiden voyage for almost every soul on board, the pervading atmosphere was pestilential. With the hull filled to bursting, every row wedged tight, each steel-framed bed loaded with gear to the gunnels, the ship's throbbing engines opened up with a roar. For a moment, in reaction, the men's groanings were silenced. Bodies tensed up as the ship's power surged. Everything shook. There was no doubt, this voyage was underway. There was no going back.

On a calmer stretch, the soft thunder of breaking waves settled into a steady resonance. Resigned to his fate, as the days merged into weeks, there was comfort to be salvaged, some solace, from the hypnotic 'swish' of the ocean. Denied any view, Ming was left with his imagination, but the only landscape he could clearly visualise, the only one he felt able to conjure up, was that of his home.

He had long-subdued the worst of his grief at being parted from his wife, but he worried like hell for her, for their children, and of course, his unborn child. Most of all, he craved his future wages, his *raison d'être* for being out here at all. Thank God, he reflected, for the good run of work he had secured in the period leading up to his departure. At least he had left his wife with a fair reserve to feed from for a while yet.

Ming may have wished that the relative calm, the successful discipline the French naval staff had been able to instil, would endure, but it was not to be. Dwelling on the survival of his family for so long, had probably given Ming the focus he needed to sidestep any trouble, preserve himself. Discontent had been brewing for some while, not least once a wave of ill health had taken hold down below deck. Several men had submitted to a fever and had collapsed to the steel floor. As fast as the French naval medics could clear them and secure their confinement, others suffered the same affliction. This swelling unrest had been in the mix for some days, particularly with the wind gusts outside tossing the boat around with an ever-greater purpose. Disturbances were erupting among the Chinese who were still fit, all now fearful the infestation around them would, sure as hell, spread their way. The French just could not keep up with it, and were now ill at ease, threatening harsh retribution in their desperation to maintain control. Had it not been for illness reducing the Chinese to helpless sufferers, the French might well have gone in 'all guns blazing'. The misery throughout this lower deck had become intolerable. The conditions unimaginable. Ming could hardly cope. Having, somehow, until now withstood the relentless passage of time, with no end in sight, Ming now craved a way out. Anything to garner a modicum of peace, a place where night time could be distinguished from the day, effort from rest. The groaning of ill men was the worst thing. They sounded like distressed animals in transit, certainly nothing resembling human noises that Ming had ever heard. Many had given up the ghost, surrendering to the miasma of the diseased and dying. It was challenging not to sink with it all.

Still, somehow, drawing resolve from his fixity of purpose, Ming just spent hours facing the hull wall to the far side of his bunk. Listless and dejected, terrified to engage with the wrong recruit at the wrong moment, he did all he could to preserve his memories of home. All those sensations, those nostalgic symbols from his precious roots, now wafted through him as, one after the other, they mercifully returned to dominate his thoughts. Then he found himself chuckling at the deceit they had all been drawn into. Dressed up for show, he assumed his wife had seen him embarking that day. She may have been pacified that her husband was in safe hands and about to embark on 'the voyage of a lifetime!' The voyage was certainly that, but not in the way she might have imagined. Then he felt some obstructive cushioning under his side. He tugged it free. It was the crumpled remains of those same smart clothes he had just been recounting, in his mind – the trim hat, the new boots, all now ruined by grime.

The Chinese had not been entirely alone on the lower deck where Ming was. It was such a vast area. Many would scarcely have noticed that a significant contingent of Senegalese had joined them, although they had been kept well away from the Chinese and, curiously, seemed not to be falling ill in such dramatic numbers as they were. If these foreigners had been infected, they certainly weren't showing it quite so graphically. As for the Chinese, they were collapsing across each other and tempers had flared. Beset by altercations, the Chinese stood out for their volatility, compared to their Senegalese counterparts. These ghastly quarters, awash with failing Chinese, resembled some ancient dungeon. It was odd. As Ming's eyes wandered across the way, he could never have known what it must have felt like to be chained in place on one of those infamous colonial slave boats. The weakest were destined to work themselves to death, if disease didn't claim them first. For Ming, such historic ignorance was perhaps bliss.

Ming amazed himself that he had managed to hang on to reasonable health for as long as he did. He put that down to his location, tucked away from the throng, but also keeping himself to himself, avoiding excessive close contact. However, it wasn't to last. With so many wilting around him, and after weeks of uninterrupted confinement at sea, he fell ill.

Desperate to feign good health, he proceeded to do all in his power to fight off the inevitable. He knew he would instantly lose his precious spot in the hull, the moment he was removed. Avoiding eye contact with everyone, most had assumed Ming was just maintaining his anti-social habit, but then the coughing started and wouldn't stop.

Sapped of any last scrap of energy, Ming dropped his guard completely. Feeling so ghastly, boiling up with fever, he now joined those who had given up before him, those he had seen writhing around on the floor. He was promptly removed, with both arms slung over the uniformed shoulders of two naval guards who had been summoned to deal with him. Hastened away, Ming felt close to fainting. Once freed from the hull, now long-reduced to a dormitory for the sick, he felt relief from the thin air as he was stretchered up endless steep stairways. He was so glad his feet were spared the ordeal. Exposed to the elements, transported ever upwards, the sudden rush of sea air made him feel alive again.

Though his condition remained critical, Ming did not fear for his life. The utter relief to find himself in a changed light, to at last be at a real distance from the constant thumping of the ship's engine room, was medicinal enough. Thanks to the occasional appearance of an interpreter, doing his rounds of the segregated Chinese, he learned that he was now among casualties destined to disembark for hospital recuperation. They could not risk spreading any illness to another vessel. Fit men had been dropping alarmingly, and the first chance to quarantine the infected would be taken. Although it frustrated Ming to learn the ship was now close to Suez – the last stretch of his voyage to France – he just needed to feel well again, and as soon as possible. A hospital, on terra firma, sounded just the ticket. A timely escape from the sea.

Part 2
'There but for the grace of God'

Ming's ongoing ordeal – January 1917

Djibouti Hospital (Djibouti was then known as French Somaliland)

Somewhere, sometime, after Ming had been extricated from the hull of the vessel, he had been settled into an area on an upper deck, but his memory had seemed to falter.

The next thing he did remember, was being stretchered along a harbour towards an awaiting ambulance truck. He could not recall any details of his disembarkation, but after that, he was fully alert. He took in all that was going on, and quickly found himself being transported to a nearby hospital, as he had expected. He was impressed with the efficient way he was now being dispatched, and he chewed over all the Ship's Interpreter had said, which included mention of Djibouti Hospital. He was destined to stay there until he was well enough to resume his voyage to France.

Once he had been taken through the initial formalities, Ming found himself installed in a narrow, metal-framed bed, within a row of fellow Chinese workers. He was surprised at the relatively small number of them, bearing in mind the speed the sickness had ripped through his deck. Ming was used to narrow, primitive beds, but not the relative calm of the ward he found himself in. He discovered he could doze more readily in this new environment, but he had not anticipated the nightmares. Perhaps he should have done, after the many traumatic weeks he'd endured at sea. For the first time, since he was a young lad, he began tossing around and yelling in his sleep.

What was different this time around, as an adult, was that flashbacks were his tormentors. His dreams would invariably isolate him in a crowded street in Hong Kong, cruelly separated from his family by a sudden surge of city workers enveloping him, mad people, pressed irresistibly against him. He could see his wife up ahead, agonisingly beyond reach, but she could neither see him frantically waving, nor hear his calls.

Ming salvaged some calmness as each nightmare subsided, but his immediate neighbour found no such repose. The man began to speak. Ming was oblivious to the impact he was having on him as he turned his head, innocently, towards him. His neighbour's words were full of threat as they wafted Ming's way, his voice suffused with malice:

'I don't give a damn for you losing sleep. You can stay awake all night for all I care, but mark my words, if you keep me awake one more time, you needn't fret about waking up at all!'

Ming went cold. It was his tone, as much as the threat, and what was he, Ming, supposed to do? The man's face matched his guttural words; he was every inch a farm hand, and a tough-nut one at that. Ming turned away, deciding any response was pointless, as was any hollow promise to cease his rants. Ming was no more in control of his sleep traumas than he was his sickness. His only hope, feeling sure this ghastly thug meant business, was to suppress his own fear. He must then, somehow, reclaim enough control to allow only benign thoughts into his head. He needed a distraction to focus on, an opportunity to channel his thoughts away from his neighbour. Then his moment came.

Whilst it was clear to Ming his life wasn't in danger from this loathsome figure, he still felt real fear at sleeping so close to him. Away from the relative safety of the working gangs he had been a part of back home, here, he alone now had to survive this irksome bully. Ming's popularity had been earned by his kind nature, his hard work ethic, but in his present sorry state those props had gone.

Ming spotted an upright, official looking gentleman, addressing a Chinese patient at the beginning of his row. He was too far away to assess him, but the man seemed to have a distinctive, angular chin and cheek bones, certainly a foreigner to Ming, and his stern tone suggested he was engaged in some formal discussions. This might be his chance. A Chinese Interpreter, who Ming did recognise, was with the gentleman, and together they appeared to be working their way towards Ming. Once close by, Ming decided, from his appearance, that this was a religious man, but from the interpreter's translation that Ming could hear, nothing remotely religious was being said. The man was, in fact, the hospital Chaplain, evidenced by his spartan attire and dog-collar. From his voice, and his features, he seemed every bit a foreigner, yet somehow different to the French.

Now in earshot, Ming could hear both sides of each conversation. Thankfully, the exchanges were all in his familiar Hong Kong dialect. Ming had hoped this might be his opportunity, to settle himself down, by spilling out his troubles to the Chaplain, but the man seemed more intent on questioning the Chinese than listening to their woes and frustrations. He was no 'agony aunt', but Ming was going to have a go. His priority was to appease his threatening, surly, neighbour, who should be able to hear Ming attempting to sort himself out and offload his complaints. He was bound to be earwigging once Ming's turn came, being directly adjacent. When Ming's turn did come, with the two men looming over him, there was something about The Chaplain he just didn't like. A steeliness of purpose that unsettled Ming. Not at all the visitation he had expected from a man of the cloth, and he had taken so painfully long to reach Ming's bedside.

The delay had melted Ming's determination to stay focused and to voice his protests. Ming's other neighbour had gone on at such length, he had seriously encroached on Ming's allocated time. In his eagerness, Ming had launched into such gibberish that the Interpreter had intervened to cut him short. His chance slipped away before it had begun, but this seemed to suit The Chaplain's purpose to take the lead. Ming had been desperate to rant about the insufferable conditions he had experienced on board ship, how sickness had been left to fester, then spread throughout their quarters until he, inevitably, had submitted to it. But no. Instead, Ming found himself being interrogated about his contract with the French, how much he knew about their, and the British, strategy, but not a scrap was exchanged about him or how he now was. Ming might have preferred a sermon!

His bully neighbour had rather more success. He was less pent up, and his gravelly tones perhaps commanded more measured handling, engendered greater respect. Either way, Ming earwigged the entire discussion. It seemed his neighbour's angst was that he desperately wanted to reach France. The assurance, that stood out, was the one confirming that, so long as any individual could show he was non-contagious, free of any sickness, he would be included for despatch to the next available French boat, which happened to be a vessel called the *Athos*. Ming's neighbour reacted with a yelp when he was told he might only need to wait a further week. Ming was also surprised to learn that the established route, via somewhere called 'Suez', and then 'The Med', would get them to their French destination, 'in no time'. So, their ocean-bound ordeal was to end soon.

That night, Ming woke with a start as his bed frame shook violently. He screamed out in a reflex reaction to it. 'I did warn you,' growled his neighbour, 'I ain't putting up with a complete raving lunatic right by my lughole, a second longer!' Ming assumed he, Ming, must have had yet another nightmare rant, but he couldn't recall it if he had. When Ming lamely protested that he 'couldn't do a damn thing about it', the man just laughed in his face. 'Well, if you can't do a damn thing about it, I bloody well will.'

Ming's neighbour stretched down to one of his bags, looked around nervously, then handed Ming a small, tightly wrapped, package, pressing his index finger across his lips, to urge Ming's silence. 'Stash it away!' Ming hesitated, sniffed it, but when his neighbour hissed at him, 'Black rice, idiot, now hide it away, quick,' Ming understood immediately. He was cornered. He had taken opium before, in safe secrecy, but here, in an official building, and in a foreign country, just having the stuff was lunacy. Now in possession, Ming hid the package away, but in a state of total panic.

'Go to the toilet, before you sleep tonight, take it in there. Use the lot. You'll sleep like a baby… and so the hell will I.'

Mistrusting his nemesis completely, Ming began taking the opium, in very small doses, for the next several days, but it didn't seem to work. Rather than let on, Ming forced himself to stay awake for extended periods of time, enough to convince his supplier that it was starting to have some effect. That kept him out of harm's way, until his neighbour insisted on seeing how much opium Ming still had left. He showed him. Ming had been rumbled. Knowing that Ming had been holding back on the dosage, the man demanded that Ming took the entire remainder that night, 'or else!' Ming knew he meant it, and as his fever had subsided considerably, with several days having passed, Ming felt fit enough to do as he was asked. The man threatened to report him if any of his supply remained unused by the time Ming retired to his bed. Ming now feared for his life, but he also desperately needed a proper night's sleep.

It certainly had the intended effect. Ming was knocked out cold for two days. He had clearly overdosed. What then transpired was alarming. When he finally awoke, he was in a huge sweat, just like the fever he had recovered from, except that this was nothing of the sort. Now suffering palpitations, fits of paranoia, Ming hadn't noticed that almost every one of the beds in his row, including his neighbour's, was vacant. Where on earth had everyone gone? Ming sat up, almost falling back again with dizziness. Spotting the interpreter, across the way, he cried out to him to come over. When the man explained to Ming, that he had suffered a relapse, thankfully sleeping through a terrible further bout of fever, and that during that time the call had come to board ship, he erupted. It was hopeless, of course. Ming had to accept the hospital's false diagnosis, or else admit to his crime.

What would be the point? The boat will have gone. When he questioned the interpreter further, he made it clear to Ming that they could not have risked including him, or the other remaining few, whilst they were still deemed to be infectious. He was sorry, but he insisted Ming calmed down, set his mind on making a full recovery. His priority must be to ensure he was fully ready for the next transportation vessel, along with the other remaining men, the moment they were called.

Ming began condemning his neighbour. If he hadn't bullied him into taking 'that wretched stuff', and a stronger dose than he should, he would've been on his way by now. 'Damn and curse him,' he muttered, having to grin and bear it, but he suspected the man had known exactly what he was doing. He just wanted his own precious sleep, and at any cost. It seemed blindingly apparent, that the surviving symptoms eventually remaining with him, had saved Ming from detection. It must have appeared for all the world to be a recurrence of his sickness, so perhaps it had all been for the best; but his perpetrator would neither have known this nor cared. Ming wished him dead for his bullying, his reckless selfishness, and vowed to himself, that he would inflict serious harm upon him should he ever have the misfortune to stumble upon him again.

German U-boat Base: HQ

A deputation of senior German officers was pouring over a large, detailed map, stretched out, held in place by some spent gun shells. Engaged in a fractious debate, their main attention seemed firmly focused on the next scheduled target for attack. There was a Chaplain present, standing in the background.

Lt. Hermann von Fischel was in no mood for prevarication. He set the tone, and few would dare to challenge his directives. Sensing restraint from the others, the Lieutenant moved from the group to retrieve a newspaper from his valise. Some grumbling soon bubbled up, in his absence, but he swiftly put paid to that when he rejoined them. Stolid, but indignant, he slapped the paper down with a thrust of his arm, insisting, in German, that they gave him their full attention:

'Take a look at this bloody newspaper,' he demanded, '*Le Petit Marseillais*!' mocking the French with an effeminate voice. 'These French dogs are making ruddy fools of us, and I'm not putting up with it, and nor should any of you!'

As he pressed his index finger along the offending headline, the others huddled around him to take note. 'Secret mass recruitment of Chinese labour by France', stood out a mile, then 'Shipped to the battlefields of "La France" under the enemy's nose.'

Von Fischel had got his message across alright, but what exactly had he in mind? None of the group could imagine how the French had orchestrated this. They feared, if the number of Chinese increased to a significant contingent, this improbable enterprise could make a real difference to their enemy. This became all the more palpable when Lieutenant V.F. swiped through to the words on the next page:

> **'Secret mass-recruitment of Chinese Workers for direct service in the munitions factories and key industries of La France.'**

The onlooking men were incredulous, but they were now fully on board. One protested that it was all the fault of the German army, losing Tsingtao to the 'Bloody Japs'. It had set the rot, gifted their enemy the perfect facility to recruit from China with Germany absent.

Now, with a captive audience, Von Fischel pulled his rabbit from the hat. He read out his latest, top secret, intelligence findings, which identified the next transport vessel due their way, said to be 'loaded to the hilt' with Chinese Workers. Recently departed from Djibouti docks, now on their final leg from Port Said to Marseille, some misgivings about this 'target' were, tentatively, voiced:

'Would this not be a blatant attack on civilian shipping?' one German comrade dared to ask. Von Fischel scoffed, tossed his head back, dramatically slapping his thigh in typical Germanic style:

'My dearest comrade,' he announced, with a peremptory grin creeping, mockingly, across his face, 'these Chinese are incidental. All we know, "officially" that there are troops on this vessel. For heaven's sake, are we supposed to interview everybody? We are at war with these buggers!' A nervous ripple of laughter erupted. Von Fischel then thrust his papers into the awaiting arms of the Chaplain.

Part 3
On Board the *Athos*

Noon, 17 February 1917 – off the Maltese Coast

Listing, as a sharp gust rocked the side of the ship, the *Athos* continued on its journey, packed to the gunnels. Cargo vessel it may have been, but this overloaded cargo shipment was exclusively for humans.

Miserably ensconced way below deck, deep down in the hull, way over 700 Chinese had been feeling the worst of it. Quartered in poor light, suffering dreadful sanitation, this maiden voyage, for most of them, had proved no better than purgatory. A French ship, and a French consignment, they had at least been mindful to separate the Chinese Workers from the Senegalese Skirmishers (The 'Tirailleurs'). Conditions down below were appalling enough without adding to the volatility of those on board by mixing 'cargo' together. (It had been much the same mix for Ming on his infamous first voyage at sea.)

These hapless occupants, closeted below, might have been forgiven for assuming that a sudden bolt of lightning, from nowhere, had successfully bombarded the ship and provoked its engines to roar in protest. Thunderous noises sound much the same from where the Chinese Workers were located, but on this occasion, they were fatally mistaken. There had been no storm at all. The ship had been directly struck, in its side, by a German torpedo, launched by *U-Boat 65*, under one Lt Hermann von Fischel.

The eruption from the blast was formidable, yet, for a moment longer, the Chinese occupants remained in a quandary. It was only once rivets along the steel panels of the hull began to 'ping', one by one, and the side walls submitted to twists and contortions, that they finally understood – the *Athos* was sinking.

Clambering over themselves in desperation, the workers began to surge towards every stairwell, every doorway. As the lamp bulkheads blew, condemning the walkways to pitch darkness, it became rapidly apparent that if any were to survive, it would be the most brutal, the strongest. Those that made it to the upper deck may have thought they were in with a chance. They were mistaken. The life rafts that existed were already full and had been winched seaward to safety. Rushing to claim any emergency gear proved futile too; the instructions were in French and there seemed not a single naval officer in sight. Having somehow survived the crush against the steel staircasing and forced their way past the Senegalese now lining up on deck, there was nothing else for it for the Chinese. They began leaping, in vast numbers, into the ocean. It was suicidal. The swell of the sea from the listing ship, had begun to suck bodies beneath it like a mighty feeding whale. This was an unimaginable end for these poor farm workers. They'd set sail on the promise of safe work, good wages, and were about to perish in their hundreds, at sea.

Looking back towards the stricken vessel, the Chinese would have been bemused to see the Senegalese, all in a long, disciplined line on the submerging deck. As the ship finally sunk, these men, without exception, stood their ground, remained rooted to the spot, to salute to the French flag as they disappeared from view.

Back at Djibouti Hospital, Ming was much restored and eager as a straining hound to receive the call to board the next ship to France. With only a small contingent of Chinese Workers awaiting despatch to the docks, they were kept well informed by the Chinese Interpreter. He drew Ming to one side, as the news about the *Athos* filtered through. As it registered, once Ming grasped that the very ship he failed to board had sunk, losing all the Chinese in the process, he broke down. Had it not been for that scheming thug in the next bed, had Ming not self-administered that final opium dose as he was bullied to do, he would surely have met his end there too.

The effect on Ming was profound. The words he had cursed the scoundrel with, under his breath, when he found himself left behind, now returned to haunt him. He had wished him dead, and he had meant it, but he had never imagined, not for a second, that his wish would ever have come to pass, and that he, Ming, would himself be saved.

March 1917: Ming needn't have punished himself with guilt so fiercely. He was about to suffer severely enough as a result of having to take a later ship. His eagerness to embark on that last benign leg of his journey to France was about to be smothered. News of the Germans' treachery, the outrageous sinking of the *Athos*, hit the French and British airwaves like a tsunami. Telegraphers, from their dedicated wartime booths, unequivocally alerted all Allied convoys to divert their onward routes away from the Med. Now that they knew German U-Boats were lurking everywhere in those waters, willing to sink any vessel they chose, 'the powers that be' had no other option.

Britain may now approach Canada, their colonial allies, for an alternative route to their destination, but France had to opt for a longer route by sea. To Ming's utter dismay, as he finally boarded, he found himself on a diverted voyage around the perilous African coast. Aside from the risks, and these were to prove real enough, months were now added to the journey. Had his cultural heritage been borne from the western world, Ming might have reflected, in a moment of penance, that he was surely being atoned for willing his neighbour's untimely death?

If Ming had assumed his voyage being extended was as harsh as his luck was going to get, he was to be cruelly mistaken. Within a matter of weeks, a violent storm engulfed Ming's vessel. This was no ordinary squall; this was a veritable tempest. Much as Ming had witnessed on his earlier trial at sea, the scene rapidly descended into one reminiscent of the historic African slave-boats. High waves surged up to pound the galleys. Anyone caught there was immediately swept away. Seawater overpowered every inch of the deck, rushing down the tilting boards like a river. Men, stranded, scurried into doorways, escaping the torrent, others lost their grip on the boat's rim and vanished. Within, the officers were mobbed to reassure those struggling that the hull would withstand the sea's force. Discipline descended into chaos. Rank became obsolete.

Yet again, Ming found himself sandwiched between anxious workers. Here he had no side wall to turn to for solace. Yet he had learned from his earlier horrors – he did not succumb to the panic of the others around him. Tempers erupted, and had it not been for the tossing of the boat, violence would have been rife. No one could gain a foothold for long enough to launch a fight. It was hard enough to survive. The yelling and barking of the men seemed scarcely audible above the clamour of the storm. This time, able to better understand the savage mood swings of the sea, Ming sensed the ship listing, being thrust upwards as unimaginable waves surged beneath it, yet Ming knew it would pass, and it did.

The next morning it became clear that the ship had suffered significant damage. It had not, thankfully, been disabled, but its powerful engines had been compromised and progress would now be impeded. Ming sunk his head into his hands. Now curled up against a welcome ledge on the upper deck, he eagerly grabbed the food and drink being offered, but his relief proved short-lived. Gathered by naval officers into small working groups, the survivors were ordered to begin throwing the dead overboard. The Chinese protested, vehemently, but Ming urged those nearest to him to cool it. He saw that the French meant business and wouldn't tolerate dissent. Ming knew why, culturally, his guys were opposed to the task, why they would react to being told to handle the dead, but he somehow found the words to console them:

'We're the lucky ones guys, take it from me, this is nothing. We didn't go down, trapped to our deaths, in the *Athos*.'

7 MARSEILLE DOCKS

Ming Arrives in France for the French

Relief swept through every man on board as the packed vessel arrived dockside. The Chinese Workers had survived, or at least the majority had, but you wouldn't think they were fit enough to disembark, looking at the state of them filing down to the quay. Most looked desperately pallid and drawn. Others appeared to have aged ten years since they left China.

It helped to be free from the rigours of their voyage and to gain their first sight of European foliage, small shady hillocks, and tree-lined roadways dotting their way into the distance.

To a man, they looked bedraggled and exhausted. Had they not been so drained of resolve, the workers might have been more alert to the throng of other arrivals, now milling around the dock. It was chaos. Literally thousands of Indian Labour Corps stood huddled in long lines, away from their moored vessels. Ming noticed a discipline about them, immediately, and they stood out for it. It was their ordered obedience that held Ming's attention, and he couldn't help feeling a sense of admiration for them. They had surely suffered too, to get here, although Ming hadn't the slightest clue how distant their land might be. All that he felt certain of, was that China must itself exist to the other side of the globe.

Ming, and his fellow Chinese Workers, were not to know why these other labour corps stood out so. They were entirely distinct because they were part of an established colonial workforce; existing, and run, as integral to their nation's contribution to Britain's wartime call. China had no such historic ties. Ming, and his compatriots, were employees on French soil, here to serve France, yet they were as unfamiliar with French as they were English, and yet these were the western languages being barked here from military mouths. Also, only the Chinese were here as an undeclared force. Only they had been hastily and artfully recruited. Inevitably, they were to be subject to mockery for their appearance and unfamiliar ways.

So, Ming and his cohorts quickly became the subject of cruel humour. They were a soft target, after all. Gathered in disorderly assemblies of hungry, tired men, bent over bowls, shovelling food with chopsticks, the opportunity would not be missed. The Chinese had already attracted curiosity for their different look to other foreign arrivals, and it wasn't going to take much to prompt mass amusement from others, after their own gruelling voyage.

For so long, themselves, at the bottom of the class 'food chain', colonial labourers could, for once, look down on another poor, unsuspecting, people. In no time, the Chinese Workers were swiftly coined as the 'strangers on the western front', and they were as readily treated as such, yet there was only so much victimisation and ribbing, even they were going to tolerate. The Chinese may have, until now, endured sustained discriminatory treatment, but away from the confinement of regimented travel, the threat of harsh punishment, being on French soil, somehow seemed a less likely prospect. In any event, their mood had hardened.

The French Officers were quick to detect the mounting disaffection among their labourers. On the brink of confrontation, the pending medicals for the Chinese were hastily brought forward. This gifted those in charge with a ready-made facility to usher the Chinese away before matters got out of hand. The medical centres were at a useful distance from the dock debarkation areas. Ideal for swift physical separation.

These would be the last invasive checks Ming's mob would need to suffer, so they were all eager to get these ordeals done and dusted. Once over, they were washed, reclothed, and prepared for transport. Ming was as bemused as the others to have his metal dog tag manhandled from his neck, removed and taken from him, only for a replacement photo ID and worker's card to be slung around his neck by a cord in its place. It would seem he and his long-suffering, seafaring comrades, were now newly branded as 'land-based cargo' for work on French soil.

French Munitions & Weapons Factory – Le Creusot

Ming could not have been further removed from all he had known. His past life in China now seemed like a distant dream, perhaps one that had never happened at all.

It felt cathartic for Ming to breathe some fresh country air into his lungs. This may not have been that familiar, dry earth smelling air, that had coursed through him from birth, the same that raked in his nostrils as a child as he scampered home craving his mother's food, but it felt good, nonetheless. He smiled as he gasped it in.

He might even have enjoyed his first flush of optimism since he departed from China. Just clearing free the last remnants of salty grime from his insides, the sting of the sea, that stultification, the feeling of being dead to stimulus, lifted him. Yet one thing Ming was still not to be blessed with, was any sense of real permanence. He hoped he might find some soon enough. Sensitive to the inordinate time the French had invested in the Chinese to get them to France, Ming detected a real sense of urgency in getting them installed in productive work. That was why they were here, finally, after all. That decisive action, dockside, hauling the Chinese away from trouble, expediting their final processing, had set the tone. There was a momentum now, and an energy-injection, and this soon fostered some order.

The Chinese were to be installed wherever they were needed, but also where it was expedient, in the short term, to employ them. Extravagant, extended, further transportation was to be avoided. The French had, wisely, concluded that these labourers had reached 'travel saturation point'. They must be made use of as soon as possible, and that was what this first port of call was designed to achieve. They had just arrived.

Thanks to the foresight and historic entrepreneurship of Adolphe and Eugène Schneider, the founders of the famous metallurgical industry at Le Creusot, it had been readily purchased, and developed, into 'Les Usines Schneider'. No wonder then, by 1915, this industry had become a major armaments factory for the French. Ming was taken aback as he was shown to his workstation. His guys were not the first Chinese to arrive. His cohorts had not expected this, although they had been warned, by their interpreter, that this was to be a temporary posting anyway. Ming felt a rush of pride to see his countrymen already hard at it, seemingly well conversant with the skill required for this work. He was overjoyed to hear their voices, the banter in his dialect, it made him feel an instant sense of belonging. What proved less joyful, however, was seeing where he was to be quartered.

Memories of those endless miles in the hull of cramped sea-vessels came racing back. Ming may have been thrilled to discover other Chinese already out here, but they, with other employees, had already taken most, if not all, of the allocated bunks. Feeling like an afterthought, Ming and his recruits were led to a tiny floor space, and thrown some rough blankets. This was where they were destined to bed-down, so they felt more than thankful to be reminded they would not have to endure these inadequate conditions for very long on this provisional enterprise.

Ming purposefully shut away his consternation in his determination to learn his new trade. He sensed this would serve him best whilst he was there. This was such an impressive working environment. Everything the Chinese authorities had preached would be out here for labourers like Ming, proved to be true here, so at least this representation had been justified. His nation's agenda, heading west, was to use these Chinese men as scouts, to return with commercial wisdom. Feeling a sense of belonging, learning in a new environment, gave Ming heart. He decided to immerse himself in his work. He had no perception what an 'Arsenal' might actually be, but having been told this was where he would next be heading, he assumed it would mean progression now that he had been initiated. He certainly hoped so. He also prayed that his next base might indulge him with a proper bed and with less oversubscribed facilities. That would surely be heartening too. Ming worried more about this than any journey he was now to face on the roads of France. He longed for humane treatment and a sense of worth.

8 YUN – SHANDONG PROVINCE
Yantai, China

Outskirts of a small township – late 1916

Yun took a break outside, in the yard of his father's machinery depot. It was as much a moment to grab a minute's respite away from his father, as it was to down some food and drink, in peace.

It was then that Yun remembered to check on his little injured bird. He had made a splint for its broken wing, a skill he had learned some years back. He delved deep within his inside pocket to retrieve it.

'It's ok my little friend, don't flutter so, It's only me trying to get you some fresh air and nourishment.'

He didn't need to whisper to avoid scaring the bird. It was perfectly tame, as were all Yun's birds once they were in his care. He just kept his voice low when with his patients, lest some malevolent toerag got wind of his vocation and found a way to play some spiteful trick on him. Yun trusted no one when it came to caring for his birds, not wishing to gift anyone the chance to rib him about his eccentricities.

For a stocky, forthright, twenty-six-year-old man, Yun could be surprisingly gentle. He had built up a formidable strength in his hands from his trade, but a fierce grip wasn't always the answer to every problem. Yun had learned this vital lesson for himself. Challenges of any kind so often demanded thoughtful strength, rather than brute force. There could be no better example than seeing Yun feeding his birds. His only regret was how gnarled and unsightly his hands had become. Wrenched from the hazards of unguarded machine assemblies, the ugly joints in his thumbs might make him appear a clumsy farm worker, which he would hate. He was proud of his status in his father's industry, and also his adept skill with his latest rescued bird.

Once he had reassured his dependant that all was well, that the sudden calm was genuine, he opened his curled palm to prompt his bird to struggle up onto his index finger. It then stared towards him. Yun then offered it seed, trapped between his lips, until his eager little friend lovingly pecked away.

What a contrast to the industry grinding away within. He could hardly find the resolve to resume his duties. He took one last glance at the appeased little bird, then returned it, with one hand, back into the sanctuary of his inside tunic pocket. 'See you later my pretty patient, sleep tight until next time.' It snuggled down tight.

Work was frenetic. Geared to be that way by Yun's tyrant father, wanting ever more from his men, yet Yun wasn't intimidated. As the eldest of four boys, he may have been an obvious target for a show of discipline at home, setting an example to the youngsters, but there was none of that here. At work, Yun could chance his luck, away from his siblings, he could take liberties here, and he was adept enough to get away with it.

His constant sport was to covertly mock his father to amuse the other men. He did it partly as a mischievous act of defiance, but also to lighten the day for his fellow workers, who he felt suffered under his father's brutish oppression too often. On a whim, Yun might swagger past the others, tutting, re-enacting his father's irascibility, wagging his finger, then deliberately colliding with a workbench with a thud. With his father still oblivious, the men chuckled in nervous amusement, but with a meek conviction. The works' foreman had a quick word:

'It's all very well for you, Yun, you'll inherit the business, but we need to keep our jobs, so we have to fall in line.'

Having got wind of his father's plan to go on one of his mysterious trips out, on foot, into town, Yun decided to follow him. It proved a fair distance to walk, and Yun had to keep his wits about him to avoid being seen.

Yun had to take an unscheduled break, but with his father also absent, he could take the risk not to be dobbed in. It was worth it in any case. Yun had to quell his own suspicions, establish for certain whether his instincts about his father were justified. He just knew, in his gut, that his father was getting up to no good on these escapades, but he needed some proof. Whatever it was, it had to offer some allure. His father was so utterly committed to his precious depot.

Yun needn't have worried about being spotted by his father. He never once turned around, so committed to his bold strut, maintaining his pace. Yun was pleasantly surprised by his father's stamina and began struggling to keep up. His father's momentum was partly aided by not being distracted.

He didn't falter to speak to anyone, or go on any other errands, en route. Yun shadowed his movements; swerving, ducking, diving through crowds, by-passing hold ups.

For a moment he lost him as he disappeared beyond an upturned wagon. The owner, now in his way, salvaging his spilled goods, sparked panic in Yun, until his attention was drawn to a discreetly sheltered, wooden building, where some smart, rather distinctive looking men, had begun filing through the entrance as though ending a break outside. Yun approached the building, gingerly, to peer through the shutters. It was an opium den and his father was inside.

Yun didn't begrudge his father a break, some respite from the pressures of his business. He worked hard, ruthlessly so, and he expected every man in his employ to do the same. Yun was relieved at that moment to find his father had not been visiting a 'girly house' under their noses. He would have hated that betrayal, feared for his mother's reaction too. It was more to do with his father's ridiculous obsession with social climbing, an embarrassment to Yun, a falsehood.

Yun's father was of humble origins which was obvious to everyone from the way he spoke, the way he conducted himself. His worst trait was his blatant pandering to men way above his social class. He was just too uncouth to carry it off, too untutored in the rules of etiquette, debating skills, to kid anyone he belonged. Blissfully ignorant that he just did not fit in, he simply blundered on regardless. To Yun and, no doubt, to those his father mixed with, he just looked a fool.

Still spying, Yun slipped, straining to see, and as the shutter clattered, some heads turned in his direction, including his father's, but Yun had ducked down. He sloped away, and nimbly vanished just in time.

That should have been that, but Yun still harboured an unresolved disquiet. His father was deceiving his family and his friends, with his opium visitations, but that really was no big deal. Yun was sure there was more to it, particularly with his father so hell-bent on impressing those he had forced himself upon. It surely wouldn't have stopped there, he was certain. With this conundrum swirling around in Yun's head, he unwittingly found himself drawn to his mother for her wise counsel:

'I just can't listen to all this, my darling eldest, I really can't,' she reacted, bitterly. 'You've put me in such an awkward position. How could you think that I could condone you spying on your father on his time on his own, you've made me very cross.'

Of course, she was right, and Yun accepted that in an instant. He should have kept it all to himself. What was he thinking? If his mother didn't, herself, harbour suspicions about his father's activities, then why should Yun corrupt her faith in him? Who was he to stir up trouble when he adored his mother and would never do anything to hurt her? It was just that she was his confidant, his best friend, and although he thought he could tell her anything, that just couldn't include confessing his mistrust for his father, nor saying anything to undermine his father's authority. Yun's mother was the only person he could openly talk to, and she knew that, but here he was venturing into fragile territory, so he hurriedly changed tack:

'I do love you mother, especially when you sound so serious,' she was his captive when he teased her, she let slip a grin.

'Look mother, here's how a no-good Chinaman tries to

walk properly when he's off his head,' at which he broke into a ridiculous stagger, pretending to upend a bottle to his lips, then stumbled over his own feet to the floor. She was an addict to his humour and he knew it. She giggled until her eyes streamed, hardly able to catch her breath. 'Stop it, Yun, I beg you, I can hardly breathe…'

Yun hugged her, then pecked her on the forehead. She was putty in his hands. He was as adoring of her as she was of him, but they couldn't always see eye to eye. His beef was, historically, that it was she who had money, not his father. He may have done well with the business, but Yun's mother had come to the marriage with money. She was of sound stock, but as tradition dictated, her dowry had been sunk into her husband's livelihood, most of it at least, but she had been shrewd enough to hold some back, just in case. One thing she had not been burdened with, was foot-binding. That was thanks to her parents' foresight; she put that down to their shrewdness. As much as she worried privately about her husband's obsessive secrecy regarding the business, she had her own private money and physical durability in reserve. She just never knew when she might need to steer the ship, so she would be ready, if and when that happened. No wonder then that she had always supported Yun honing his skills at the depot, yet making certain he had other strings to his bow.

The demands of his job had kept Yun insanely busy. He suspected his father had deliberately organised it that way, if only to frustrate Yun's efforts to pursue his language studies with the missionaries, which involved significant periods of absence from work. What it had meant, was that Yun had been denied the time to keep tabs on his father whenever he crept away. It hadn't starved Yun's fertile mind from speculating though. Something he had unearthed about those men and their opium societies, was that these were invariably linked to gambling. Betting was a Chinese 'disease', endemic, but Yun learned that those with a higher status, or those that aspired to it, were prone to rather more ambitious wagers. This was an accepted symbol of status, in itself, and so opium smoking and gambling became intertwined. So, Yun may be right?

It became inevitable that Yun's father ultimately suffered a catastrophic loss. He had almost put the business on the line, in a last-ditch act to recoup a run of losses. He had been so certain he would win, so sure he would prevail and be acclaimed for his courage. Instead, he hit the buffers, worse than any collision, and his fatal miscalculation was to change everything.

He had lost before, as had many, but nothing like this. In his desolation, he sought solace in his opium parlour, determined to show a brave face, falsify the truth. But things were to get a great deal worse. The word had spread like wildfire. He had fallen prey to a perfidious society, one he had so staunchly believed he was a part of. He soon discovered that he was not.

To his astonishment, he was refused credit for the first time in his life. Then he was handed his final supply of opium, told that this was 'his last', and that he was not to darken their doors again. Somehow, they seemed pleased to see the back of him. He hurled his abuse at them through the slammed door: 'Damn you all, curse you dogs to your graves, all of you!' He had finally broken from deference, but all too late.

Taking to the side streets, away from anyone that might recognise him, someone sought his company but he had failed to hear their footfall. He had been tailed, and now in the obscurity of a gloomy alleyway, they pinned him by his neck, to the wall. He had seen mobsters before, from a distance, but close up these thugs made his skin crawl. As the leader made 'his client's' demands for cash clear, he had to live by his wits. Then he remembered the British recruitment posters about sending young men abroad, and their offer of generous wages sent home to their families left behind. He pleaded, 'I have a foolproof plan for payment,' now gasping for air, 'I know the British Government will pay.'

Swayed by his audacious claim, and his apparent desperation to choke out a plausible solution, they released their grip on his throat. He spelled out his scheme as convincingly as he could. Still thinking on his feet, to save himself and his business, he assured them that his eldest, Yun, was more than eligible, and that the British recruiters down at the docks were offering the bulk of each man's wages, earned abroad, by direct regular payments to the head of each family. He claimed he had already made enquiries and had garnered some influence. They strode away.

The family were seated, ready for dinner, awaiting Yun's father until in he burst. Clearly under the influence, he failed to disguise it as he stumbled towards his place at the head of the table. Grim-faced, bedraggled, he could scarcely raise his glass to his lips. You could have cut the atmosphere with a knife. Everyone remained silent as Yun's mother began serving up the food. With typical poise, she tried to break the tension with some random gossip about their friends, how their lives had been that week and what their children had been up to… that was until Yun's father broke into a choleric rant:

'Damned business, how can an honest working man hope to make a living, pay off his debts, when the cost of everything's gone through the roof!' A strand of spittle broke loose from his lips and the boys grimaced. 'Our wretched Republic's gone to the dogs, and we'll be next! No, I'LL be next!'

Yun might have held his tongue, as he knew he should, but his father's conduct was an abomination and so he felt for his mother. He knew nothing of the guilt eating away inside his father's head. Seeing his mother's tortured face, as she pleaded for him to hold back, he tried, but only until the next tirade erupted, and this one was directed at him:

'… and you're no use either,' he barked, scowling at Yun. 'Ya mother's filled your head with useless stuff about education, taken you away from real work to go to those ridiculous missionaries; what the hell's the use of English and French in Shandong for hell's sake? Ya might as well dig the earth for the money that lot's gonna earn you, mark my words.' He didn't draw breath or sense the indignation, the rage, that was, by now, welling up insatiably inside Yun:

'It's all your mother's fault, she's the one that thinks working for me's beneath ya, well I can give it to you straight; you need to work hard to make your mark in the world, couldn't agree more, but it ain't gonna be through any soppy schooling, that's a fact.'

With his mother's gesticulations, pleading with Yun not to react, Yun held, falsely calm, but just could not resist striking back with a taunt, 'Oh, you're so right, isn't he mother? But thank goodness those 'soppy' missionaries don't disgrace themselves when they're telling us about the world and how it should be…' But before he could add any further fuel to the fire, his father exploded.

The boys rushed towards their mother as the crockery began to fly. Yun just sat there, hoping not to get struck. Only when his father had finally run out of things to throw, and he had stormed out of the house, did Yun react. Yelling expletives about his father, words his mother had never ever in her life heard from Yun, let alone directed at his father. He burst into a choking fit of tears and rushed away to his room. The boys remained glued to their mother, all three sobbing, uncontrollably.

Yun's mother had so wanted to weep too, but she found she could not. Something, fundamental, changed deep within her that day.

9 THE SOMME OFFENSIVE
July – November 1916

The True Horrors of WWI

A mischief of rats had found strength in numbers, succour also from the newly abandoned rations of the British troops. Here, in the trenches, war had become the ultimate 'leveller'. A trench proved a snare into which rats would inevitably tumble, or humans would find themselves 'tethered', struggling too for their existence. Incarcerated together, this is where endangered, war-blooded lives, would either survive or perish. Right now, in this particular trench, the rats had got the upper hand.

When any living being finds itself trapped between two cliff faces of a trench, a ready meal becomes currency. Somehow, in barely a minute, the sound of feasting rodents, massing over edible spoils, had triggered a furore. Like a rallying call to a distant mob, a frenzied mass of rats had appeared, from nowhere, and were now scrapping over an open tin of Fray Bentos, sticky with jelly, and the burst remains of a Huntley and Palmer biscuit pack.

The mischief scattered as a revolver round struck one rat through the head. The echo clattered away down the curve of the trench run. A bunch of bedraggled squaddies, trudging back to the spot, cursed how these 'bleeding rats' had butchered the grub they had hurriedly abandoned. The rats had, somehow, upturned the brazier, spilled over their provisions, and gorged the lot.

A soldier went to raise his revolver again, then realised that this creature, now struggling in the muck, was just a toad. The trench had sucked in every living thing, helplessly tumbling, like spiders, into a huge bathtub. Once inside, existence soon pares back to nothing more than swamp-life, submerged in a morass of mud deep below an elusive, narrow, grey skyline. Here, for these hapless creatures, the entrenchment becomes a prison. For their human counterparts, captivity too, but for them a welcome hideaway from 'singing' bullets, whistling shells and the pounding of maelstrom ordnance.

'George took one in the face, right beside me, as he went over,' one guy ranted, now running his dirty thumbnail along the seam of his trousers, for lice. This unit was so young. The last uniforms they had worn were school issue.

'Both Harry and Tommy too mate, got torn up trying to haul some injured bugger to safety,' cursed another, sobbing.

A siren went off, jarring their nerves, testing the resolve of these already beleaguered troops; and then that dreaded call, bawled out from some distant Sergeant, '...Gas! For Christ's sake, gas! Boys, get ya masks on and leg it...'

Before the sloshing boots of the last troop to scarper had finally gone silent, the rats were back, to finish their meal.

On the first day alone, 20,000 British troops had perished. Crippling losses had afflicted The Allies during these first two years of conflict, but nothing of this magnitude. The Somme had forged links of this ghastly war into one mighty, choking chain, and the headline news had become shocking. Obsessing about the decimation of British troops, rumours were now gaining traction that the Allies may, unthinkably, be losing the war. How were they going to replenish their fallen?

Debates in Parliament were growing ever fractious. Churchill seemed alone in his insistence that China held the key.

Still smarting from his tarnished reputation from the disastrous Dardanelles Campaign, young Winston had a point to prove. Never blaming himself for the scorn that had been harshly poured upon him for this debacle, Churchill was on a mission. Blindly arrogant, or self-assured in extremis, it mattered not. He may have sat back, sullenly submitting to Lloyd George's reticence, but Churchill was neither swayed by this politician's prejudice against non-colonial support, nor intimidated by the narrow-minded Unions who had long lobbied against outside paid help. He was immovable; Britain and their brave fighting men came first:

'We will win this damned war, if it means booting the backside of every feeble idiot that gets in the way of blindingly obvious solutions!'

With cigar ash flaking to the floor, his fist thumping, his finger wagging accusingly, Churchill wasn't letting up, not this time. In retreat, in the sanctuary of his private chambers, Lloyd George had sunk his head into his hands. He could stand Churchill's tirades no longer, and he would just have to soak up the Trade Union's hostility, survive the wrath of Parliament for his capitulation once they had got wind of his decision; for capitulation is what he had finally submitted to, and that would be clear to everyone. Churchill, a true military man, had won through; resentment would be rife.

Yet might some form of disguise be found? Might Lloyd George yet be gifted a covert way of ducking these lines of fire?

Way behind France with their decision, Britain struck a deal, privately, for Chinese labour. They knew France's recruitment had faltered. It had certainly got off to a hesitant start. Britain was determined to do better by learning from French failings. At the very least, Britain must do that. Liang's masterstroke, for the French, had been the adoption of The Huimin Company as a commercial façade for Chinese recruitment. Inevitably this now paved the way for a similar strategy for Britain, and they were far better placed to make this work. Armed with their territorial advantage, blessed with their naval supremacy, Weihai docks was theirs to use, and it swiftly became the obvious candidate for the first, British, recruitment centre.

The Chinese enrolled in vast, ever-increasing numbers. Churchill's persistence had paid off; Lloyd George may have continued to nurse his wounded pride, but he had found cover.

Dressed up depictions of an awaiting, glamorous voyage for the Chinese, issued from other shores, whilst Britain's own propaganda was hurriedly despatched. Recruitment films were shown repeatedly to reach rural, illiterate workers. The British deliberately targeted labour from the Shandong region. A masterstroke of sorts. The men from here were chosen for their known strength and resilience, and it suited Britain's purposes that most would remain blissfully ill-informed, shielded from the now raging protestations elsewhere. These men could not have guessed how testing their journeys were about to be, how far away their destination, how challenging the climate, nor how perilously close-by the theatre of war. As the women in their lives waved their tearful goodbyes, they had no idea either.

Chinese desperation for decent, paid work, was the dominant force for these sanguine men. Ironically, it was the mothers, the women, the stalwarts in their lives, they were the ones who would suffer the most from their absence, they who offered that crucial, telling, encouragement for them to go.

10 DARK CLOUDS GATHER OVER YUN

Back at their home, it had seemed like the end of any other, normal, working day, except for Yun's father's dark mood.

They had all become used to his grim demeanour. Since that tumultuous outburst, when half the kitchen had got hurled about, very few words had passed between him and Yun. That was probably for the best, but it had made their time together at work extremely tense, and the men had felt it too. For now, only the boys were chatting together, discreetly, as they all tucked into their evening meal.

Something drew up, with a clatter, outside the house. Curiously, Yun's father stayed put, his head, oddly, lowering. As the sound of heavy feet made their way towards their door, Yun gazed in the direction of his mother. She shrugged, still eating, but when the loudest 'thud' on the door shook the room, Yun jumped up to deal with it.

'Are you the eldest?' the man demanded, as Yun opened the door.

'I am, but why are you asking?' Yun replied suspiciously, quickly glancing back, questioningly, at his mother, but she knew no more than him. Within seconds the man had gestured to the others hovering behind him, and they were all over Yun. He had no chance to think, not now that his arms were being held fast behind his back, and he was being bullied towards the door.

'What the hell's going on, you monsters?' Yun wailed, outraged at being manhandled by a bunch of thugs in his own home. With his father seemingly rooted to his chair, not even raising his head to make eye contact with these intruders, Yun suddenly grasped the situation, alarming though it was. This visit was by The Triad, feared by every Chinese soul.

'You're despicable father! How high and mighty do you feel now?' he yelled bitterly. The boys now huddled, snivelling, in their mother's arms. Still his father said nothing, did nothing, his head set downwards. He knew, all too well, why the mob had shown up. He knew their ghastly faces, their brutal purpose. Yun had managed to clutch the door jamb, just gaining a precious moment to scream some sharp insults in his father's direction, making certain the family knew what he had suspected all along:

'So, they've finally caught up with you, have they, the bleeding mob! Your smoking and gambling have brought the business to its knees, and they want blood, my blood!' As Yun spat out these words, he fell silent, let go his grip, with a sudden realisation that, indeed, the mob had come for him and not his father. So how the hell was 'seizing' him going to be an 'asset' that might save his father's skin?

The family were inconsolable. Unbeknown to Yun, his father was now weeping like a child, slumped over the kitchen table. 'Oh my God, I'm never going to see my eldest son again…' he sobbed. 'What have I done?'

The mob then wrestled Yun towards their vehicle, struggling to bind his hands along the way, but he erupted into a rage. As Yun attempted to launch his fists at them, he was swiftly overwhelmed. Beaten and kicked to the ground his tirade evaporated. Bundled away for transport, grimacing with pain, Yun had no illusions. He was just another hapless mug, entangled by the debts of another who had failed to pay up. He hadn't wanted to accept it, but he now knew full well, and the reality of it screamed in his head, 'Curse it, for hell's sake!' There and then, Yun resolved never to return.

With not one of his questions being answered en route, not even a dismissive 'grunt' being offered, Yun sat tight, deep in thought, biding his time. As a well-educated, well-read Chinese man, Yun stood out for his maturity. He had heard all about the British drive for manpower; he had read the posters that had been going up everywhere, like an epidemic. He had been suspicious, naturally enough, but with the security of work at home, his future in his father's depot, he hadn't had to agonise any further about any of this, or so he thought! It was only since he had rumbled his father, found out for sure that his habits might be crippling the business, that he had begun to worry about himself at all.

Yun was well-travelled. He knew the route well towards the British base at Weihai docks, but this wasn't where he was currently heading. The thugs may not be communicating with him, but they made no attempt to shield him from their own banter to each other. Under no illusion that he had been press-ganged for recruitment, he quickly gathered his captors had grossly miscalculated by giving Yun such a beating. He was now too injured to pass the stringent British entry medicals! With no other choice, and at a location Yun didn't know at all, he was thrust into a cage until 'deemed fit for presentation'. With nothing more than a bleak offering of a bowl of rice and hot water each morning, time dragged by agonisingly.

'So now I'm in a human cage for a prison!' Yun lamented, 'even a bird wouldn't sing for its food stuck behind these bars.'

With not a soul to console him, Yun dug deep to stay sane.

Yun was far from feeling fully recovered when the day arrived for him to be moved on. This said, he didn't complain or attempt to resist. At least now he recognised the journey, the direction they were taking, or so he hoped. At last, there might now be some prospect of humane treatment, and proper communication.

As they arrived at the British base, Yun was then frog-marched towards the recruitment yard flanked by two thugs. It would seem these brutes needed to make certain, before they left Yun there, that he would be accepted. More to the point, that his British wages were secure too. Yun was apprehensive, but also intrigued. How had his father bargained him into this with his creditors? The British officers now dealing with Yun, seemed uncannily familiar with what was going on, and they were processing his papers with purpose.

In spite of his fluency, Yun hardly bothered to read what he was now being asked to sign. He seemed to salvage calmness by just accepting his plight. Marking time, seeing how events might now unfold, seemed wise. Once he had signed, the mob withdrew. Yun didn't care to turn around to see them go.

He dismissed the thought of them, his father's ugly role in it all, condemning the lot of them to the very back of his mind.

Yun had quickly gleaned from the assurances the recruitment officer had given to the mob – his father's creditors – that the lion's share of his future British wages would indeed be remitted back to China. Needless to say, the creditors had already put in place diversion arrangements that would ensure these wages would go to them to pay off Yun's father's business debts. All that Yun had salvaged, his sole 'inheritance', were his language skills, and these had been gifted to him solely by his mother. It was her wisdom, her foresight, that must protect him now, and he thanked her from his heart for standing so steadfastly by him. Her love, and that of his little brothers clinging to her, would remain his only memory of home, the last vestige from that previous existence which would echo in his mind.

To any other recruit, by now terrified for their lives, the dreaded 'sausage factory' would have been a final, fatal, blow. Not so for Yun. He had heard all about it; the humiliating stripping off of clothes, the scrubbing and shaving, the 'dog tags' being clamped to their wrists, so he communicated with the officers conducting the procedure. (Yun was not to know that his French-recruited comrades had suffered the less uncomfortable neck-bound IDs). You can imagine their surprise when Yun was able to engage in some banter during an, otherwise, demeaning process. Making light of it, he stood out a mile. As he had hoped, this also singled him out for 'mentions in dispatches', and he was quickly separated away from the other, regular recruits, once the enrolment process had been concluded. He tested his humour:

'Sir, I guess these numbered wrist tags are there to help you find our owners if we get lost foraging for food on board?'

The Lieutenant taking down Yun's details looked up at him in astonishment, chuckled, then nodded to a fellow officer as though to 'endorse' his findings. The officer asked Yun to 'stay put' as he then wandered off to locate some fresh paperwork. He promptly returned, announcing he had a 'more appropriate' contract for Yun to check through and sign. He didn't insult Yun's intelligence by bullying him to sign immediately, as was the norm, but Yun read it quickly enough. Not too swiftly to notice, and ignorant of the French five-year commitment, this was a three-year agreement and with harsh terms. He was to be subject to military law, like the troops, but for him he was to be given superior duties as an Interpreter, with better quarters. Yun smiled, feeling he had already earned himself a better existence in France, but he grimaced to see, in black and white, just as it had been in the first document, that 90 per cent of his pay would be remitted 'home', to China, and he knew who would get that!

The Lieutenant had mumbled, during the signing process, that had Yun been selected for Interpreter duties from the outset, they would have dispensed with the imposition of a wrist band. Yun shrugged.

It had helped that Yun was able to exchange words with the Brits when he needed to, but also to engage with fellow labourers, in their dialect, as they struggled past him. This flexibility wasn't lost on those that mattered, but he already had his 'promotion' papers, and he had every intention of using his apparent privileges whenever he could. Nonetheless, he shared his comrades' discomfort, and their fear, for what might yet confront them. He may have got the upper hand when compared to the other recruits, but he too had never been to sea, nor travelled any great distance beyond his home in China.

He was asked to wait by the ship's bridge, whilst some other formalities were being finalised. Yun started fiddling with his wrist band. He was bemused by the long ID number. He smirked at the thought of ever remembering it off-by-heart. He also wondered if he could stand this blatant branding for the next three years. He rather doubted that he could.

He was watching the others boarding, in a long line. Like him, they looked rather smart in their new kit, some, optimistically, pushing barrows full of belongings, but, unlike him, they were not smiling, far from it. It made him reflect how lucky he was, until he overheard two officers chatting:

'Poor, naïve devils. If the war doesn't kill them, the journey to get there probably will!' Yun looked on, aghast, but he swiftly disguised his eavesdropping, turned his head away. A sharp stab of fear struck Yun in the chest. It was the worst he had felt since he had been forced away from his home by the mob. How bitter he now felt as his hatred for his father burned away inside him.

He was beckoned to board ship, but not before posing briefly with the final group, in front of a camera set on a stand. He could see that the gentleman in charge of the equipment was an officer of some description, but having removed his cap to operate the camera, he betrayed a greater age than the others. There was also something less officious, less commanding, in his manner.

11 THE TANK DEPOT AT ERIN

Northern France, 1917

He had been irascible before, but it was becoming almost part of General Alan Thompson's personality. His men had got used to him, learned how to keep their distance when the word was that he was 'on one'.

At least the General had just announced some heartening news; well, that was the way the General saw it.

'I know The Somme's been a bloody nightmare, leaving us ridiculously short of good men to tend these tanks.' His face had flushed up, as it usually did, whenever he was suppressing his frustration. He twiddled his moustache and continued, 'But the news is, managed to get some foreign recruits, skilled technicians to help out, quite a number of them, been told they know their nuts from their washers!', a rare joke from the General.

His men, of course, exaggerated their appreciation. Yet the announcement caused more disquiet than they would ever let on. 'More bloody foreigners!' one tank guy had muttered. 'What the hell would they be doing with our tanks? They'd better know a bit more than twiddling a screw, or holding a mallet.'

The General strode briskly out of the depot. He was never one for Q & A's, wouldn't think to grant that opportunity. So, the men at the depot were left to gossip among themselves. With absolutely no experience of skilled foreign technicians anyway, they could only speculate that the 'powers that be', and General Alan Thompson in particular, knew what the hell they were doing. If this was pure desperation, with British skills for these demanding tanks now almost extinct, the men's reactions must soon take a turn for the worst. For now, they were prepared to 'wait and see'.

The trench contingents were not so wet behind the ears when it came to foreign recruits working alongside them. Granted, colonials were the norm, and the Tommies had found themselves communicating with them. They were a known quantity. Most understood where they came from, and why, and they had been briefed on how to tackle them.

The going had become particularly tough working the trenches. Like the tank depot guys, men in their thousands had been moved forward to take on front line duties, leaving depleted numbers to dig and maintain the channels. In a particular trench, the dreaded order to drive forward, en masse, had been cabled and the men, dishevelled and miserable, were just resigned to joining the front to face their probable ends. Stacking their tools against the dugouts, the clang of steel set nerves on edge. Entrenching spades, pick-spikes and mattocks, all got slung onto dedicated storage-stacks, as the men prepared to relocate forward to meet their fate.

The shock revelation as to who the new recruits were was palpable as the first Chinese contingents arrived, in long lines, and the British CLC sergeant attempted his pidgin Mandarin. It was a joke, and the men, the new arrivals,

Once the CLC had got stuck in, applied themselves to their work, they proved every bit as effective as their British, and their colonial counterparts

just frowned towards each other, bemused. The British were desperately short of interpreters, particularly those conversant with the different dialects. Comical sign language had been tried and had failed. In spite of the horrors of their journeys to reach France, the stench from the open latrines here even made the Chinese wince, not to mention the spectre of uncleared body parts. Persistent inclement weather, had set them afloat on the congealed muck, making them impossible to clear.

Once The Chinese Labour Corps, The CLC (as these Chinese recruited by Britain had come to be known), had got stuck in, applied themselves to their work, they proved every bit as effective as their British, and their colonial counterparts. In the absence of any praise, the CLC were not to know this, but they seemed to thrive on hard work. Perhaps that was just from the relief of getting to France in one piece! Many didn't make it. More likely, the work ethic of these resilient, and brave, men set them apart from any visible working groups.

General Thompson might well pray that the Chinese men he was destined to inherit at the tank depot – the new arrivals – would indeed prove to be every bit the equal of each trained Tommy they were replacing.

12 YUN'S ORDEAL FOR BRITAIN

March/April 1917

Part 1

Yun's Rail Transportation Across Canada

Britain may have long enjoyed their superiority of the seas, but the ever-present German threat lurking in deep waters, had proved a constant menace. The sinking of the *Athos* was devastating, but a tragedy of this magnitude had been a long time coming, with political heads buried in the sand. The reaction to the sinking was the more extreme for that, and the alternative options a real conundrum.

To thwart Germany's ruthless ambitions, with their successful attack on the *Athos* bolstering their ego, Britain had a dramatically different plan to try and prosecute. At a top-secret summit in Vancouver, with the Canadian Chief Censor, Col. Ernest Chambers, Britain negotiated a dedicated train route traversing the entire width of the country. A dominion ally, Canada may be, but here they were in the driving seat, and this was no 'soft' agreement. Anything but. Canada had already met their wartime duties as allies.

Never admitting to the importance for Britain, nor the urgency of completing their Chinese labourers' transportation, the fate of this daring enterprise was entirely in Canadian hands. Canada was Britain's 'get out of jail' card, and the edges of that card were soon to suffer wear and tear to get this deal over the line.

Canada had their own legitimate concerns. This wasn't just political brinkmanship. Their historic use, their established engagement of Chinese Coolies had, inevitably, resulted in a significant settlement of Chinese communities in Canada, and they did not want this latest concession to swell those ranks. As ever, when immigrant labour is needed, the appropriate accommodation is put in place, but when that need vanishes, the host country is often left with a foreign population they never really wanted but cannot easily remove. Again, the protective cloak of secrecy was to be the facility that would free-up the participants to proceed.

Canada was the mid-way point for Britain, the obvious awaiting bridge for them to cross. They knew they must, somehow, reach those safer waters on the other side of Canada and bring their recruits ever nearer to France. If successful, there was absolutely nothing the Germans could do about it, if they heard about it at all. For Canada, their past with the Chinese aside, a diaspora of any alien population across the entire country was unprecedented, but this was exactly the solution Britain was demanding from them.

When a telegraphed message safely arrived from the Canadian Prime Minister, Robert Borden, confirming his agreement, Ernest Chambers was free to finalise a deal with Britain, but this would be on harsh terms. In a rare act of authoritarianism, The War Measures Act had already been passed, which enabled Canada to 'gag' the press, 'muzzle'

The RMS *Empress of Russia*

them completely, whenever they chose, and they were about to do precisely that. There was to be outright censorship, on the back of wartime necessity. Britain's unwanted Chinese 'cargo' must remain securely on board for the duration of the 4,000-mile journey. With the press outlawed, the Chinese arrivals prevented from fraternising with Canada's Chinese inhabitants, this was an embargo.

As Yun and his bedraggled comrades disembarked from their fateful ship, *The Empress of Russia*, an ocean liner requisitioned twice by the British Admiralty during WWI, they could never have imagined, in their worst nightmares, that their greatest test of endurance was, in fact, yet to come. Already familiar with their awaiting medicals, the brutality of them, these seemed now like benign initiations. That dreadful loss of dignity they had loathed, reactions to the intrusiveness had gone. At least the compound they were next herded into was in the open air. Crammed though it was, they could see about them, and they just had to hope that wait for onward transportation would not be unduly protracted. The makeshift communal baths, laced with disinfectant, became a positive luxury, as was that feeling of security with their feet back on solid ground.

Yun overheard some Canadian officials. Apparently, even as foreigners in colonial hands, Yun's mob were not to be classed as 'immigrants', in any circumstances. Yun hadn't grasped the implications of this, not yet, in any case. He had heard them mention that no 'head tax' would be levied against Britain, so long as every single Chinese '…was kept locked in his "little prison" until he fell out the other end!'

They were still able to peer through the open window sections. It wasn't to last

As the Chinese were marched along the platform to the designated carriages of their awaiting train, everyone, to a man, must have felt a tinge of excitement at the prospect of a rail expedition, but Yun knew better. He had overheard enough to realise there was rather more to this scheduled journey than just a train jolly. He was certainly not alone in noticing that every single window had been 'blacked out'. This wasn't obvious to those Chinese already on board, because they were still able to peer through the open window sections. It wasn't to last. Just long enough for, yet another, of those curiously posed photos to be taken, but from a discreet distance.

When Yun's turn came, he was horrified. Upwards of fifty men seemed destined for each carriage, including his – yet surely the maximum capacity should be closer to half that, and for a somewhat shorter trip? Yun panicked, but kept nimble on his feet. He had alone spotted the substantial open bolts to the outside of his carriage as he stepped inside, and the location of the latrine and cooking stove, so he turned away to secure his spot at the opposite end. He could not have been proved more shrewd. He quickly estimated that most benches would convert into four-berth communal bunks, but his was only a two-berth one and it was tucked away. He could see that his choice brought him close to a double-guards' position, where two were already hovering, but he sensed he might yet take advantage of that in the fullness of time. Better to have a further loss of privacy than have to endure the stench of the latrine and any cooking whiffs from the carriage stove. It all seemed so horribly toxic.

When the moment approached for the train to pull away, the true horror of what lay ahead became clear to Yun. Prompted by official orders bawled out from further down the platform, the heavy doors slammed shut and the iron bolts to each were drawn across outside. With the windows now shut fast, the resulting oppressiveness was the new reality.

The escalating 'huffing' of the engine, the sounding of the whistle, the screeching of steel wheels slipping on the rails, combined to send a pulse of fear through Yun that constricted his breathing. The erupting complaints within the car were futile. The once calm guards, two to each end, were suddenly in military mode, and they were not to be messed with. The wartime tenet: '...better to be dead than dying', rather found resonance for Yun as he slumped back heavily on his bench. Once it became clear that there was to be no outside exercise for the duration and with no space inside to 'swing a cat', the disquiet within festered. Yun wondered, privately, how long his comrades' indignation could be contained.

The nights could be unbearably cold across Canada. Unbeknown to the hapless train inhabitants, their journey would soon take them through a landscape smothered in heavy snow. Chaotic as they were, meal times, from the single carriage stove, at least maintained a tolerable temperature for the men. When the guards allowed it, the Chinese would keep the stove lit, even stoke it up, just to gain a few precious degrees to help everyone sleep. Huddled together provoked antagonisms, but, keeping warm, quickly became a priority. Yun's seemingly effortless ability to converse with the guards at his end of the car, was conspicuous. What could have instilled mistrust for Yun – his ability to understand and engage in English – wasn't viewed that way at all by the other men. Yun passed on their grievances, got their questions answered, and whilst most improvements to their lot simply weren't possible, they at least felt better for airing their complaints. The guards were quick to see the value in Yun. At the very least, the initial threat of altercations had been averted by Yun, certainly in his car, which granted everyone a degree of peace. It was a stressful enough ordeal without trouble.

Once Yun had fallen into an easy familiarity with the guards, he felt more able to feather his own nest. All that brusque officiousness of the guards subsided. Before too long, details about the journey, the conditions that lay ahead, all were let slip, but Yun was sensible enough to keep much of what he learned to himself. He certainly didn't let on to his guys, that a few cars down, the travelling officers were enjoying rather more exotic conditions, in 'tourist' class, with their own chefs and a diluted number of occupants and in far warmer conditions. One time, when the latrine froze over in Yun's car, even Yun feared his intervention might not be enough to quell a revolt. It was often touch and go.

Perhaps what ate away at Yun the most, the thing that upset him terribly, was that the first glimpse his comrades should have had of The West – the anticipated witnessing of a superior way of life – was to be 'blacked out' from view in a locked train. They truly had become a 'cargo of human freight' for Britain, and many felt completely betrayed. It didn't ease that sense of injustice to learn that they were 'valued freight' either. Yes, Yun had gleaned there was a contractual penalty imposed on any British contingent for the loss, in transit, of any Chinese worker, but that was hardly a vote of respect for human life.

Fate would have it, just as Yun had begun to agonise how

his comrades might be coping in more tightly packed carriages than his own, the train dramatically slowed to a standstill. Within moments, just as the men around him had broken into fractious rants about this unscheduled stop, their carriage door slung open and Yun's name was barked out.

The rush of air, his first ever sight of glistening snow, here in broad daylight through the open door, was a blessing. It certainly was for Yun, and he felt the more exhilarated by the bleakness of it as he stepped down from the train. The carriage door hurriedly slammed behind him as he hobbled along the low, white-strewn platform. His guard warned him that a 'scrawny CLC', already gaunt and withered from the ordeal of rail transportation, had given up the ghost and had 'damned well gone and died on them'.

It was having to exist in such close proximity to their dead comrade, propped-up and sheeted over, for several hours since he passed away, that had provoked the other men into a tinderbox of revulsion. Where they were now was the first available stop, and a Canadian transport truck had been wired to collect the poor fellow, as a matter of extreme urgency to 'quell a riot'. Until the truck arrived, Yun's orders were to simmer down the carriage mob before the guards were forced to raise their rifles. It took all Yun had to shout the odds at his people, whilst he himself suffered a sickness cramp in his stomach at the despicable situation these men were in.

Wrapped up in heavy jute sacking, a pair of guards bundled the body onto the platform and marched it away to a collection point. However, before they could resecure the carriage door, a naked CLC leaped out through the opening. Screaming like a banshee, a thing possessed, the desperate man made a dash from the train, through the deep snow, waving his arms above his head as he went. Two guards made chase, clumsily, but soon enough brought the poor fellow crashing to the ground. Yun's mind raced as he was ushered back to his carriage, wondering if the overwhelmed CLC, now returned to the relative warmth of the train, would survive his ordeal.

Yun had already witnessed the distressing deaths of several men back at the quarantine camps, where their ghastly journey across Canada had started, but those trials were well managed. The men lost, back there, had fallen to fever, or had conspicuously succumbed to sickness. They had been removed, swiftly, for hospitalisation. Trapped with a dead comrade, inescapably locked in with him like a spectre, was the worst of all nightmares for the already beleaguered Chinese.

This ghastly episode prompted Yun to question the adjacent guards in his carriage with ever-greater vigour as his journey resumed across Canada. Less inclined to hold back, and with Yun's reputation as a mediator enhanced, the guards disclosed many other instances of Yun's comrades' suffering. The most prescient symptoms of intolerable stress, it would seem, had been the alarming disintegration of the men's psychological state in the carriages. It haunted Yun to hear of the extent to which succumbing to madness had increasingly gripped the CLCs.

As non-combatants, hired to engage in support of a warring faction, they were destined to become unarmed allies in a shared war zone. Yun could but reflect, as the Canadian journey finally drew to a merciful close, and once they had been shipped to Britain, that the only assets he and his men might ever be able to resort to, were the ones they had owned themselves – their courage and their wits, their hands and their feet, and an unrivalled history of human civilisation.

Part 2

Liverpool Docks – en route to France

Yun reached Britain's shores expectant on a new life. Whatever his fellow Chinese may be feeling, he was full of optimism. He had survived the treachery of his father, the loss of his inheritance, the ultimate test of endurance at sea and by rail. All he had experienced, all he had to show for the thousands of miles that had been conquered to get here, was the traumatic memory of hostile seas, unstinting oppression, and a blacked-out train passage across Canada. As he journeyed from Liverpool to Folkestone, for once able to see, and enjoy, the passing scenery, breathe in the untainted fresh air, he was in seventh heaven.

Yun looked with fascination at the sheep and cattle grazing, in unison, all pointing steadfastly in the same obedient direction. He smiled to see the pacified expressions on the Chinese faces, their transformation, all gazing in wonder at England's fertile fields, shelving their way down to the sea.

As they arrived at the southern coast of England, heralded by those magnificent white cliffs, the men were still a protected secret cargo, but Yun couldn't care less. Whatever the British sensitivities were about the arrival of thousands of Chinese workers on their precious soil, whatever restrictions his guys may yet have to tolerate, Yun was just thrilled to have made it this far. He was at peace. There were some minor disturbances among the Chinese when they learned that they had still not arrived in France. Yun quickly put paid to that, and the British officers could not have been more impressed with him. Rather than try to explain to them, in words, exactly where they now were, Yun just gestured towards the glimmering French coastline beyond The Channel. It proved enough to have pointed the men towards France. The waters between these two countries hardly compared to those they had struggled across to reach the inspiring British Isles, and now their destination was visible to the naked eye.

In sharp contrast to that endless seascape they had been forced to endure, Southern England offered alluring beaches and the sight of massing white gulls rising on cushions of misty air. Their memory of intimidating, crashing waves, was now replaced by the assured hiss and drag of shallow waters on shingle.

The utter relief at reaching Folkestone, so tentatively close to their intended French destination, was swiftly countered by further Chinese losses. Yun was heartbroken to learn from a British officer, stationed in Kent, that one, particularly young, Chinese CLC had passed away, and that his older brother, in his desolate state, had to engrave the headstone of his grave. Yun weakened to sobbing in private, on hearing this rending account, yet this proved to be just a meagre sample, mortifying though it was, of the terrible attrition the excessive demands of their journey here, from China, had imposed upon them all.

Yun attended the funeral of no fewer than six Chinese souls at the Shorncliffe military cemetery whilst awaiting the final embarkation call to France from England's shores. As Yun averted his gaze, reflecting on the vast accumulation of his compatriots in their concealed, tented quarters along the Folkestone coastline, he found solace in the impressive

The savage manifestation, the true face of this war, unfolded

numbers of men that had survived. A fervent rush of pride gripped him as he looked on, wistfully. With not a single engagement to date in the war itself, and not a step yet made onto war-torn French soil to begin their assigned contracts, the CLC had, nonetheless, suffered the same rigour and privation of disease and death as their combatant British counterparts.

Part 3

La France!

They scarcely noticed the 'hop', by boat, across The Channel. Before they knew it, they were in trucks and on their way by road, towards their destination. Yun could hardly imagine there was a war going on here at all. He certainly couldn't yet hear or see one! Yun, in a small wagon, enjoyed chatting to the officers in the front, and they seemed bemused to hear a Chinese man speaking English at all, let alone as comfortably as Yun. Things were really looking up for him. He enjoyed the mischief of cracking jokes, in English, and seeing his guys looking on in admiration. They certainly felt in safe hands with Yun, so able to converse in a foreign tongue. It put them at ease, and the officers in charge. A great start.

As his journey into the heart of Northern France continued, Yun's impression of a benign war, one that had not yet shown its hand to him at all, swiftly altered. The savage manifestation, the true face of this war, unfolded. Individual houses, sometimes entire villages he passed, had been decimated. Unable to tell when these devastations occurred, Yun was consoled to see locals in amongst it all, determined to return their homes to good order, equally resolved to resume their previous lives. Yet he agonised for them, the families, the mothers left on their own to cope. These poor souls had made it through, but what were their lives worth now with their homes destroyed? With his mind racing, the stark impact of these horrors struck him in his heart, sent a shudder ripping through him.

It wasn't just buildings that had taken the brunt, the

countryside had too, and this was sickening. Charred remains of trees, entire woodlands, seemed more like the ugly backcloth to a violent play. With row after row of sterile spires, once thriving trees, images of utter desolation, it sank home, but the sight, up close, of wounded and mutilated troops distressed Yun the most. He looked on as the truck had slowed, to a crawl, to navigate around a long line of invalided soldiers. They were beyond struggling. It was painful, pitiful, to see. Many heads were bound-up in stained bandages, others were limping on sticks; their stooped postures betraying missing or smashed limbs. As Yun agonised over these dreadful scenes, haunted as he was by them, a sudden realisation struck him.

The officer driving them had announced their destination was approaching. So exactly how far away from active warfare were these Chinese workers destined to be? Pretty close, Yun feared. Yun reflected, nervously, that everything he had just seen along the roadside, was just a tiny part of the ugly reality that every active soldier had to face in this war. This was the tip of the iceberg.

Yun had only ever experienced the sight of injured birds, first hand, and that was the sum total of any suffering that he had ever witnessed. Yes, he had come to feel for his birds' agony, and he had devised their best possible rehabilitations, but what living thing could survive the wanton assaults that had struck here? No able-bodied bird, out here, could remain immune from these perils for long, Yun was certain of that now. At least, Yun pondered, his feathered friends had a choice, so long as they could still fly.

'What sane bird would ever decide to linger here, even if it had spent its entire life here until now? We humans do not deserve their dainty trills upon our ears whilst we mindlessly fight on and destroy their, and our, homes.'

As the transport truck began to slow, as it chugged down the main street of a small French village, Yun sat up to take it all in. They passed some barracks, saw groups of marching men pass by, then they took an abrupt, sharp turn. They were then heading up a steep gradient, through a mature woodland. Yun guessed, correctly, from this sudden deviation, that they were now close to their appointed quarters.

13 THE HAUNTED WOOD

Modern Day France – 1990s

Break-time at a village junior school in Northern France

Escaping through the rickety school fencing into the forbidden woods on the hill had become a regular enterprise for this motley bunch of wayward boys. They were perfectly concealed. Dense clumps of gorse, now in fervent yellow, obscured their secret world like a screen, and muffled their frenetic voices into the hillside.

Rampant among ancient trees, they were beside themselves with revelry. This was their own private war-zone and they loved it. Gripped by the thrill of rule-breaking, as only young boys could ever be, this was their adopted battle ground, their fantasy theatre of war, and they were in full flow acting out every famous conflict from WWI.

'Pierre, idiot!' Ahmed yelled in provocation.

'Come on big boy... try and take my rifle from me before I lance you through with my bayonet... ahhh,' he barked, more like a guard dog than a ferocious front-line soldier.

'*Pas de problème...*' Pierre responded bravely, taking on the challenge, plump though he was... but Ahmed had legged it, mischievously taunting Pierre to take chase, which he did like a clumsy hound after a wily fox. Now striding in his heavy awkwardness, with no chance whatever of getting close, he screamed, with his lungs burning from the effort, '*Ça c'est la guerre, ma guerre*, and I shall kill you Ahmed like any Moroccan immigrant deserves.'

'You couldn't spear a dead mouse fat boy,' mocked the ecstatic Ahmed now way up ahead, deliberately slowing to allow his pursuer to catch him up. Then he swerved adeptly at the very last moment to avoid a concealed hazard that only he knew was there. Along blundered the pathetic Pierre in hopeless pursuit, sweating like a pig, pumped up like a balloon, until his leading boot struck, full on, the old, perfectly concealed tree stump.

'Ahhh...' The pain was immediate, as was the thud that rang out as he collapsed in a heap clutching his foot.

Not quite expecting his prank to work out quite so perfectly, nor expecting such wild screams, Ahmed turned back wondering what he should do next. It was his trap, and now it was his problem. Pierre's yelps had become squeals, most unsoldier like, injured though he was.

'Now you've done it!' Robert thumped Ahmed's shoulder in frustration; 'Gone too far, *maudit marocain*, as usual, you just can't think like a real French soldier, can you. Now what the hell are we going to do, eh?'

'Lay off, how was I supposed to know the fat idiot would go and break his damn foot... it was just supposed to trip him up, that's all, bloody hell!' But Robert was inconsolable.

'What the heck got into you Ahmed... we're bound to get rumbled now; this racket could wake the dead!' Ahmed went ashen. 'You could have heard Pierre screaming in Paris!'

'Not my fault he's a clumsy oaf... and everyone knows about these stumps up here, just gotta keep your wits about you if you're chasing The Hun.' Ahmed knew only too well he was now caught in his own snare.

Everyone had heard the rumpus. How could they not? Pierre's protestations could only be the wailing of an injured wild boar or, more predictably, the screams of a child in agony. Any hope that the distant playground noise back at the school, would mask their own commotion way out here, was a forlorn one. The Head had been told and he was over the old fence in a second.

Spotting him coming, Robert sounded the alarm, louder than he intended: 'Quick guys, scarper, the Head's coming... run for it.' However, Ahmed, slow off the mark as always, froze, rooted to the spot. Stuck fast, the full might of the Head's grasp lifted him up on his toes.

'What's the damn ruckus about Ahmed, you scamps have alarmed the entire village... and what the hell are you doing up here anyway?' Mad as hell, now yanking Ahmed by the arm towards his wounded friend who was, by now, yelping even louder to his new audience.

'Strictly out of bounds you monkeys... *interdit*!!' The Head was fuming.

'Yes sir, sorry sir,' Ahmed snivelled as the Head let go his grip.

Pierre, disabled, caught in the act, stuttered out a pathetic explanation about being a soldier in the First War and how his parents, back home, would only get stressed out if they got to know he had been injured by The Hun. Kicking some old tree stump, rather than falling in the field of battle from an enemy shell, would be his ultimate humiliation, he explained.

'I am happy to hang on for my Court-martial, sir, I know I've got it coming, but my ankle, sir... I think it's busted,' he resumed his pained, over-egged agony. Meanwhile the Head despatched Ahmed back to the school with a flea in his ear, to sound the alarm bells and get the medics on site.

'Come on now Pierre, pull yourself together lad, you're a big boy now...' (The others giggled at the irony, the Head's inadvertent barb.)

'Let's get you propped up so that we can see exactly what you've done to yourself.'

'Oww, ouch... sir, that really hurts.' The Head sensed his chance to extract a confession, if he could just stop the injured 'soldier' sobbing his words.

'Now, think that's eased the pain a bit for you until the ambulance guys arrive.'

'But will it be a proper army medic, sir?'

Feeding on his fantasy, the Head stepped up the pressure, 'If you want a medic rather than the military police you'd best tell me what on earth you twits were doing up here, out of bounds, in the first place... serious act of trespass way up here in the woods, you couldn't be in more trouble young scamp.' The Head now cowered over him.

'Well, sir,' Pierre grimaced, on the brink of dobbing in his mates, 'the old beech carvings up here are our battalion HQ you see, sir, strictly schtum of course.' The Head offered a patronizing nod. 'It's where we do strategy, sir, and draw up battle plans...' The Head now raised his eyebrows, feigning admiration.

'Wouldn't come up here at night, sir, no way, haunted by war-ghosts; well known to those who know, that is, the walking dead we calls them... cos that's what they are... them carvings are messages from the tomb...'

The Head stripped down his large handkerchief and bound up Pierre's ankle, still pretending not to pay attention. He spurred him on. 'Carvings, eh my boy, so what sort of messages are they then?'

'See for yourself, sir,' he then yelled out – 'Julien, take sir to the haunted wood and show him the work of the devil,'

Doubting every word, but duty-bound to check the story out, the Head followed Julien up the slope. As they pushed through the undergrowth, Julien beckoned the Head towards a group of huge old beech trees, towering above them.

'Don't be scared, sir, the carved trees are just here, sir, and I don't think the ghosts are around at the moment... at least I can't see any...' starting to spook himself.

'These look like magnificent trees Julien, '*d'énormes hêtres*', but why the excitement?'

'No, no sir, wrong side, this one's the biggest and here, look, round this side, them's the written proof that these are the devil's own trees.'

Shuffling around the tree, the Head still struggled to see what Julien was going on about.

'Here sir, here, the written proof... just like I said... we've known about these forever sir... spooky!'

Still unconvinced, but too intrigued to give up, the Head struggled to see anything, until he got close up. Still expecting a prank, his cynicism then drained away into the woodland floor. Utterly taken back by what he saw: 'Wow, what on earth are these carvings doing here – *mon Dieu*!'

The Head's jaw dropped, now oblivious to Julien, or the distant groaning of Pierre left way back, still holding his ankle. Now, with his nose pressed close up to the first beech tree, the Head began to run his fingers along the outline of a series of carved images, captivated by the detail and the intricacy of the work. He did the same to some inscriptions, almost as if they were in braille; bewitched by every intriguing depression in the bark.

'Amazing, truly incredible – these aren't the work of ghosts, but I'm guessing they originate from a distant country, that much is pretty certain.'

Julien gawked back at him, not really understanding why the Head hadn't yet mentioned the devil at all.

"Well, well,' the Head went on, now in the zone. 'Aren't these two carvings of boats, and not just of any old vessel, *pas du tout*, these look all the world like Chinese Junks... yes, that's it.' And on he rambled, to Julien's confusion, then wandering from tree to tree as though in a trance, still oblivious to the furore now building back at the accident scene. Mesmerised, the Head's prolonged absence wasn't lost on Pierre who, by now, forgetting his injury, had ceased clutching his strapped ankle. Distracted by having been left alone, Pierre began to crane his neck as far as he could to see what on earth was keeping Julien and the Head for such a long while.

'What do you make of these phantoms, sir, are they chanting anything? It must be the devil, mustn't it, sir?' Now shadowing the Head, Julien peeped around him from a position of safety.

'Well, I never... and here's an elephant's head and an inscription above, curse it, can't read a word, foreign lettering and all too widened by tree growth... a Chinese symbol I think?'

'Chinese ghosts do you mean, sir?' Julien's voice began to wobble. 'Don't think so, sir, a British phantom maybe, or even a ghost of our own, never Chinese,' now looking smug at having corrected the Head's inferior logic.

'What do Chinese ghosts look like anyway, sir?'

'You know I'm really not sure Julien, not sure at all...' Julien looked puzzled, not expecting a reply, and equally uncertain he had been given one.

'Not sure about what, sir...?'

'...but Madame Sangler will know, for sure, no one knows more about our history than her. I shall get Madame up here right away...'

'Oh good, so she's a ghostbuster... ooh,' Julien whooped an owl hoot; the Head still ignoring him, still too preoccupied.

Then it sank in, for a moment, that his gang might now lose their secret world. 'No rush, please, sir... these ghost carvings have been here forever, sir, as long as I know anyway,' angling to put the Head off taking things further.

'That's just it, Julien, they are so old, the bark has almost grown over the original work, so there is some urgency, we're only just in time to see them at all... we must find out what they all mean.' Julien looked glum.

'Blimey, sir, and what about Pierre, sir, is he going to die out here and join the Chinese dead?'

'Oh, good Lord, Pierre! Thanks, yes, Julien, I completely forgot.'

Just then a couple of uniformed medics appeared in the distance to where the long-forgotten patient was still clutching his leg. They called out to the Head, 'Where is the patient, Monsieur?'

Grabbing Julien, the Head marched them both down to the accident scene but the Head still clearly had only one thing pressing on his mind, 'Why did I never know about those amazing trees?' he muttered.

'Pardon, Monsieur,' questioned the medic, overhearing him, expecting to hear the Head's instructions about the injured Pierre! The Head just mumbled, now feeling rather stupid that a bunch of errant kids, acting out their fantasy war games, may have stumbled on a significant historic discovery.

It was no surprise, therefore, once Pierre had been stretchered off, and the boys were being led back to the school, that the Head returned to the trees for another look.

'Right under our noses, *incroyable*,' he exclaimed, now alone, back tree-side, again running his fingers along the outline of each carving. He tried to fathom out what it all meant. Now it was his turn to let his imagination run riot! He too began to wonder if this wood on the hill might indeed be haunted by ghosts, even Chinese ghosts… and why not? Who knows what these people, so far from their homeland, were doing here up on this hill and what fate they may have endured?

'Leave the patient with us,' shouted one of the distant medics, back towards the Head. 'We will get him x-rayed in Hesdin, sir, let you know if there is anything broken.'

The Head heard the shouting, but remained distracted. He just raised his arm and waved back.

As the sun began to peep through, sending fresh light across the shiny bark of the beech tree, the elephant's head became a completely highlighted image, and the junks gleamed like newly constructed craft, sharp as the day they were carved. The Head felt a tear run down his cheek, drawn into the wonder of it all, now feeling he too might yet play his part in history.

14 ARRIVAL

Yun Reaches his First British CLC Base

France 1917

Yun wasn't sorry to get out of that truck, finally. Yes, he was still reeling from all that he had seen along the way, but physically, every bone in his body now ached. Transportation, over land, seemed more than tolerable compared to seafaring, but getting shaken and shunted, confined in a rigid truck on rough roadways, was punishment enough. The unforgiving bench-seating had crippled his back, but the ordeal had been a distraction too, one that he needed.

Then the moment came, and it would never desert Yun's psyche. He found himself trailing at the tail end of his small group. They were just a handful of new arrivals. Yun had held back to sort out his gear. He had already been registered, so he sloped away towards a small spinney of trees near the compound entrance to straighten himself out. Now, beside the trees, something about them caught his attention.

At first, he couldn't quite decipher the markings he had observed within the bark of each tree. He had spotted the etched outline of some images, but not clearly enough. He drew closer in, took a proper look. Yun then gasped in astonishment:

These were no ordinary tree carvings. Yun knew that immediately. The images Yun was now face-to-face with were the inimitable work of a Chinese craftsman, someone who understood his homeland intimately. In a state of helpless bewitchment, Yun began tracking the shape of an elephant's head with his fingers. It was stunningly depicted. Then there were a pair of Chinese junks, at sea, floating on wave symbols. Yun loved these, as he did the sinograms. So entranced by the work, Yun did not, at first, hear the British sergeant's rasping voice from somewhere behind him. Chastised for wandering off, he was now being ordered to return back into the line.

The moment was shattered. Yun rejoined the group. Not a soul among them could have had the slightest clue what he had just been through. Yun could have been back in Shandong, body and soul. Those carvings, for the briefest moment, had sent an irresistible rush of longing straight through him and his resistance had melted away. These were the emblems of his childhood, the vestiges of his home. Too transfixed, it would not have entered Yun's mind how local children might fantasise over these in the future mists of time. Yun could have wept, there and then, as his mother's face appeared, smiling, in his thoughts, still clutching his brothers as she had been during that furore, when he had been dragged away from his home.

'Well done compatriots, and well done to you, the craftsman, who created this work. You have gifted us a powerful reminder of who we are and what we have left behind us. The "powers that be" may lie to us, but we shall never be untrue to ourselves.'

The ranting continued, at pace, in his head: 'Curse

Shandong and to hell with my father and his precious business. I'll make the most of all I'm left with, out here. These trees will give me heart, every time I pass them by, or each time I think of them.'

As much as Yun was smarting from his nostalgic whirlwind, he was overjoyed that it had happened. It had left him feeling a deep empathy for his fellow workers, and all that they had been put through to make it this far. Every one of them was just doing what they could to cope, doing their level best to survive.

One Chinese guy spotted Yun staring towards the top of the perimeter fencing as he passed. He had noticed the stressed look on Yun's face, his eyes straining to fathom the height of it. In that briefest of moments, the man had read Yun's thoughts:

'Hey, you there, no need to fret; they may have fenced us in, but they'll never imprison our souls!' he cackled, Yun smirked.

Yun had not appreciated, from the entrance area to the Chinese camp, just how extensive this designated area was. As they were being led towards the far extremity, the sergeant ordered Yun's group to stall, just alongside a Nissen hut. A motley gathering of Chinese had been lined up outside and Yun's mob were to wait until they were dismissed. Looking on, now at a standstill, Yun's group stayed put. This was yet another, curiously, posed photography moment. They had themselves endured these many times before, but this time they were just onlookers. Still not understanding the process, or what it might mean, waiting there gave them the chance

Yun had not expected just how extensive this designated area was

to take it all in, just for that passing moment.

Yun could see straight through the false expressions of these workers, having been told to 'smiley, smiley, happy faces' by the officer-photographer. Stooped over his apparatus, he couldn't care less. His task was quickly over, and the men were then as rapidly dispersed. Only Yun's group would have understood those men as they bickered after the event. They had clearly hated being herded around for a purpose they neither understood nor cared a damn about. They had felt like objects of amusement.

Yun had been taught, by his mother, how to read people from their facial expressions. He adored her for her innate wisdom. She had tutored him how to detect, and then how to interpret, tell-tale signs. It had already paid dividends for Yun on this expedition:

'Look carefully at their faces, see past what others only see on the surface. Once you sense people's moods, their real intentions, only then will you make your best judgement about the people themselves.'

If Yun's allocated billets were to be the same as the shabby hut he had just seen, close up, he feared for his sanity. He had grilled the sergeant about these structures. They were the template for every building within the camp. They had, apparently, been named 'Nissen huts' after their inventor, a shrewd innovator serving the British military. The only thing that was shrewd about these structures, so far as Yun was concerned, was that these were ready-made to cram full with bodies, animals or humans, and no one outside would be any the wiser.

Yun could see straight through the false expressions of these workers, having been told to 'smiley, smiley, happy faces' by the officer-photographer

Yun quickened his pace, to get alongside the sergeant. He wanted to glean more general stuff from him. 'Any hits up here, sir?' he dared to venture. 'Any enemy shells made it into this camp at all?' Yun had decided to pry into what he feared might be sensitive:

'God no, no chance, tucked away up here; you Chink lads can all sleep "snug as bugs", safest spot in all of France!' His slippery grin wasn't lost on Yun. It surely betrayed a lie, but Yun couldn't yet tell how big that lie might be. He held his tongue. In any case, they were now, at last, heading steadfastly towards, what had to be, their designated billets. Predictably, another one of those Nissens, and they were all fearing the worst. They were ushered inside. Amazingly, they were to be pleasantly surprised by what they then saw:

This was as good as these men could possibly have hoped for, given what they had witnessed on their march here. Though the same as all the others, from the outside, these quarters had clearly been configured for greater comfort. To the far end of the camp, the other residents might have less opportunity to learn of this preferential treatment. There were far fewer beds, more than adequate cooking and washing facilities, and there were even some Chinese musical instruments hanging from the rafters! Yun breathed a sigh of relief.

Yun's sense of reprieve, however, wasn't to last. He should, he reflected, have predicted that would be so. No sooner had he released his bag onto his designated bunk, when an officer's lackey appeared in the doorway calling out his name.

Yun was being summoned for a formal initiation into his posting, whatever that might now turn out to be. He knew what had been promised, but he wasn't going to hold his

This was as good as these men could possibly have hoped for … There were even some Chinese musical instruments hanging from the rafters

breath. He was keeping an open mind, just in case. Now being ceremoniously trudged all the way back through the compound, he was at least free from the burden of his backpack. He had also secured his bunk. He felt remarkably less oppressed by the towering camp fencing. The relief of his superior billets, the relative comfort of them, must have raised his spirits. A lighter mood was welcome. He suspected he might need to be in the right frame of mind rather soon in any case.

Leaving the confines of the camp revitalised Yun even more. Alone, behind his accompanying soldier, gave him time to observe, to look around the vicinity. They route marched across the outskirts of the village which nestled below the CLC camp hill. He passed a row of solid, traditional buildings. They appeared entirely intact, which was heartening. Spotting some symbols, chiselled into sandstone walls, he viewed them enough to realise these were the insignia of some resident British troops. How starkly these contrasted with the artistry carved into the bark of those trees. These army symbols were destined for permanence, the Chinese depictions left to the mercy of the passage of time. This cruel irony, the poignancy of these tangible contradictions yelled out at Yun, and upset him deeply.

A fully laden trailer was parked to the side of the roadway ahead of them. Yun was taken aback to see that the labourers unloading the payload were in fact Chinese. He assumed they must have been from his own camp. There wasn't time to exchange words with them, and he might have been rebuked for distracting them, so he looked on, eagerly, as his march-by progressed. With one guy up on the trailer, a pair of Chinese on the ground below him, a consignment of gun shells was being offloaded. Yun felt concerned by the speed

Oh, those Chinks used to blow themselves up, now and then...

of the exercise, but admired the men's efficiency.

'Come on, come on,' bullied the British guard in charge, 'can't wait all day, let's get these shells stockpiled, sharpish".

Yun was all too familiar with his men's forced subservience, yet he winced as he heard 'Go, go, go!'

Knowing both languages, Yun knew the Chinese had instinctively misinterpreted these barked commands as '*Gou, gou, gou*', meaning 'Dog, dog dog!' an insult reserved for maximum effect in their language. The officer in charge then marched away.

It troubled Yun all the more to see munitions, fresh gun shells, being manhandled. He feared for the safety of his compatriots. 'Looks like a chancy operation sir,' Yun pressed his officer up ahead, choosing his words, 'surprised the shells don't go off in their hands sir, chucking them about. Hasn't anyone ended up getting killed?' He chanced a false naivety.

'Oh, these Chinks used to blow themselves up, now and then…' the officer responded cynically, oblivious to Yun's ethnicity, '…but not near as much as they used to!' The soldier mocked, boorishly pleased with himself. Yun felt sickened.

A short distance beyond the working Chinese labourers, Yun arrived at what appeared to be a form of army HQ. Ushered through the entrance to an impressive, framed, canvas tent, Yun was taken aback by the grand interior. The formal trappings on view unsettled Yun. He just hadn't expected it, nor the daunting height, or the appearance of the General now confronting him. He cut an austere figure, sporting a stern-looking handlebar moustache, an imposing khaki peaked hat, and an extensive array of badges and stripes;

enough to prompt any subordinate to buckle instantly. This General epitomised everything Yun had come to expect from Britain's top brass. He had seen stylised moustaches before, and he had learned how to distinguish Generals from other officers by their apparel – their insignia – but this General carried himself with a distinctive countenance, an assured gravity, so when the General began to speak, Yun froze:

'Now, let's put things simply, CLC,' raising his eyebrows like an owl, the ends of his moustache quivering, Yun's confidence sank ever further, his legs wobbled. 'All jolly well having ya lingo skills, damn good show, but got despatches that ya'r a dab hand with mechanicals too.' The General was clearly reading from a report, with his eyes lowered towards his desk. Then he looked back up at Yun. Battling with his nerves, Yun mustered a reply, enough to confirm he had a suitably proficient mechanical background. He hoped he hadn't over-egged it. He hadn't regained enough composure to craft a balanced account of himself.

'Excellent, excellent,' the General seemed unreservedly satisfied. 'Point is, CLC, ya wasted here, complete nonsense when me old colleague, General Alan Thompson, needs fellows like yaself at his tank depot at Erin. Bit short d'ya see?'

So now Yun knew all that he needed to. Barely installed at the CLC base, he was now being moved on. As much as he liked the thought of being singled out, and he had hoped, from the start of his exodus, that he would be, he also balked at the prospect of being uprooted and put back on the road all over again. Yun hadn't heard of Erin but prayed that it wasn't that far away. He had heard of tanks, or at least the traditional meaning of 'tanks', but the General was quick to put Yun straight despite the secrecy surrounding this bold innovation.

He clearly intended to extol, even exaggerate, their virtues:

'If Thompson's tanks don't bust the Hun, nothing will,' he boasted. 'Sooner we get them properly underway, sooner we shall win this bloody war,' and at that he produced some papers from nowhere. It would seem Yun had already been reassigned! Yun signed where he was told and, without further ado, he was dismissed, ordered to be taken back to his base to await his pending transport orders to Erin, however long it might take for these to be notified.

Within moments of leaving HQ, a massive 'bawoom' erupted nearby. Both Yun, and the officer with him, hit the deck. Somehow neither of them had been struck, close by though it clearly had been, but the Chinese Workers were less fortunate. The cruel reality quickly became apparent, as mayhem broke out in response to the blast. The trailer, with its last shells still on board, had, it would seem, self-detonated into oblivion. The explosion lifted the trailer and the Chinese men into the air on a fireball. So, Yun's fears had proved fatalistically exact; exposing anyone to these risks was utter madness, criminal.

The British priority had been to check HQ and the General. They were untouched. Yun was restrained from getting involved. Consumed with rage, it had taken three attendant troops to bring Yun to the floor. Had they failed, had Yun got his hands on the officer, the one who had chosen to so readily deride Yun's people, who knows what he might have done. Yun was utterly inconsolable. Yun's agony worsened when he learned that these new shells were known for their fragility, their instability. With fatalities and ghastly injuries having already been recorded in the recent past, it was only a question of time when the next such calamity would follow. No doubt the Chinese Workers would, regardless, continue to be assigned to shift live shells, by hand.

The resulting blaze forced everyone back from the scene of the atrocity in any event. Once the firefighters arrived, what remained of the trailer billowed up into the atmosphere as a caustic cloud. This may just as well have been a direct enemy hit for the carnage the blast caused. Yun left the scene harbouring one hateful conclusion; this was no symptom of the brutality of war, this was death by negligence.

'Birdman' Yun

Yun trudged back towards his billets, absolutely spent. Once the officer leading him was satisfied that Yun's anger, spiked by the incident, had quelled, he had conceded some space between them.

Yun was left feeling sick to the pit of his stomach. He was now oblivious to the soldier way ahead of him, save that he had allowed Yun to slow to an amble. Yun kicked his boots, disconsolately, through the spent fire traces that had settled way beyond the incident site. He was still haunted by what had happened. Some tepid ash coughed up his legs and stung his skin through the splits in the cloth, but he felt nothing. Yun had been broken by the experience, sapped dry, then something caught his eye.

Yun's focus fell on something struggling in the ash. It was only a tiny disturbance, almost under his feet. It stopped him in his tracks. Yun stood fast, staring down at it. Could it really be? It turned out to be the tiniest bird, black as the charcoal around it, having somehow survived the inferno. Then, as if by some miracle, as though prompted by Yun looking down at it, it mustered a little, brave, hop and there it was. A small sparrow, clogged in soot, trying to shake itself free to fly away. Yun still stood there aghast. Then it took one more courageous hop, caked though it was with grime, until it nestled against Yun's toe caps, turning its beak towards him as though ready to exchange experiences from the war.

Suddenly Yun felt alive again, blessed by the smallest living thing imaginable. Yun crouched down, as smoothly as he could, so as not to alarm his new acquaintance. There it remained, resolutely staring back at him. Silent, yet sending out the clearest cry for help – 'Please rescue me'.

Did it realise, could it possibly know, that in its desperation it had just hopped towards the only human being in France who knew everything about lost and broken birds? Yun was a legend back home for his magic touch with these injured, defenceless, creatures. He hadn't become known as 'BIRDMAN Yun' for nothing! Every bird found injured in his neighbourhood, or any just needing a loving hand back to health, was brought to Yun. It had become habitual, back then. Whilst all that seemed a very long time ago, right now it felt like the only relevant skill Yun still had intact.

'My little beauty, did some mystical being tell you about me? Have you flown here all the way from China, seeking me out for healing?' As he whispered his words, Yun so wanted to weep, but found he could not. His clogged face had blocked every gland in his skin, every facility to feel or to function.

Introductions over, Yun held out his cupped hands and, in an instant, as though it had been slavishly rehearsed, it popped straight into his palms like a fledgling into its nest. Yun crouched right down to take a closer look. With his fingers, he gathered a trace of warm blood from his scratched forehead and gently brushed its feathers, clearing away the worst of the clinging dirt. Yun wanted to inspect it for damage, praying it was salvageable. He could see that one wing had been completely bent back, so he gently manoeuvred it, manipulating the joint as he did so. The brave little sparrow neither squawked nor struggled, though Yun could sense it was in pain. The more he examined it the more he was certain. Tiny though it was, it must have managed to catch part of the shell-blast, a fragment of shrapnel, enough to make certain that its flying days were rendered well and truly 'over'. Yun was of no use to it out here, so he snuggled it deep down into an inside pocket of his tunic. He sensed its precious body quiver with relief, until it settled, and with it, Yun's pulse calmed back to normal. He smiled, contentedly. Their friendship was complete.

The attendant officer, up ahead, had been patient, but seeing Yun scratching around in the dirt, he had decided he'd waited long enough. Hearing him ordering him forward, Yun responded. His focus now was to get started on his new patient's recovery. He prayed he could at least save its life. For that he needed to get it back to the safety of his base. Yun was certain he would need to keep his bird a strict secret from his fellow residents. One or more might well complain should they discover there was an injured bird in their billets, a threat to hygiene.

Yun quickly crafted a meticulous routine. The bird's greatest asset, it transpired, was that it remained steadfastly silent. He had never known an injured bird fail to make a sound. He hadn't expected it to sing, but not to utter a single note was exceptional. This curious introversion might yet save its life!

It also proved a perfect 'pocket-guest'. Covertly resident, it seemed content to stay hidden. This habit persisted wherever and whenever Yun had to move or be transported around. He scarcely knew it was there at all. He had never known a patient like it. Yet Yun did worry about the creature. He suspected, from its silence, that not only had the violence of the explosion busted its wing, but it might also have broken its spirit. Not a murmur came from its beak, nor did it show the slightest inclination to hop around when Yun gave it the freedom to do so. Yet it was totally content to be handled, which facilitated a firm splint to be fitted to its wing. It was almost as if Yun's new friend had resolved not to speak until it was well enough to thank Yun properly! Each had come to each other's rescue. Yun adored the bird for that.

As it happened, Yun needn't have worried about any adverse reaction to his bird. Inevitably, in spite of Yun's determination, the bird's existence did become common knowledge in the camp, as did Yun's reputation as a 'bird healer'. Most came to admire him for his compassion and for his skill. They looked up to Yun as the resident bird medic. Even the officers got to hear about him. Seeing the supportive reaction from the Chinese themselves, they left Yun to his own devices. They were wise, as it happened. When it came to the day of the funeral for the Chinese workers who were killed, Yun and his bird, in attendance, brought calmness to the proceedings. It might well have been otherwise once the group attending saw the Union Jacks and not, at least, some distinctly Chinese drapery, some sensitive symbolism, to cover each of the coffins. They had, after all, managed such empathetic

The group attending saw the Union Jacks and not, at least, some distinctively Chinese drapery, some sensitive symbolism, to cover each of the coffins

representations at the Chinese hospital at Noyelles. The Chinese were not colonials.

These men were more than hardened to a lack of tact from their British employers. Everything seemed that bit less distressing knowing that Yun, with a tiny, permanently disabled, survivor in his care, like a message from above, had been gifted into their midst for both comfort and hope. It would thus go on to stir up some consternation amongst them, once the news broke, that both Yun and his bird were soon to move on.

Within days, Yun was indeed transferred to the tank depot, at Erin, in accordance with his dispatched papers.

15 WARTIME WORK FOR ALICE

Gas Mask & Fabrics Factory – Northern France

Alice could but smile, as she looked around from her workstation. With not a man in sight, she really had begun to wonder if she was destined to remain single. Yet row after row of working women did have some compensations. She thrived on the gossip, the prattling, the laughs, but she had always preferred the company of men.

One quality Alice was blessed with, was her optimism. She had a zest for life, an irrepressible enthusiasm, and that made her popular with most people. Her pretty looks helped too, and she had recently become far more conscious of that, within herself. As for her strength of character, her determination, well, that was all down to her mother. It was these aspects of her DNA that had pulled her through the hardest of times.

The women in the factory seemed drawn to Alice for banter. Her background had exposed her to quite a course sense of humour, and she herself resorted to this, every now and then when the moment demanded it:

'Good job there aren't any men around us here,' Alice announced, impishly, then one took the bait.

'Why's that then young Alice?' fully expectant on a fruity answer. She wasn't to be disappointed: 'Because they fart all day, and then we'd have to wear these masks the whole damn time!!' Alice stuck out her rear, pinched her nose, then gestured with a mask, pretending to put it on. The women broke into fits of laughter.

Gas mask assembly was a monotonous affair, but it was this kind of wartime work that had come to bolster the position, and influence, of European women beyond measure. For the first time in their lives, they had found their hands firmly placed on the building blocks of power, and they felt immeasurably stronger for it. They could be irreverent, even bawdy when they dared, just like the men. They were handed their weekly take-home wage directly from their employer, just like the men, and they were in sole charge of what should be spent and what should be saved. This said, it certainly focused the women's minds on their level of pay.

Alice found she could share her frustrations with some of her colleagues. She had been naturally drawn to the bolder women, for their fortitude and bluntness. They could moan openly with each other, garner their support, let slip some confidences to check the others out for their views. It helped that each had their own take, their own stories to confess to, but Alice sensed, in her gut, that she held the greater secret and that it might serve her best not to 'tell-all'.

In this company, Alice ventured a crafted lie about the father of her child rather than risk being looked down upon as an unwed mother. Yes, in the heat of the moment, her confessed truth might garner some passing sympathy, but such transient reward was no match for her quest for respect:

'If he hadn't died on the battlefield, bravely fighting for

La France, if he'd abandoned me for any other reason, I'd have strung him up faster than he could blink!' The women gasped at her stoicism, her barbed recount, helped in no small way by Alice, somehow welling up, then choking as she added, 'All very well being brave on the battlefield for his country, but that's fat use to me and his son now!'

It was all down to her mother. It was her calm guidance, her sagacity passed onto Alice, that instilled that same mettle in her: 'Remember, my darling, we are immigrants, trespassers in a foreign land. War or no war, we need to strive harder than most, shape the truth when we need to, somehow salvage an advantage when it's there, and if we can add some borrowed patriotism to the mix, all the better!'

So, Alice continued to hold back the truth. Her mother had, after all, counselled such skilled navigation in her. 'You just cannot, should not, trust outsiders when it comes to the really personal stuff, not completely.'

Alice had so often wanted, and at times been sorely tempted, to let on that her lover was a ranked British officer and not a dead, brave, French soldier, but she never weakened, no matter how much she desperately wanted to perform to her listeners. It eased her frustration to conclude they might not have believed her anyway.

Alice was fortunate indeed that her mother had been able to take Maxime into her care each day. She would have been stumped without her. It tore Alice apart not to be there to bring her little boy up properly, give him the full life she so wanted him to have. It was bad enough to be a war child, but a fatherless one too was heartbreaking. So, with the best interest of her son, and herself, in mind, she could live with her conscience that she had dressed up her account to enhance the women's perception of her as a stoic survivor of the war.

What Alice also held back were her true feelings about her son's father. She had to, somehow, strike a balance if she was going to be both believed and respected, yet any woman left on her own, at a time of dire hardship, had ready licence to deride her absent man, even one said to have fallen in the line of duty. It would not have served her blossoming role as a grandstander to confess how she had loved her man, truly, and that she had thought of him often. Neither did she think to suggest, for a moment, it may all have been an infatuation, and that was all it could ever have been for her. Her English officer had been everything an aspiring, young, French woman could have wanted from a lover, yet he had proved as calculating and fickle as any passing soldier away from home. So, Alice only allowed herself, privately, to cherish her memories, foolish though they may feel to her now. He was, after all, the father of her son, and that was a bond she could never break, nor would she ever wish to.

Maxime was compensation enough. He had become a strapping toddler, and she utterly adored him. As with any good mother, her guilt might have destroyed her had it not been for her own mother stepping into the breach. It crushed Alice, every time, to struggle home after each gruelling working day, too late to see her son into bed each night.

Now that Alice had come to know the sweet taste of independence, she wanted more, and this could only be satiated with better pay. Her posting at the factory, getting any paid work at all, had been a godsend, but that initial euphoria had quickly passed. Stoked up by her fervent clutch of like-minded agitators, her hunger for higher wages was growing:

'Alice,' one woman advised, 'I've just got word that our pay is crap compared to other industries out here.' Alice was all ears. They sloped away from the others, free from the clamour of machines. It would seem this woman's mate was posted at a munitions unit, and it was her who had been shouting the odds about how far more prosperous she was.

'She's a "Munitionette", Alice, at an armaments factory, not so far from here, and she's getting way more money than us.'

'Wow!' exclaimed Alice, 'but how can that be, I thought we were being well paid here?' Alice hated appearing ignorant.

'Oh, I think it's the risks, you know, shells and bullets and all that, and they are doing longer hours,' she explained, vaguely.

'We're taking enough risks here anyway, aren't we? Every chance of being stretchered away, cracking up from boredom!'

She loved Alice's humour, but reminded her that equivalent British women workers had become known as 'Canary Girls', because the TNT 'yellowed' their skin. Alice, so intoxicated by the thought of far better pay, made light of that remark too.

'Ah, that's good, always fancied myself as a Chinese woman anyway,' she slanted her eyes, 'rather exotic, don't you think!'

If Alice had aspired to become ever more like her mother, she had succeeded way beyond her own expectations. She sensed it, every day, through her actions and her thoughts, with that inner resolve to feed on her mother's fine qualities to help her ease through any tribulation life might throw at her.

Now obsessed with the prospect of enhancement improving her lot, Alice couldn't get the idea of moving-on out of her mind. Her mother, with her innate motherly skills, reassured her that the munitions factory wasn't far enough away to threaten her caring for Maxime, so it was just down to her to decide. As much as she had become immersed in this new world of female liberation, it still went against the grain for Alice. She had been brought up to encourage men to go out in search of better pay, but she didn't have a man! Here and now, Alice was the provider, as well as the one that had to keep her home going, tending to her child. Yes, of course, her mother made a huge difference to her, and her father's wages were enough to keep her parents afloat, but Alice had been lured into a man's world, felt the drug of independence, and it tingled through her veins. Her preoccupations were thoughts of ambition, determination and she could feel herself gaining self-confidence by the day:

'To hell with Maxime's army father, wherever he is, I'll teach my boy all he needs to know about the virtues of love and honour, and I will make my mother proud.'

Munitions Factory – Arsenal

It was the news that the munitions factory was recruiting large numbers of unskilled workers, that finally prompted Alice to make her move. The escalating demand for more supplies had reached a fever pitch in the war. With production now straining industry at its seams, labour became vital. These were government-run factories, and they had been prioritised.

Alice hadn't fully appreciated just how fluid these work opportunities had become. As ghastly as the losses of the war now were, and so destructive, the world had opened up for every woman who felt able to step-in and take advantage. She knew she had to be both flexible and courageous. The men had learned, over time, how to manipulate the harsh, murky workings of the labour market, but these were different times, and many men had either died or were risking their lives elsewhere. Alice, and young women like her, were learning, on the hoof, how to duck and dive, how and when to stay, or to move on. She could reflect, now, how brave her parents had been to uproot themselves from the comfort of their homeland, from the familiarity of their origins and their friends. Her mother had understood the meaning of opportunism, even if not the word. It was instinctive, seeing the light in the distance, sensing when the time was right to set off to reach it. They had fled to evade hardship, with all the risks that involved, in the hope that better times were out there, and were there for the taking. Only now, immersed in this uniquely 'upturned' existence, did Alice feel her true strength rise up inside her. She had become resilient, a determined young mother, a woman to be reckoned with.

There was a long queue at the munitions factory entrance. The word was clearly out, and the demand for work was as strong as the Government drive for recruits. This was part of the Arsenal Warehouse, an impressive building, housing vital production units. If the imposing size of the place was anything to go by, she could imagine why better pay may lie in waiting here. She could also now fathom, callous though it might sound, that masks were less 'valuable' than shells; they saved some from dying, but they couldn't kill, or defeat the enemy, and bringing forward an end to this destructive war had become all that mattered.

The most intimidating time for Alice was finding herself in amongst would-be women recruits that she didn't know. She had been tireless in mixing-in with her previous cohorts, and it had taken time and effort, but here she would have to start all over again. Here, among strangers, she reverted to her natural reticence. She ignored the tittle-tattle about wages and conditions. Those others in her line, close by, would have no better idea about all that than she would. No, she was going to wait to find out the full picture for herself. She queued patiently, kept her eyes focused firmly up ahead.

Once her turn came, and she learned from the recruiter, that her pay would be at the rate of 4–5 francs per day, she could hardly contain her joy. Breaking her insularity, turning to a total stranger behind her, she whispered under her palm, chuckling, 'That's double what I was getting at the mask factory!' The woman gestured, approvingly, with her eyebrows, a sharp French mouth-rasp of her lips, not wanting to betray her surprise prior to getting the same offer, if indeed she did, when her turn came.

Thrilled to have got the job, Alice launched herself into mastering every aspect of it. Only once she settled, was she able to gawk at the sheer volume of gun shells throughout the warehouse. Then she felt the danger. It was real enough, as were the days and hours her work-rota was to demand of her. Once the adrenalin had subsided, the exhilaration of better pay, the real challenge of her new work started to take its toll. The shells themselves were heavy too. It would be tough to expropriate the men when it meant lugging these damn things around, she could see that from the start. Alice quickly felt the strain, the prospect of exhaustion. For the larger ordnance, handling the requisite shells put untold duress on the back and shoulders, and by the end of a long shift, an unthinkable payload had been handled by each individual.

That sparkle, that lightness of foot, began to fade in Alice as fatigue set in. Each night she could barely manage the long trudge home. Her parents would be there, which took the pressure off her, but she longed to give Maxime that final goodnight kiss, in her arms, even though he would sleep through it, blissfully unaware that she had been with him at all. It helped her to stay sane. It was when she had suffered the beginnings of a nagging cough, from toxic air impurities at work, that she began to feel drained, yet it was more her fear of waking up Maxime that concerned her the most.

It was in those precious moments at night, alone with Maxime, that she could smother him, unashamedly, with motherly kisses whilst he slept on. She heaped her excesses upon her precious son, driven by a single mother's lonely guilt, as she prayed for forgiveness in the eyes of God, for failing her fatherless boy. If she succumbed to weeping, with Maxime sleeping in her cradled arms, it consoled her to feel her falling tears washing through his blissful innocence, soaking into his tiny frame, knowing he would never know nor feel her pain.

Her mother worried deeply about her declining strength since she had changed jobs, but there was no deterring Alice. She now had more money, and she wasn't going to part with that extra pay. Her mother was anxious, yet so very proud of her daughter. For the first time, she could see in Alice that same resilience of purpose that she had. Sacrificing everything for a better life, never giving up her fight for her family's betterment, struggling for their survival. Woe betide anyone who dared to get in her way. Her mother's job as a guiding hand for Alice, ever watching over her, was all but done. She felt both the joy and the sadness of it, as only an adoring mother can.

The Strike – 1917

Once word got out at the factory about their pay comparison with the men, everything changed. The treadmill of incessant, long, working shifts had already paved the way for festering discontent. The growing awareness of the dangers of the job just added to it. A recent recruit she may still be, and in spite of her physical fatigue, her cough and a growing skin irritation, Alice had still found the resolve to make herself known as a force to be reckoned with. She had encouraged a key group of working women to make their intentions crystal clear – if things remained as they were, with the men's pay grade at almost double theirs, there would be serious repercussions.

The problem, at first, was that the authorities had absolutely no experience of female-led revolts in the workplace, nor of any spontaneous threat of strike action, not triggered by a union. This was completely new territory. Not only were the workers exclusively female, but their spokesperson was female too! The factory owners, and the politicians, may have retained their scepticism, but the unease among the women was palpable, and it really did become clear that theirs were not empty threats.

War or not, their anger had reached fever pitch for these toiling women. For now, they were either single mothers, with mouths to feed, or women left alone to fend for themselves. There was no status distinction between them and their male counterparts. Their ultimatum was simple – grant them equal pay and conditions, or they would 'down tools'. Once one of the women had been taken to hospital with rumours of 'toxic jaundice', there was no stopping them.

The authorities were rocked by the unrest and the growing incidents of injury and respiratory complaints emanating from the women workers. With the exile of men to the front, this was a collapse of conventional gender roles. Suddenly the label 'munitionette' had a demeaning connotation. The Government, thinking ahead, may have preferred to see these young women adhere to their primary roles as mothers and home keepers, but they couldn't have it both ways. Munitions, right now, was a vital industry, and these women were making sure they were running to demand. Striking was no longer the sole preserve of male workers, so those that mattered would just have to sit up and listen. There was a nervousness, from above, about what to do.

Alice again found herself among the leading women agitators. She had become a powerful champion for their cause. They demanded parity of pay and an increase in living allowances. Faced with a stubborn resistance, the workers abandoned their posts and took their protests to the street. They called for solidarity from their fellow workers, strutted in proud groups, singing the Marseillaise. It was as stirring a wartime scene as you could imagine. Whatever the outcome,

Alice could sense that this was a telling moment. She, and her courageous working mates, had feminised a space that had, until now, been the sole preserve of male workers. They had only set out to secure decent work, but they had, it would seem, unwittingly ended up igniting a flame, an historic movement, for a wider emancipation.

The women were clever also. Alice had to rely on the more experienced rebels for their guile and sophistication. They began to employ the strategy of '*débauchage*'. This meant leaving their posts with the intention of encouraging other workers to join the strike, then forming committees if their demands were not met within a few days. They cunningly deployed the traditional French rhetoric of their 'double sacrifice'; they were not only workers, but the female dependants of mobilised men. This resonated well with the traditionalists within Government, and with the press. They quickly gathered momentum, then something else happened.

Watching from the sidelines, looking on quizzically, a leading politician had covertly been assigned to check things out in person. He was chatting, discreetly, to the factory owner and a senior Government mediator. The politician took them into his confidence:

'Do not worry unduly gentlemen. The word is that a significant consignment of some, 500 or so, Chinese Workers are on their way.'

'So might we then be able to threaten the replacement of these women once they get here sir?' the mediator asked, mischievously.

The politician shrugged his shoulders, raised his brow. The others smiled, wryly. They dispersed as surreptitiously as they had arrived.

16 MING MEETS ALICE

What confronted Ming, as he was shown into the Arsenal base, threw him completely. The place was awash with female workers. All the new Chinese arrivals felt the same. The women, turning, to take a good, long, look at their strange new foreign additions, unsettled them completely. They felt totally intimidated.

The arriving Chinese found it extremely disorientating, irrespective of their initiation at the Le Creusot works. This, here, was clearly a female stronghold, and the immediate atmosphere was one of suspicion and bemusement. As it happened, this was a genuine reflection of how these women were feeling. They had not been told there were mass recruits coming, and certainly not that these would be Chinese men. There were questions to be answered, but, for now, they put these on hold, because they were being directed to settle these new recruits in.

If Ming had, instinctively, expected to at least be segregated from these women, he was quickly proved mistaken. It became immediately clear that the Chinese were not only destined to work alongside these established female workers, but they were also expected to share work positions with them too. In Ming's case, his posting was to be alongside Alice. With his scant familiarity with French, a little more with munitions, he wondered if he was going to be able to engage, effectively, in any work with this female stranger at all, let alone communicate with her.

Alice felt much the same way, but with her background, she was always going to be the more confident of the two. Sensing her gang may have just been wrong-footed by the factory owners, Alice was quick to extract all she could from Ming:

'I'm Alice,' she ventured, exaggerating a broad smile, offering her hand to him. Ming bowed back, tentatively. Alice glanced at a female, beyond Ming, whilst deliberately keeping her hand out, and still smiling. She persisted, 'What's your name?' clenching her palm, she now pointed at Ming, but he froze, frowning back in puzzlement.

'I'm Alice,' she repeated, patting her chest, insistently, '… and you are…?' once again, pointing back towards him. To Ming she was as exotic as a prize canary, but with a haunting song of kindness and femininity thrown in, and it scared him.

At last, he fell in. At first bewitched to confusion, his stern expression melted. He announced, meekly, 'Ming', patting his own chest, with his heart thumping within. A gentle smile stole across his face. Alice giggled, moved a little closer to him. She began showing him some components, whilst Ming's eyes remained glued to her.

Alice, on her next break, began to chatter to the other women from her line. She was clearly animated. Freshly linked-up with one of these new Chinese Workers, she had a great deal to bounce-off the others, to get their views:

'Girls, listen,' they gathered in, 'this could be a game-changer, for our bosses, can't you see?' They drew in closer. 'With these Chinese guys turning up out of the blue, we'll never get what we want, what we've been fighting for. They can kick us lot out, whenever we say we'll strike. Replace us, with the very people we've been asked to train!'

She had certainly been quick off the mark, and shrewd enough to get the others thinking. Their efforts to force the factory into submission, to meet the women's demands, had really gained some headway, and they desperately didn't want to lose any ground. This sudden glut of new recruits was a serious blow to their aspirations, but they weren't going to roll over. They were in no mood for conceding or losing momentum. But what could they do?

Alice began to find herself at the forefront of the women's cause. It wasn't that she was the most forceful of her group, because she certainly wasn't, it was more that she had given their plight the most thought. She hated the idea of being outmanoeuvred by their male bosses, perhaps that was born from her own isolation with her son. More than that, she wasn't to be outwitted without a fight, but she needed to find an angle they hadn't thought of themselves, hadn't factored in. Then she had a brainwave, a light-bulb moment, and she quickly announced it to the others:

'We women must find a way to bring these new Chinese co-workers of ours onside,' she ventured, solemnly. 'I wonder how much money these poor, foreign, devils are being paid for doing the same work as us?' she added.

It was a shrewd question. Alice had learned to make her own luck. So, perhaps, she might find good fortune here. It wouldn't be for want of trying, and her workmates admired her for her tenacity. It would take time, and patience, and more than a little helping of guile. The more she thought about it, the more Alice convinced herself. These Chinese Workers must be on a poor rate of pay, she didn't yet know just how poor that might turn out to be. They all agreed and made a pact with each other; they must do all they could to find out the level of the Chinese' wages, and they could only hope to do this if they remained banded together.

The next day, Ming was assigned to a quantity of stacked shells, ready for assembly, at the far end of the row. He had been there, at first, with a couple of fellow Chinese, but he was now on his own. Alice spotted him and went over to help him out. She was already more than conversant with the assembly process, so this was the moment to tutor him.

Resorting to hand signals, gesticulations and mouthing her words, Alice took Ming through the entire procedure. Showing him a tin of powder, getting him to finger through it, with her, she then beckoned him to the empty shells. He visibly relaxed, putty in her hands. He had clearly been daunted by the thought of facing this task all on his own. Alice tapped into their growing intimacy. He was enchanted by her femininity in such a masculine setting, yet it hurt him deeply to remember his young wife. Her softness, her strength, and how he adored every part of her being. He buried these fruitless longings with every resolve that he had in him.

After mimicking the next step, she began guiding his hand, with hers, by tipping the powder into the shell, then stemming it down, firmly, using broom handles and soft mallets. There was clearly a knack to it, and Ming was open to this brief apprenticeship. This was his first intimacy with any female since he had left home, and the stimulus toyed with him, mentally, but he showed no emotion. He did drop his guard, at one point, by smiling broadly at her when Alice insisted on repeating the entire procedure, being ever-more overtly tactile with him. When it came to dealing with the shells, Ming could see the toll the repetition of effort was taking on Alice, particularly when she winced, so he began to keep an eye out for those moments so he could step in to help.

From that moment onwards, the two began their own private ritual. They agreed to salute each other, whenever they were reunited, after being apart. It helped Ming break away from his servile bowing, made him feel less conspicuous for his differences, his traditions. Alice just revelled in their growing familiarity, and she was proud to have fostered this with body-language and signals, having been denied her usual reliance on her 'gift of the gab', to tempt someone onside. For Ming, Alice had become his angel, lighting up the gloom in a foreign world that he neither liked nor understood.

Pay Day

With the threat of a resumption of strike action, pay day had become an incendiary ordeal for the factory. There was a seditious atmosphere, and even though the authorities considered they had regained the upper hand, with the arrival of the Chinese, they were far from feeling smug. The disquiet amongst the women, now lined in their separate queues for their pay, was palpable. The paymaster could sense their pent-up tension. The women were still biding their time.

Meanwhile, the Chinese workers were, dutifully, waiting in their lines for their wages, keeping themselves to themselves.

Seeing Ming wandering away, with his pay packet, Alice made a beeline for him, breaking away from the other women. She prodded his packet, playfully, gesturing that her envelope was far bigger than his. He reacted with a rare moment of frivolity, by miming his struggle to carry his pay packet as a heavy load. Alice feigned a belly laugh, pandering to Ming's primitive humour. Then, with her heart in her mouth, she decided to take a real chance.

Still playing the clown, Alice opened her packet, gesturing that she could prove her pay was way better than his. She used teasing dramatics to draw Ming in. This was his first pay day, so, in that moment, he was clueless how to decipher the figures. Through admiration, and a growing addiction to her, Ming had come to place his trust entirely in Alice, his new guardian. Alice, cockily, began playfully flirting with her pay slip in his face.

So used to Alice offering a guiding hand, almost out of habit, still ever-reliant on her for her counsel, he handed his slip to her, without thinking. She hid her joy, and her now shaking hands. Alice managed to glance at his wage, enough to see it, then handed it back, mockingly, as though beneath her dignity to have to witness such meagre pay. Her strategy worked to perfection. Still not suspecting her performance had been entirely contrived, Ming's demeanour began to change. With Ming now frowning, gesturing to see her wage slip, Alice had to change tack. This moment was key, and she knew it.

She had suppressed her delight well enough, but she now knew Ming's wage was, indeed, some way lower than hers.

Now she had to adopt a serious manner and exploit the trust that Ming had so completely placed in her. Still feigning her own surprise at his ignorance that she was better paid, Alice held up both slips, side by side, clutching her wad of money to visually illustrate their wage difference. After some grimacing, and grunts of frustration, Ming finally understood. His mood sank.

What Alice had failed to learn from Ming, or understood about him, was the underlying mental turmoil he was already suffering from. She had expected a degree of outrage about his poor pay, to have upset him sufficiently to stir up his comrades to join the women's revolt. She had miscalculated. Ming had another, more pressing mission to attend to. A cause of his own to pursue. Even though Alice had, so craftily, fostered a tender bond with Ming, she clearly hadn't courted him enough to understand him fully. Seeing Ming's change of spirit, she backed off.

Ming had been waiting, desperately, for his first wage with only one preoccupation in his head – he must send money home. Yes, he was furious and upset to learn from Alice that he had been fobbed-off with a derisory wage by the French, but that would have to be a grievance to address some other time. For now, he had his primary duty to attend to, and this he would tackle entirely on his own. This said, for the first time since he had arrived at the factory, for once he could not rely on Alice, but his next move would place him in the hands of his Chinese Interpreter, first and foremost, and then he would be at the mercy of The Factory Controller. Deciding only to hold back a fraction for his own subsistence, Ming had resolved to commit his long-awaited, precious pay to the formal workings of the war postal services, and the honesty of its handlers. He was now on his own in a perilously unfamiliar place.

Ming had made his wishes and his concerns, crystal clear. The Interpreter had assured him several times, that he understood, and that he had made certain that the Controller did also. Everything had been done to ensure his package of cash posted home would be safely, and promptly, despatched. Ming had urged, forcefully, that it was a matter of life and death for his family. He had pushed his luck, as a subordinate, to the limit with his assertiveness. Now he had done all that he could, all he dared to express.

Alice advised her women agitators to hold fire. She needed longer to fathom Ming out fully. They expressed frustration, but they were swayed by what Alice had counselled. She was clear that they would be compromised if they acted without their Chinese counterparts on board. They needed to wait, to bide their time, hold tight, yet how patient might they prove to be?

17 THE TRAPPED BIRD

At first it had been a welcome distraction, but then it had become clear that the bird was hopelessly trapped.

It hadn't caused any concern for a while, so the dear thing had been left to its own devices. It had flapped around, preened itself, content enough up in the rafters of the factory structure but eventually, in its bewilderment, an agitation had set in.

Unable to ascertain exactly where it was, or where it had come from, the bird had taken to swooping, low down, over the workstations, and the women workers had begun to panic. Once a few desperate squeals had erupted, more and more workers had abandoned their posts for fear of finding the bird entangled in their hair. The Works Controller had stepped in. He hadn't much of a clue what to do about it, but he now felt compelled to take action.

Clutching a long broom, he took a couple of wild swipes at the bird as it flew past, but that just made matters worse. Starting to fluster, there was a new urgency in its efforts to flee, the bird dashing to and fro in the hope that an escape route might reveal itself – but none did. The bird couldn't recollect, for the life of it, how it had got into the building, nor why an inhabitant had suddenly taken to it with such an irrational hostility.

Inevitably, as a last resort, and with the only available light filtering through the far-end window, the bird launched a final, desperate, dash towards it. Honing its flight, one final time, over a now cowering audience below it, this was to be the bird's last-ditch chance for freedom. It had wagered everything it had left upon it. It failed.

The collision emitted a remarkably soft impact, considering the speed the bird had generated. With more of a muffled 'thud' than an ear-shattering 'smash', the poor bird had not anticipated any obstruction, and nor did its committed purpose shatter the glass. Instead, the defeated creature crumpled, and flopped pathetically earthbound, until there it lay, an undignified heap of feathers.

Alice was first to rush over. A country girl, born and bred, she alone had not recoiled as the bird had broken into panic. Quite the contrary. She had ruefully pleaded with the Controller to desist from frightening the bird throughout the entire episode, but he hadn't listened. He wasn't to know any better, but she had urged he was making matters worse.

The Controller had, as it happens, long taken a shine to Alice. He both feared and resented her involvement with the women's unrest at the factory, but he had found her irresistibly compelling. This, ultimately, won over his favour. Now, with the once acrobatic bird reduced to pitiful immobility, Alice had scooped it up, intent on saving its life. She rushed around frantically in search of a suitable box to house the bird whilst it was still unconscious. A fellow worker found one and launched it towards her, across one of the working lines. Alice lowered the bird into safety. Chance would have it, the bird miraculously began to stir, instinctively resisting any fruitless struggle that might make matters worse. It must have sensed its new enclosed state was a place of relative safety.

The moment seemed to have prompted a round of applause from the workers. Alice blushed, oblivious that she had, all along, attracted a significant audience. Meanwhile, still unaccustomed to clapping, the Chinese bowed towards her.

Things were not going to be plain sailing at the factory. The more vociferous of the agitating women felt they had waited long enough for Alice to announce that the Chinese were securely on side. They had lost faith in her directive, even though she had urged them that her ongoing efforts, through Ming, needed more time. He remained their only real contact so far as exercising influence on the Chinese Workers was concerned. No one, other than Alice, seemed blessed with the tenacity to get anywhere with these unfamiliar men, or perhaps they just lacked her resolve. So it was, inevitably, that a breakaway band of discontented women revived their demands. This time, Alice kept out of it. She was confident these women would just hand back the advantage to the factory officials with so many trained-up Chinese now working in amongst them. These men were still too new in their postings to want to join in any rumpus that might provoke trouble. Crucially, apart from Ming, they were also still oblivious to the poor level of their pay by a simple comparison with the women, so it should have been no surprise that Alice still resisted the call. Her gut told her these men would obey the factory call, when it came, to replace the striking women, when push came to shove. She didn't want to be part of any losing cause. So, for once, she held back.

Things played out well for Alice when she delivered her boxed bird to the Controller's office, requesting his urgent help. He was far too distracted, under pressure from the rebel women, to engage with Alice on such an utterly trivial subject. She didn't let the request go. She pressed him, seductively. Had she persisted like this, at any other time, even with the Controller so enamoured with Alice, he would surely have told her to 'get lost'. Sent her back to her station with a flea in her ear, demanding the bird be disposed of. Yet instead, in sheer exasperation, he practically ordered her to leave and to deal with the problem herself:

'Remove the damn bird, take it out of my sight, dump the thing up at the British CLC camp,' he announced, beside himself. 'There's some idiot Chinky bloke up there, one of their Interpreters, got himself known as a "bird fixer", bloody madness.'

He was as much enraged that a single bird might take precedence over his present troubles, as he was that the British, in their stupidity, had accommodated a foreign worker's eccentricities. The only thing stopping the Controller from going off the rails completely, was his relief that Alice had, for some reason, made it clear she was no longer part of the women's fight.

The Controller's astonished face was a picture as Alice launched at him and pecked him on the cheek. She left, in haste, with her bird.

Alice had absolutely no inclination towards the Controller. She had, unashamedly, used him and she had loved her victory. Yet she feared, in that moment, that she had perhaps contrived an awaiting future snare for herself. He might now assume she was fair game, and who could blame him after that episode. As a thin, unsettling little man, he was anything but attractive to her, but he was a key personality at her place of work, and that mattered. She put all that to the back of her mind as she left the building, with a skip in her step. She had, miraculously, been granted temporary leave, and she was hopeful her bird's salvation was that bit closer.

She hadn't realised just how confining her work environment had become until she breathed in her first, delicious, gasp of morning air. Her breathing, and her persistent chest discomfort, had left her in a weakened state, so access to fresh air was more than just a mental tonic. She was 'off-shift', with only her injured bird for company, and she could hardly imagine in that moment, there was a war raging on at all.

She wondered what her little boy would think of her. She was sure he would giggle at his mother's nerve at her workplace, or perhaps, more likely, he would just be excited to see her bird in the flesh. He would surely also wonder how the mysterious man she was heading to see could possibly save its life. She began to agonise, 'You will have everything, my darling boy,' she gritted her teeth, her mood hardened, '...everything, I promise.'

How she then clung to her boxed bird as though it were Maxime himself. 'Your army father will pay, one day, for his "crime of desertion".'

It felt like a country jaunt as she turned to take the path towards the Chinese camp beyond the village. It proved quite a way. She questioned why any support force would be based so far from the other barracks. She was even more bemused when she first caught sight of the camp, that it was encircled by such high perimeter fencing. '*Mon Dieu*!'

she gasped, partly also from being out of breath from the distance she had walked, 'this looks more like a prison camp.'

She had been mindful not to rock the bird around too much, with her enthusiastic stride, but the dear thing hadn't moved at all. Arriving at the Camp gates, she explained her situation to the guard. Charmed by her, and her eccentric request, he dutifully went off to get Yun. In spite of her poor English, he seemed to know what she wanted. Sporting her box and mention of 'The Birdman' proved enough. Yun appeared within a few minutes. This was the first meaningful contact Yun would have had with any female since he had left China, let alone such a pretty one, just as it had been for Ming, and ironically, with the very same woman. Yun was immediately unsettled by this unscheduled, endearing encounter, but he purposefully betrayed nothing in his demeanour.

Proud to posture as the 'bird doctor around these parts', Yun took the box from Alice and lowered it to the ground. He crouched, gently lifting up one of the cardboard flaps to take a look. Alice seemed, involuntarily, to be shadowing his every move. Their heads were now touching, both crouching-down, facing each other. Yun then played his trump card; he spoke to her in French:

'*La pauvre petite*,' he whispered, overtly softly, keeping his line of sight on the bird. Alice jolted her head in amazement. He didn't react, but continued, in French, 'Wow!' she whispered back also in French, 'What wonderful French, Mr Birdman, *quelle surprise*!' He still kept his cool countenance, not wanting to drop his cloak of professionalism. Then, after examining the bird, and with equal assuredness, as he confidently returned the bird to its box:

'*Ça y est!*' he murmured, as though, naturally, assuring

himself. 'Now I see,' he added, as he took the boxed patient into his care.

'Will it survive?' pleaded Alice, taken in.

'Yes,' he responded, 'it's miraculous, the dear thing has injured its back, but it will, with luck, still have a chance of flying again.' Yun mentioned nothing of his permanently resident sparrow, still nestled snug within his tunic. One patient he had not been able to restore to its former self.

As she wandered back towards the factory, Alice couldn't get Yun, and his treatment of her bird, off her mind. He had been so kind with the creature, yet with such powerful-looking hands and arms. His efforts, at French, had just entranced her all the more. She had wondered what Yun thought of her. Did he think her just some pathetic, foolish, French girl, unable to help the bird herself? Only the second Chinese man she had ever really met, he was so different to Ming. Self-assured, masculine; she had taken to him. They had almost forgotten to introduce themselves to each other, but did so as they parted. Yun needed a week, or so, with the bird.

Alice could think of nothing else from the moment she resumed working. In her impatience, she was back at the CLC camp in days. Now firmly in favour with the Controller – whose infatuation with her had only deepened – she took full advantage. Yun wasn't there. She was told that he was on urgent duties at the tank depot. Distant thundering from some significant salvo had shaken the ground beneath her, on her way there. As though expecting Alice to show up prematurely, he had left a note with the guard. In it, Yun explained, now that he had made, and attached, a splint to the bird's back, he was 'Very optimistic that a further couple of weeks of recuperation, assuming the bird would begin feeding again, would see the patient through'. She smiled, handed back his note, having scribbled on it –'*Merci*'.

She began to dream about Yun as he did about her. For Alice it was all wonderment that swept her away as she slept. The bird appeared as a graceful dove, flapping triumphantly over her head, and Yun a mystical prince from the East. For Yun, his apparitions were entirely masculine. The kind that taunts men, promising sexual bliss, then vanishing, just as satisfaction seemed a certainty. Yet, deep within him, partly out of affection for his mother's memory, he saw beyond his lustful drive for the first time in his adult life. A maternal hallucination it may have been, but Yun saw in Alice that same strength of purpose his mother had, that fortitude, and he loved Alice all the more for it.

By the time the two met again, with the bird ready for its final inspection, there was an air of easy familiarity between them. Having only actually met the one time, it must have been their obsessive preoccupation with each other, in their thoughts, that had progressed their mutual feelings. Alice was fired up, tingling with anticipation, as Yun opened up the box. The camp guard had said they could venture away to a safe, calmer, distance from the entrance, to give the bird its best shot at not being spooked. This had gifted the two some privacy too. The distant rumblings of war had, for that moment, ebbed away.

Yun beckoned Alice to handle his patient with him, side by side, to celebrate this as a joint venture. They proceeded to share the endeavour together. Now pressing against each other, rather awkwardly, the two cupped their hands to raise it from the safety of the box. Alice noticed how gnarled, and slightly deformed his thumbs were, a detail that seemed incongruous with Yun's soft touch. With the bird held high over their heads, Yun signalled for them both to open their palms, in unison. They did just that, but the bird remained still. Yun had seen this act of hesitancy a thousand times before, so he whispered they must both maintain their outstretched arms a while longer. It promptly became a moment of intense intimacy. They were as close to each other as they could possibly be, breathing in each other's air, feeling one another's heartbeat. Then, just as the muscles in Alice's arms had begun to burn, the moment finally came.

As the bird raised its wings, as though testing its back for strength, it began to beat them through the air with an increasing vigour. Then, but only when it was ready, up it rose, and in moments its innate flying instinct kicked in and off it raced into the distance. She tried to suppress her emotions but found she could not. Alice sank her head into her palms and sobbed with joy. Without thinking, now on automatic drive, Yun instinctively stooped down towards her and kissed her forehead. For the first time he could taste her, smell her skin, and he desperately wanted the magic of it to linger. He needn't have suffered any such longings. Sensing his lips, mere inches above her mouth, Alice raised her head, offering her mouth towards his. They kissed, passionately.

Little was said between them. As they parted, Alice waved back to him. He waved in reply. There was now a bond, the beginnings of love, but neither had the slightest clue what this might mean nor where any of it might lead. Both knew, full well, how strict the governing rules were, prohibiting integration between their disparate peoples. For the French, the Chinese were here under sufferance, whilst they needed them to labour alongside their female workers. A degree of 'fraternisation' was inevitable but actively discouraged. Any thought, any fantasy, that an act vaguely resembling an attempted courtship could be kept as discreet, was optimism at its best. If it were to flourish at all, it would take every drop of stubborn determination by both. Perhaps, in such contrast to a sterile war environment, the drive of passion might yet prevail.

The British were free to adopt an entirely more rigid approach, and this they applied with a dispassionate determination. Yun's Chinese contract tied him to military rules, so he realised he would have to resort to his, apparently, raised status, to craft further opportunities. Alice rather dreaded risking more flirtations at the factory to win repeated leave to stay in touch with Yun, so she had, instead, begun to milk her poor health as a new leverage to sway the Controller onside. A convincing coughing fit, as she approached his office, pressing for exercise breaks and fresh air usually did the trick!

Alice and Yun's fragile prohibited new romance was to be severely tested in the days and weeks to come. They were in fate's hands. The vagaries of war might yet play a telling part in this along the way.

18 MING MEETS YUN

The strike, by the hardcore band of women, had come to an end. It wasn't an official truce. As Alice had predicted, the 'powers that be' had privately cautioned the women's spokesperson, that those intransigents who did not accept the terms now being offered, would be summarily sacked and replaced. With Alice no longer one of the leading voices, and a significant body of doubting women wavering because of her absence, a capitulation was the inevitable outcome.

Even though Alice had been key to the progression of their strike action, and every female worker had, ultimately, benefited from these efforts in their pay packets, Alice no longer held much sway with them. She felt the injustice of this deeply. She took it personally. It would seem she was resented for deserting the women to suffer a compromise deal, when she had warned them, all along, that they should wait. She had cautioned that the factory officials would use the Chinese to counter their threats, and this is exactly what they did!

Alice hated any unpopularity, no matter how ignorant and petty it might be. It was ill-conceived, that was the truth, a complete injustice, but there was little she could do about it now. She felt both sad and bitter. She was pleased at the pay increase, for what it was, and if there was a shift in the dynamics within the factory, she decided she would just draw closer to Ming and his people. They had, in any case, remained blissfully ignorant of the murky workings of all that had come to pass between the women and the factory, and Ming remained preoccupied. They were bemused anyway. Working alongside women, seeing them protesting for better pay, these were things of total fantasy back in China, anathema to Chinese men, so they had instinctively kept well clear of it all. In any event, a world away from all of this, when the day of reckoning finally arrived for poor Ming, everything changed for him, both body and soul.

It had taken forever, but a letter eventually arrived for Ming. It was from his wife, but he had no means of knowing what it said! The two were both, of course, utterly illiterate, so Ming knew full-well she had not written the letter herself. She would have enlisted help from somewhere, and now Ming needed the same support to read it for him. His mistrust for The Interpreter went deep, so he resolved to say nothing about his plight to him, so he remained utterly stranded. His dilemma ate away at him, relentlessly, and whilst he hung on to his determination to keep this to himself, the strain of it began to show in his conduct. Alice, sensitive and astute, had detected the deterioration in Ming's demeanour for quite some time, and she had become increasingly concerned.

The first sign was when Ming had failed to respond to their, mutual, saluting ritual. They had established a remarkably tender rapport, so this sudden estrangement had upset Alice, but she had taken it as a symptom of a passing mood. Then his conduct at their workstation became alarming. Ming had started to clang down his tools, loudly exclaiming Chinese words in a cursing manner that suggested choice expletives. His compatriots had glanced over to him, looking shocked, reinforcing Alice's suspicions. With a tangible agitation brewing all around Ming, Alice resolved to do something to break the tension.

She chanced her arm, during every private moment between them, to press him to confess his problem. With every gesticulation she could muster, she urged him to let her help him or he would soon fall into real trouble. Finally, he cracked. During a work break he handed the letter to Alice. With an empty gesture of his open hands, an agitated mix of facial expressions, shoulder shrugs, comical attempts at acting charades, Alice gasped as she finally understood. What a relief for Ming. At last, someone he trusted was aware of his problem.

Now that Alice had seen the letter and realised it was from his wife, she empathised with him completely. He was beside himself, not knowing what the hell her news was! So, this was the cause of Ming's misery. Alice so felt for him, it was heartbreaking, but what could she possibly do to sort this out for him? She began to rack her brain. 'How dreadful for poor Ming,' she reflected, now that she knew. 'How devastating, having waited for so long to hear from his dear wife but having no clue what she had to say.' Alice could see from his face, that Ming's imagination was running riot. 'Was she ok?'; 'Were the children safe?'; 'Had he sent her enough money…?'

Ming was now entirely in Alice's hands. He had accepted that, and had also taken on board her gentle request to give her space, alone, to think. It had been enough, for him, to have offloaded his angst, his burden, so he granted Alice the time that she needed. It took a few days and a great deal of soul-searching, but when the answer crystallised in her mind, Alice just kicked herself for not conceiving the solution from the outset. 'Yun, of course, idiot,' she chided, 'Yun will resolve this mess, I'm sure he will.'

She came to Ming with the good news, but he neither understood nor cared, in his present state, what she was chattering on about. He had learned that if Alice was happy, better still, enthusiastic, only good could come from it. He had at least grasped that a Chinese man, called Yun, might be key to his agony. He was a fellow countryman at least, but he neither knew the name out here, nor his purpose. He'd also not anticipated, at all, that whatever scheme Alice had cooked up for him, it would involve leaving the building!

Once more, Alice had to grovel to the Controller. It wasn't in her nature to be obsequious, overly deferential, but it was completely in her to do what was needed to get her way. Again, luck was on her side. Engrossed in something, enough to stop him considering her request with any proper scrutiny, he dismissively gestured his consent. He hadn't grasped at all that this would include Ming. Had he realised, the outcome might have been completely different. Alice hadn't mentioned Ming at all, but he was standing with her at the time, looking suitably meek and bemused, so he just steadfastly clung to her. She didn't dilly-dally.

Then Ming held back. Now outside, where on earth was Alice taking him? He knew, full well, leaving the building without authorisation, was a strict breach of the rules, but had Alice in fact gained permission for him too? The Chinese were only ever given leave in limited circumstances, invariably connected with a works detail, and he feared for any retribution. This said, seeing Alice in no mood for anything other than temerity, Ming fell in behind her, but only with a very heavy heart. His paranoia about his unread letter proved the greater force.

Alice had, naturally enough, been hankering after an opportunity, any chance at all, for venturing out to see Yun again. She hadn't used Ming, not as such, but her drive to help him had been given an irresistible boost by her desire for Yun. She accepted, but put to one side, the likelihood that she would get no chance at all for any private intimacy on this visit. Yet it was better than nothing and, who knows, something miraculous might happen? She had so desperately missed Yun.

As it happened, 'fortune favoured the brave'. As Alice drew up close to the CLC gates Yun was already in the yard tending to a delivery of parts he had been asked to rationalise ready to go to the tank depot. His and Alice's eyes met immediately. A flush of joy went through them both, it had been an agonisingly long while, but this time there was a Chinese stranger in tow? Yun got an informal pass to chat to them both outside the gates. Alice restrained her feelings, as she dutifully introduced the two men to each other. Alice explained Ming's dilemma to Yun. Ming looked totally nonplussed, hearing the two converse together in, what he assumed, must be French. Things didn't get any better when Yun then turned to Ming and began to prattle away to him in Mandarin. Ming waved, manically, at Yun to stop. He could only understand his own dialect! They both went silent, there was a momentary, uneasy pause, until they both burst into unrestrained laughter.

Alice pressed them to 'keep it down'. Thrilled, though she was, that they had hit it off, they were attracting unwanted attention, but Yun explained the moment to her. She giggled at the irony, but then pressed the letter into Yun's hand, urging him to focus, to study it promptly. He read through it, carefully, twice. Being only vaguely conversant in Ming's tongue, Yun contrived to convey his wife's messages to him with a combination of words, hand gestures, and symbols written on his palms. Ming was slow to grasp it all, but, oddly, that didn't seem to frustrate him. Ming had clearly found the whole process very engaging. He had been offered a lifeline to ease his torment, and he rather loved the feeling of being at least on the fringes of literacy, but once that novelty wore off, the enormity of what the letter actually said struck home. Ming's shoulders dropped, his face changed, he slumped heavily with his stare set downwards.

Ming now knew, to his utter consternation, that his money had not reached his wife at all. Now she was suicidal and, worst of all, her health had seriously declined since Ming left his family behind in China. She berated him, in a state of despair, for letting her down, leaving them penniless. She said that she prayed he was safe, and that there was an entirely rational reason why she had heard absolutely nothing from him, but that no explanation was of any use to her now. Ming choked with despair. His body tensed up, began to shake. In his agony, his desolation, he went to throw a punch at Yun, but the others both restrained him.

He had, instinctively, wanted to 'shoot the messenger', which Ming realised, just in time. He cursed getting the letter at all. He would rather have known nothing. Then, as his mind raced, he reached the only conclusion that he could. Those evil officials back at the factory, those he had never trusted anyway – The Interpreter, the Controller, the whole damn lot of them – had cheated him from the outset. They had taken his cash.

Yun assured Ming he would compose a reply, even lend him the replacement money to go with it, but Ming was having none of it. With his face drained ashen grey, his eyes lifelessly dark and menacing, Ming turned away, setting off for the factory alongside Alice. Alice stole a glance back towards Yun, smiled affectionately, reassuringly, but this had been a miserable encounter for them all.

Ming had parted from Alice, after a long shift. She had lost sight of him but had then congregated with a group of women, outside. Both she and Yun had suspected from Ming's mental agony, his transformed state of mind, that he was hatching something but they had no idea what.

Noticing the Controller was away from his office, Ming had grabbed the moment and crept in to search around. He'd decided, that if his cash had indeed been stolen, it might still be intact, in its original pay-packet, stashed away for future use in the office safe. He found the key in the desk drawer and then spotted the safe. Certain of what he would find, he turned the key and opened the safe door, then plunged his hands inside to rummage through its contents. He had been reckless, too fired up to take proper care. Not only did the Controller turn up and catch Ming red handed, but the two soldiers he was with were able to arrest Ming there and then. As fate would have it, the Controller had been in a briefing with some top brass, and they had sent him back to his office, with these troops, to discuss transport arrangements for their latest batch of assembled shells. It couldn't have been a more facilitated arrest.

Alice was alarmed to see Ming being escorted by the military from the factory. They marched right past her group, but with such conviction, such a forthright purpose, she was stunned into silence. What on earth could have happened from mere moments ago? She feared the worst, knowing his desolate state of mind, but became resolute about getting to the truth, and sharpish. Alice rushed into the Controller's office begging him for an explanation. To her amazement he gave it. Her heart sank. The mad fool had been a naïve and reckless idiot. She cursed herself for not keeping a closer eye on him. Both she and Yun knew the impact his wife's letter had inflicted on him. In her exasperation, her utter chagrin, she pleaded with the Controller to mitigate for Ming, explaining his state of mind with his wife suicidal. Alice was desperate to help, but the Controller was unmoved, saying, 'He is nothing but a common thief.'

Even with The interpreter there, at the hastily convened Criminal Hearing, Ming didn't understand a word of what was being said. He didn't dare spell out his suspicions about the theft of his money because he knew only too well they would have laughed in his face. He was the thief, and he had been caught in the act. Anything else he might have claimed, shouting the odds, would have been dismissed as total fantasy and an unacceptable swipe at his employers. No, he was guilty, and that was that.

It was only when Ming was being led towards, what looked like, a firing squad post, that he went berserk. Surely the verdict that had been read out to him, none of which he had understood, had not been one condemning him to death? He wasn't strong enough to break free, but he had given it all that he had, enough to provoke one soldier to strike him on the back of his head with his rifle butt for good measure. He flopped to the ground. Numb and exhausted, he was then tethered to the post, more securely than they might have previously done. They left him there. So, this was his punishment. He was not going to die. He was relieved, but he was still resolved to murdering every factory official for their treachery, even though he hadn't been shot on the spot as he had feared. He was only guilty of being recalcitrant, he hadn't attempted to 'steal' anything. He had just wanted to retrieve his own money, to prove that it was they who were guilty of theft, and not him. It was not to be. He had been ridiculously impetuous, too despairing to think rationally.

As it happened, the so-called 'field punishment' location, where he was now incarcerated, was immediately to one side of the perimeter fencing to Yun's Chinese Labourers' compound.

It wasn't long before Yun recognised Ming through the wire and began communicating with him. It proved tricky for gesturing back this time, with Ming's tied hands out of commission, but Yun gathered enough from him to despatch an urgent message to Alice telling her where Ming was being held. As soon as she heard, she really began to chance her luck, using every seductive charm she could muster to sway regular forays away from the factory. Never suspecting her purpose, Alice managed to smuggle out food and medical applications, past the Controller, to ease Ming's hunger, and treat his head wound back to recovery.

Thanks to his two, kind friends, Ming had not suffered quite as he might. By the time of his release, he was eager, and fit enough, to return to his posting. His Chinese comrades welcomed him back, but not without a serious dose of ribbing, and a fair share of berating for being a reckless fool. Ming didn't venture to explain his motives, his suspicions, not even to them. There seemed no point. As for the women workers, they had mostly been puzzled by Ming's actions, though some sided with Alice, believing he had reasons for acting as desperately as he did. The factory officials were another thing entirely. Ming was, to them, a pariah, to be treated like an outcast. A Chinese thief who was to be watched like a hawk. To them, he had got away with murder.

A few weeks in, there was an air-raid. It was thought the German bomber had messed up, flown past its intended target, and dropped its remaining ordnance wherever it could. It had nearly 'struck lucky'. One shell had missed the rear of the factory, taking out a shelter and ripping a gash in the factory wall. The resultant smoke-surge smothered any view of the building, so it was impossible to judge, right away, what it had hit. It had struck during a busy shift. Ming had just finished and gone outside for his break, but Alice had got behind and was still inside.

It looked worse than it was, but Ming wasn't to know that. With the siren clattering in his ears, he had panicked when he realised where Alice was. He wasn't going to wait for the fire guys to show. He ripped a length of cloth from his tunic, tied it around his mouth and nose, and hurried inside. It was impossible to see a thing, but Ming had always had a facility for seeing in poor light. He struggled, but somehow navigated his way towards his workstation, where he hoped Alice would still be. She was. He recognised her cough, her nasal voice, he yelled her name for reassurance. She had remained where she was, unable to see which direction would take her to safety, and not towards the source of the smoke. She had managed to stay calm, but all the while she thought only of her son and how she must survive. Just as she had begun to panic due to the lack of any breathable air, Ming had led Alice to safety. Now outside, Ming's immediate instinct was to go back in, to help the others he had seen, but as he went to do so he was hauled back by a bunch of officers who were making way for the fire fighters who had just arrived on the scene.

Miraculously, damage to the factory itself was minimal. Even the arsenal, the component parts, hadn't been touched. They needed a serious cleaning-up. Mercifully, and despite the heat, none of the assembled shells had detonated. Had they done so, had any of the stored powder ignited, it would have been an entirely different story. Alice was passionately grateful to Ming. Several of the women also voiced their gratitude. As for the factory officials, they made their position completely clear. Ming should have stayed put, not risked his safety, nor that of his fellow workers, by his 'idiotic act of bravado'. If he thought he had, somehow, immediately cleared his name by his actions, he was wrong. Those that mattered in the business hated him, and far from acknowledging any credit earned for his latest actions, they simply viewed Ming as a low-life who had sought to steal from them.

This just compounded Ming's torment. He feared he was already too late to save his family from doom. Alice feared what he might do next.

19 THE PHOTOGRAPHER

Yun quickly made his mark at his new posting in Erin. It proved to be a combination of his mechanical skills and his value to The British as a competent interpreter, that had helped him swiftly build a solid position.

He had become known as 'Birdman Yun' to his compatriots; an eccentric, imaginary, 'badge' he had come to sport wherever he was billeted. As with any quirky epithet, the word had got around generally, but Yun kept this side of his reputation as quiet as he could. For now, he needed his official attributes to earn him some accolade.

This said, his newly adopted sparrow, the one he had so poignantly rescued from the ashes, became his permanent resident once Yun was certain it would never be able to fly again. It had never left his inside tunic pocket since that time, nor was there any sign that either of them would ever consider a time they might be parted. The circumstances of their meeting, the shock aftermath of that fateful explosion, had been formative for them both. They were now as one. Yet another 'innocent' caught up in this war, Yun would never desert his disabled friend.

Having been mentioned in dispatches, from his last CLC

base, Yun had hit the floor running at the tank base. Yun couldn't remember, not exactly, what he had been told, or what he had learned for himself about Britain's classified data. So many of the British Officers assumed that none of the arriving Chinese spoke a word of their lingo. In this environment Yun gathered much that he needed to know, enough to realise, all too well, that the British tank was a vital new addition, their great new hope. The fresh innovation to turn the tide of fortune around in their favour. Blessed with this knowledge, Yun was set on exploiting their importance in every way that he could.

Yun's first sight of the Mark IV tank took his breath away. Standing idle, awaiting their time, these monsters were a formidable sight. Yun could see, now he could witness them in the flesh, why they might 'scare the pants' off the enemy. He could picture these steel creations, panelled into a fearsome assembly, looming large across the battlefield, intent on crushing everything in their path. Aside from his ambition to make his mark, he was impatient to fire their engines. He figured he wouldn't have to wait long. He had immediately been placed in charge of a select contingent of Chinese workers and most of the tanks required their urgent attention. Yun would need to stay on his toes.

Back at the CLC compound, Yun salvaged a precious moment to tend to his war-beleaguered sparrow. He knew he hadn't long until his next shift at the depot, but he realised he had neglected his long-suffering companion. What Yun hadn't noticed, was that all the while, his CLC camp Lieutenant, Bill Hawkings, had been busy setting up some camera equipment a short distance away. Pressed to tend to his bird, now up on his feet, Yun proceeded to feed it from his mouth; 'Come on my little friend, time for food, you've waited long enough.'

Utterly captivated by what he could see, Lt Hawkings turned his lens towards Yun, to capture the image. Only as Yun was shuffling his satisfied companion back into his tunic, did he spot Lt Bill Hawkings at all. Fearful he'd been rumbled, his covert relationship exposed, Yun wandered over to confront him. Then, realising who the man with the camera actually was, and his rank, he panicked. Yet he needn't have because the Lieutenant seemed immediately sensitive to Yun's feelings of vulnerability, and Yun was quickly reassured by his benign countenance as he approached him. Yun had no understanding of cameras, but was aware of photographs:

'What a remarkable endeavour!' the Lieutenant remarked, in English, dispelling Yun's concerns. 'I'd heard some Chinese were known wizards with birds, but I've never seen anything so touching as your intimate treatment; you've just gifted me my best image of the war!' He seemed to know Yun would understand, which quite took Yun aback.

Caught in the act, yet feeling increasingly relaxed, Yun chanced a conversation. The Lieutenant seemed entirely up for it. He introduced himself. Yun was fascinated to learn it was this man who had brought the last contingent of Chinese here for tank-work deployment. Close up, Yun could see that not only was this gentleman possibly in his forties, which set him apart anyway, but also he had none of that abrasive army manner Yun might have expected from him. Yun eyed him up curiously. It transpired Lt Hawkings was a volunteer to the British cause. He was here to willingly contribute to the war effort, allocated to be with the Chinese on account of his familiarity with Mandarin. What the Lieutenant was not here for, was for taking photographs, and he was clearly sensitive to this. He had cause to be. Photography was just his hobby, he was an amateur, and since only the official cameramen were authorised to take strictly controlled wartime images, always having to toe the propaganda line, Lt Hawkings was, in fact, a bit of a schemer himself, chancing his arm with his pursuit. Now that they had rumbled each other for their unauthorised obsessions, they both had a secret to guard!

As they parted, it troubled Yun that the Lieutenant had made no remark at all about his English. It was almost as if he had expected Yun's fluency. Did he already know who Yun was, he wondered? He hated unsolved conundrums, the more so whilst he, Yun, felt he had been masterful with his manoeuvres to ascertain who everyone was and who might matter. Yun's mind was whirring as he hurried back to his duties. Then he became certain, as he reassembled the past in his mind, that if this gentleman had indeed been snapping images of the CLC from the outset, it must have been him he noticed, doing exactly that, when Yun first boarded ship in China.

General Alan Thompson had recently been advanced to Major General. His name had lodged firmly in Yun's mind, his reputation having been so heavily emphasised at his last posting. He was known for being 'hands-on', but this recent promotion had spread-wide his remit. Now rarely seen at Erin, yet he was well known to all as being in overall command. Yun figured it would serve him well to know

Lieutenant Bill Hawkings

more about him. There was one, fleeting, moment when an encounter with Yun did take place.

It was mid-November 1917. Utter mayhem had broken out at the Erin tank depot. Yun had understood enough to realise that a pivotal, a possibly 'make or break' campaign, was on the brink of being unleashed. Yun's depot was to be in the eye of the storm, or at least it certainly felt that way. Yun had explained to his team, as best he could, that inordinately extended shifts were about to be imposed and there might be no let up for several days. Already overwhelmed, the news wasn't received well by his men. Yun had to quell a protest, and it took all he was worth to avert a full-scale rebellion. With his tongue firmly lodged in his cheek, Yun assured them all that a period of leave had been alluded to for the aftermath, but it was down to them to 'ensure a victory'. The encounter took his mind lurching back to that wretched train ordeal across Canada and his extreme efforts there to rein in his comrades.

The British in charge could see, and duly noted, Yun's impressive communication skills. An incendiary reaction was anticipated, certainly once the shifts were issued, but there was relief when Yun diffused the situation. Forewarning their new work regime was one thing, tolerating the reality of it, when it came, was quite another. To Yun's horror, every single tank was to be deployed in the forthcoming campaign, fully 'war-worthy' or not. This made no sense to him whatsoever. He may still have a vast amount to learn about these new beasts, but he already knew enough to know this strategy was flawed. If every machine was to be involved from the outset, what on earth did the British have in reserve? Yun's comrades may, just about, perform a minor miracle whilst the machines were base-bound, but once in the field on active engagements, these tanks were 'on their own'.

It wasn't for Yun to question the orders. They were emphatic and that was that. Why should he care anyway? That said, Yun did rather fear, cynically, that if there were to be any significant mass engine or mechanical failures during the engagement, his men were likely to take the full rap. With that foreboding speculation lodged, menacingly, in his head, Yun pushed his men, intent on driving them to the limit if he could get away with it for long enough. His reputation, and the preservation of his hard-earned status, were his priority now.

At the most critical time, during the chaotic preparation, Major General Alan Thompson appeared at the depot. Yun hadn't noticed him at all. Yun was crouched over some lower tank-tracking, cursing about an elusive obstruction, when their eyes met. The Major General had been strutting along the working lines, belting out orders, berating the lack of progress to his attendant officers. He had been told Yun was the man to ball at, for results, to bully progress:

'Do your damn lot realise how vital these tanks are?' he demanded, irascibility writ large across his face. 'Been assured you're the man to set things straight with these Chinks, so can I rely on you, man, to bark that out to them loud and clear?'

It was a ridiculous tirade, scarcely meriting a respectful reply, but this was the top dog standing before him, Yun knew that all too well. Despite the din belting out around them, the oil smears, and the grime smothering Yun's face, he gave it his best shot:

'Yes sir, of course, sir, do my best to stir them up, best

I can, sir,' then his dry throat got the better of him, he choked. 'Best!' came the response, 'Your best or *their* best?' he challenged, not expecting a reply. He didn't get one.

So, this was the Major General. Yun had expected to catch sight of him at some point, but not at close quarters, and not right there and then. Certainly not whilst he, Yun, was in such a dishevelled state. Yun cursed the timing of it, but then laughed off the encounter as a fiasco anyway. Alan Thompson certainly cut an impressive figure, not least for his cantankerous temperament thrown in. Yet, there again, in the thick of it, the riot of rivet-working, machines roaring above the bark of working men, any well-turned-out man, in authority, was bound to appear imperious. He was every inch a top brass, and Yun prayed he might just have noticed his fluency and attempt at being forthright. Yun had wanted to make his mark, but also to take a closer look at him, whilst he could. He had been caught unawares. He thought he had detected red hair beneath his cap, a moustache, perhaps, but by the time Yun had looked up from wiping his face, ready to examine him properly, the Major General had moved on.

ZERO HOUR: 6.20am – 20 November 1917
Cambrai – Northern France

'The Trial of the Tanks'

The German frontline troops, were exhausted. The third Battle of Ypres and the sanguinary horrors of Passchendaele, had taken its savage toll. The Allies had suffered horribly too, but Britain had been brewing a master plan for a long while, and now, oddly, seemed the perfect time to execute it – to break the territorial trench deadlock.

Dug deep into their trenches, along a six-mile stretch of their infamous Hindenburg Line, the German troops thought little of the occasional deep rumble, wafting their way from the static Allied positions. Even the surprisingly low flight of some British aircraft over their heads, didn't raise any great concern. They were light aircraft, perhaps on reconnaissance, and with up to 100-yards deep of well-crafted, picketed, barbed-wire defences, the Germans were entitled to feel smug and secure. They could not have known, nor be blamed for not suspecting, that these 'token' British fly-pasts had been launched partly to smother the grinding giveaway sound of 474 British tanks, the largest ever assembled force, taking up their strategic positions under cover of night. In any case, with no familiar 'shock and awe' bombardment raining down upon the German positions, to soften them up, there was no reason on earth to suspect that anything major was about to happen.

A German guard, on watch duty, peered through the mist, certain he had felt an ominous, steady, juddering through the trench wall and the clay beneath him. By the time he had spotted the advancing British Tank Corps, in vast numbers, it was too late. The resilient Germans stayed put, securely dug-in to defend their positions but with absolutely no notion of the formidable force now heading their way. Under the command of Brigadier General Hugh Ellis, the planning of the British Tank Corps advance had been meticulous. The leading tank formation crushed the German wire defences like matchwood. Considered impregnable, until now, the multiple rows of treacherous, barbed, entanglements were no match for the steel tracking of these brutal 28-ton beasts.

This battle ground had been well chosen. Relatively virgin territory, the British machines, the infantry and cavalry behind, progressed unhindered by craters and hazardous shell-holes from past battles. Avoiding severe cratering had been a well-considered reason for resisting the customary pre-battle bombardment of enemy positions. The solid, resistant ground, was a godsend. With a flattened pathway in their wake, the next run of tanks reared up like giant stag beetles clutching their prey in their talons. With a front-loaded payload of brushwood fascines, each six-feet deep, down they plunged into the German trenches, breaching them for the next arriving tanks to securely lumber across. German stalwarts were either crushed for their foolhardiness, or captured. The infantry, and the awaiting cavalry, traversed the trenches, now compromised with fascines as though they had never existed at all. Whatever became of the enemy troops imprisoned deep down, might only be revealed by future archaeologists.

All on this first fateful day, the British had punched a five-mile hole into German territory and taken 7,000 enemy prisoners. Ephemeral though this victory proved to be, it was far from a pyrrhic one. Yes, for myriad reasons, the British were unable to take full advantage and one they so deserved, for securing this outrageous initial success over their 'immovable' enemy.

Church bells pealed, in celebration of their victory, all over Britain for the first time in WWI. The British Commander-in-Chief, Haig, desperately needed this immediate news of a stunning advance, as did the entire country. This may have been just the first day of the Battle of Cambrai, a mere one-day snapshot, but it was going to be milked for all its worth, whatever happened next. As ever, Churchill had been in the background pressing for the tank's development, and deployment, for some while. Now the day for a proper test of this newly adopted war machine had arrived, all eyes were on the British Mark IV tank.

The legacy from it was to prove invaluable. Experience gained for the Tank Corps could now be deployed with increasing confidence, and effectiveness, in the many battles to come. The tank had come through its first 'trial' with flying colours.

Were it not for the timely expropriation by the Chinese, of the vacated British postings at their Tank depots, not least at Erin with men like Yun and his CLC compatriots, the ultimate course of WWI may well have unfolded rather differently indeed. Many have speculated, without daring to assert, that the war itself may have rumbled on for much longer had it not been for their contributions.

The tank had come through its first 'trial' with flying colours

20 THE PERILOUS PATH TO PEACE

It had taken a long while to locate a suitable safe haven for Yun and Alice to elope. It wasn't just a problem of where to meet, but also how to coordinate that elusive time together. It had become a tortuous task for them both, but finally, the moment had arrived. It was really all thanks to Yun.

He had stumbled on a partly derelict house, between their two locations. The property was empty, deemed unsafe, but Yun had sneaked around and found a lean-to to the rear, discreetly hidden. It must have been a store, annexed to the house, but it had been stripped bare. Yun had contrived a means of securing it and, by smuggling some cushions and blankets away from his billets over a number of visits, he had made the space really rather cosy. It was damp, but at least the roof didn't seem to leak. For Yun it seemed just perfect, and he was on his way there to meet Alice.

The war had been kind to him that day. With a lull in hostilities, there was an eerie calm in the air. He had heard the sound of a gramophone, hardly audible, just muffled waves of music issuing from a distant officer's quarters. It sent his pulse racing. He fantasised the melody was for him and his secret lover. He wished their affair had been clandestine for reasons other than yielding to a strict, non-integration directive issued by both their employers. How demeaned Yun felt, categorised as an unwanted foreigner, here purely for wartime expediency, yet a vital component for the British. As for Alice, she was a prized young woman, surely destined for a high-ranking army officer! Well, she had failed on that account, all on her own. Now all she wanted was her Chinese lover. She no longer hankered after the excitement of risqué encounters, where a chance for security might lure her to someone beyond her reach. Now she craved simplicity, the pureness of compassion and love.

There were no windows, but with the gentle glow from the makeshift stove, it was not entirely dark. How else had he managed to view the perfect silhouette of her naked body as she released her loose clothing to the floor. Yun could even see flashes of anxiety across her delicate face as she drew towards him through the gloom. Her meek, yet resolute, countenance made him want her all the more. That sense of fear, never feeling safe enough to show their affections to each other, not knowing when they might be caught, fuelled a surge of lust. Their longing for each other rose up, urgently, as they pressed together.

As her fingers stroked the soft skin of Yun's chest, feeling his powerful arms around her, she could scarcely accept that this warrior, gripping her, was that same gentle being who had fixed her broken bird, or one that had nursed countless other compromised creatures back from the brink. Yet she was now one such vulnerable soul, helplessly in his care, and she felt his strength. Such a different romantic encounter to the steely conduct of an insensitive British officer. Yes, Yun made love to her feverishly, yet she could sense he had so wanted to be controlled, restrained. Yun felt terror at the thought that this moment might be denied him at the last second, like some cruel prank. With her feminine intuition, she realised this in him too, and she loved him all the more for it. She gasped as she held him to her, frightened, yet strangely comforted by his unfamiliar, muscular frame. He was every bit the lover she craved, the more so for their enforced separation, forbidden to fraternise in plain view. A secure affection had grown within her, and she treasured the fragility of it, and the newness. She consigned her officer to her reckless past.

'We've done it, *ma chérie*, we've outwitted them all, *finalement*,' she gushed, sweating, and trembling. 'But now we must leave here as though nothing ever happened between us at all.' He knew she was right.

Their determination to protect their hidden shelter proved the stronger instinct. They parted, separately. Alice first, floating like a ghost from the scene, Yun, more sullenly, cursing the transience of this, their first precious act of passion. This may have felt like the fulfilment of every yearning he had ever had, but the only single desire driving his thoughts right now, was how to make this happen over, and over, again.

Even Ming noticed, through his established closeness to her, a distinct change in Alice, suspecting something had taken place between her and Yun. He felt a pang of jealousy, naturally enough. If his instincts were right, it only served to deepen those longings for his absent wife, revived by the impact of that single letter. With no further news from home, no sense of any safe way of reversing their fate, he chose not to question Alice, not wanting his suspicions to prove true and their happiness to be rubbed in his face.

Yun and Alice did continue to see each other, but only when it was safe. Alice insisted no risks were taken. They must not excite any suspicion. Yun's status at work served him well, whilst Alice's continued 'charm offensive' with the Controller masked her elicit purpose. Yet it upset them both never to be able to stroll freely in each other's company, have anything close to a normal loving relationship, but such was the inescapable nature of each of their disparate, wartime, predicaments.

Despite the enforced distance in their relationship, Alice knew, full well, that the subject of her past romance and the birth of Maxime, would soon have to be broached as their relationship progressed. Alice was acutely alert to this, and she was dreading it. What explanation would she offer Yun? Would she peddle that same well-trodden lie that had served her so well thus far? Either way, a decision had become inescapable, with Yun starting to scheme how he could take leave to visit her parents, so she took the plunge at the next opportunity.

She was in unchartered territory, yet she was clear in her head, that the relative fragility of their improbable union did not allow much elbow room for total honesty – 'not yet at least' – was her calculated thinking.

Yun didn't seem to react, not noticeably, but then Alice had embellished her account of the past, for safety, to match the tale she had peddled at work. She felt she just had to stay consistent, to protect herself, her son and her reputation. She explained how her son's father had died on the battlefield for 'La France'. He had done his duty, and she was proud. 'Maxime is all I have to remember him by.' If Yun found it odd that Alice showed little sign of any visible grief, he didn't say so. Perhaps he was just in awe, once he knew, that she had proved determined and resilient in the face of a shattering loss for her. For him, these might be the admirable facets of a woman defying the disablement of sudden widowhood, for the sake of her young child. Yun's love and admiration for his own mother had become so much a part of his perception of all that was worthy in a woman, and in a devoted mother. Yun seemed to accept what he had been told, even admiring her for it. That was all that mattered to Alice, for now.

Late 1918

With every sign that the war was, finally, drawing to a close in the Allies' favour, Ming agonised how he might break his French contract. It was crucial for him that he did so. Set for a five-year term, an end to the war would not mean an end to his contract. He was contracted to stay put. The French had calculated, from the start, that these Chinese recruits would be essential way beyond the ravages of war. As the host nation, someone had to clear up the mess for them on French soil.

Yun faced a diametrically opposed dilemma. His British, three-year term, was about to expire. He knew he would face removal from France as part of the agreed, compulsory, repatriation back to the country he had abandoned. Conversely, Ming still urgently craved a dramatic home-coming if he wasn't already too late to save his family, whilst Yun was set never to go back. Yun's lover, his new life with her and her son, lay here, in France, so Yun was going nowhere and he would stake his life on that resolution.

It was whilst the three of them were, by chance, together, that a seemingly improbable notion entered Alice's mind. She hadn't thought it through, not properly at all, yet she had opened up about it, without preparation, voicing it to the others in vague terms, as a fleeting idea.

'If only there was some way, Ming, that you could *become* Yun, and Yun could *become* you. Alice chuckled at how fantastical she sounded. 'It's only that you both want what the other already has, and ne'er the twain will meet!'

Alice's choice of idiom was rather more apposite than she could have realised. Oblivious to this, Yun burst into life:

'You're a genius Alice, a wizard, why on earth didn't I think of that?' yelped Yun, now pacing like a madman to and fro, as though obsessing over some master plan that might save the world. As it transpired, he was doing something quite close to that, for the three of them at least. Alice was falling in, gradually, but none of these antics had yet registered with Ming at all. Still with his shoulders shrugged, his head stooped, Yun's explosion of energy did, miraculously, stir him back to consciousness. What on earth were the two of them wittering on about?

When Yun spelled it out, slowly and meticulously, a look of astonishment, and a fair helping of fear, crept across Ming's face. Was Yun serious? He could tell from Alice's smirk that he must be.

The War Finally Ends

On the 11th hour, of the 11th day, of the 11th month, the cessation of hostilities of WWI was finally declared. It was over. The culmination of a coordinated Allied offensive, extending over 400 miles of the Western Front, after four long years of bitter conflict, resulted in an overwhelming advance forcing the enemy towards their ultimate end. So, what now for these three protagonists in this trilogy of lives?

21 THE DECEPTION

Yun knew a comrade, an able mechanic at the tank depot, well enough to trust him completely. It was vital that he did. What Yun had persuaded Alice to condone and, crucially, Ming to agree to, was unquestionably illegal. Alice had to accept the risk, after all she had provoked the idea, but it would equally implicate Ming for taking part should either of them ever get caught. Ming was entirely complicit, an essential accomplice, so Yun had gone over every detail, meticulously, with Alice, until they both concluded that it was their best, and safest, chance.

With the war at an end, there was a transformed atmosphere about the place. It felt unreal to everyone. France, for so long an occupied theatre of conflict, you could almost hear the earth straining to suck in, then spit out, its final sodden lungful of corrupt air. The sooner the instruments of war, the troops and their armaments, vacated French soil, the sooner this wounded nation could begin to rediscover its soul.

In this atmosphere of relief, and disbelief, no one would ever even notice, nor view with any suspicion, a diminutive Chinese Worker on his way from the tank depot sporting a small backpack of specialist tools. A safe haven for Yun and Alice, for so long their secret hidden love nest, was about to serve its final purpose. Both Yun and Ming were already inside, waiting, when Yun's comrade showed up. He had been delayed by the glut of departing British troops and equipment, now trudging homebound, down French roads for their final time. Yun had kept Ming calm, but only just. The suspense had made Ming agitated, and Yun feared he might lose his nerve, but he did not. The plan was reckless in extremis, but neither felt they had any other choice.

Yun had picked his comrade well, if only for his skill and efficiency. Starting with Yun, on Yun's direction, he held Yun by the wrist, and pressed it down onto a neat, solid board he had stashed into his back-pack. Then, with a small 'jimmy', raising Yun's ID wristband, offering-up the rivet clasp, he deftly snapped it free. Yun gasped as the old rivet 'pinged' through the air. Yun sensed utter relief at feeling free, at last, from his permanent symbolism of servitude.

Within moments, and with even greater fluency, as though their accomplice had conducted the same operation countless times before, he proceeded to re-rivet Yun's removed band to Ming's wrist. Ming looked anxiously at his photo ID/work card as he removed it and placed the cord around Yun's neck in exchange. Yun saw his concern, reassured him that their difference would never be noticed:

'We Chinese all look the same to them, if they bother to check us at all!'

The crime was complete. They felt like 'prisoners' all over again, but prayed they had, in fact, just been gifted their tickets to freedom.

Yun's Escape as Ming

Yun and Alice wasted no time in orchestrating their escape.

Alice offered her mother only the scantest explanation for collecting Maxime earlier than usual, and none at all for why she had so hastily packed both their belongings into a single, inconspicuous valise. With her rushed assurance that she would contact her mother 'as soon as she could', and that 'everything would be fine', she then rendezvoused with Yun. An old hand at dramatic departures herself, her mother betrayed a knowing smile.

Thanks, in no small part, to her many crafted forays to meet up with Yun, Alice had fought off the worst symptoms of her previous poor health. Now, with a final escape in view, she planned to restore herself to full fitness in a transformed environment. She owed it to her family, and to herself, to be resilient at this crucial time for them all.

Shrewd as ever, Alice had done her homework, well in advance. Through her cautious enquiries, she had been told of a farm in a nearby village, where unskilled workers were being recruited. This was backed up by two French women she had heard gossiping in the street, bemoaning this was taking place, and how scandalous it was that 'any old' person could get work there. There were to be many such opportunities, now that hostilities were safely at an end, but the terms would be harsh. This particular farm suited them as a family, down to the ground, but Mme François, the farm owner, a forthright single parent, had insisted on meeting Alice and their boy, before making her decision. Luckily, they all got on like a house on fire.

Mme François needed a farmhand with mechanical skills, but also with an ability to tend her hens. Alice knew only too well how vital these birds had long become to France, with local laws protecting hens from theft or poor treatment. Once Alice explained 'her husband's' combined skills with both birds and machinery, the deal was struck there and then. Chattering away together, in French, both women laughed with amusement as they watched Yun and Maxime playing with the hens, getting to know them. Alice had clearly charmed Mme François. She didn't even bother to question Alice as she explained that her husband was Chinese and had been prematurely discharged from his wartime contract, continuing that they now needed both work and accommodation. Alice didn't dream to press for better pay at their meeting. The deal was such a perfect fit for them.

Shrewdly spotting a questioning look in Madame's gaze towards Maxime, Alice seized the moment:

'He's all I have, Madame, from his dear Papa.' She tugged out her handkerchief, wiped her eyes. 'He fell like every brave soldier should, willingly for La France.'

Taken in, as though perhaps with some personal resonance, Madame promptly leant forward to squeeze Alice's arm.

Enthused that her only son, Paul, might, at last, now have a friend to play with, Mme François called him over to say 'hello'. An energetic, open-hearted young lad, Paul bounded over and immediately took Maxime's hand to show him the farm. As they disappeared, Mme François led Alice and Yun to the cottage where they were to settle. It would seem they had magically slipped the net of the French authorities.

Alice had held her nerve. This was the biggest risk she had ever taken. For any other 'contract' – one offered in response to a job application – Yun (acting as Ming), would've been subjected to strict authorisation procedures in order to officially 'end' his French contract and work elsewhere. Governed by The Colonial Labour Organisation Service (CLOS), created by the French War Ministry, this was the regulation Yun would otherwise have had to face. Mme François had shown such enthusiasm to snap up the family, she had dispensed with every formality.

Until now, Yun had not needed to 'lie', officially at least, to anyone. Their conscience was clear so far as Madame was concerned. She had just gained, extremely cheaply, a genuinely skilled employee, more than qualified for the job, and a ready-made companion for her son. No, it was the next, formal stage, that Alice feared the most, for it should be she who would have to orchestrate the process. She had the necessary CLOS forms, she had filled them in, and now she knew she must submit them. This was the only legitimate way, for their security and their future, that Yun would be able to be permanently free from his 'assumed' French contract. At the very least, Alice needed this, for her peace of mind. She simply viewed her immediate success with Mme François as the first hurdle to overcome.

Now Ming was entirely alone, and what he had just done weighed heavily upon him. He had invested everything in his friendship with Alice and Yun. Breaking that golden proverb, that modal logic, 'never put all your eggs in one basket', the self-confidence he had mustered since these two had entered his life now began to slip away. The timing of this realisation could not have been worse. Ming would need every ounce of courage, and self-belief, if his next move was to succeed.

Ming remained in his post, at the munitions factory. He kept his head down, knuckled under. It was tough without Alice there, but he had plenty else on his mind now. He prayed that no one would notice that his French necklace ID was missing, nor that a bracelet ID had suddenly appeared on his wrist. Until questioned he needn't torture himself. Meanwhile, he took care each day to somehow keep posted as to when the first British CLCs were due to be called to leave France. It wasn't quite Ming's time, not yet, but the moment of truth was just around the corner. He was beset with trepidation.

22 FATE OR DESTINY

Lt Bill Hawkings was, perhaps, more relieved than most, that the war was finally over. He felt he had certainly done his time. Having completed two additional trips back to China, both to collect fresh Chinese recruits to add to those already in his care, he had surely had his fill of seafaring at the mercy of thousands of miles of ocean. In any event, he had long planned to see something of Europe once the war was over.

By late spring 1919, Lt Hawkings had concluded his last 'shift' at the British CLC camp, leaving those in charge to finalise the transportation of the Chinese to the docks, he felt his job was done – but was it? He still had the daunting task, one he had put off until now, to pack away, for transport, his accumulated photographic gems of his labourers from China. He had at least completed his review of them, spanning three war-years, which proved no mean feat.

Lt Hawkings decided that he could embark on that European tour he had long-dreamed about, having by then almost concluded his ominous task of rationalising and packing away his treasured images. It would give him the encouragement he needed to finalise all of this, spurred on by his planned trip sitting there waiting for him.

He could have done without the disturbance, but when

Major General Alan Thompson burst in, unannounced, what option did he have? It turned out, he had only dropped by to bid Bill, his old acquaintance, farewell, and a safe passage home, on his way to collect his wife from the Boulogne-Ville railway station. Relieved this was to be brief, Bill left the room to fetch them both a drink. Whilst he was absent, the General wandered around, restlessly. He happened to notice the open trunk overflowing with photographic plates. He ambled over to take a closer look. Intrigued, he held one of them up to the light. It was a striking image of a Chinese man, holding up a tiny bird, feeding it from his mouth. Bill reappeared with their drinks, but reacted with alarm to see his privacy invaded.

Undeterred, the General persisted, transfixed by the composition, now holding the image right up, for better scrutiny:

'What an utterly charming photograph, Bill, old chap, a tender moment in a brutal war, don't you know!' He broke into a boyish chuckle, amused by his own eloquence, assuring himself he was only feigning empathy, a tactful reaction. 'I knew you had a bit of a penchant for photography, but all these, old fellow, when on earth did you find the time?' He began shuffling some photographic plates on the top of the pile. Acutely embarrassed at being rumbled, Bill began to stammer in his panic to justify his accumulated photo haul:

'Oh, just a hobby Alan, something I did "just for me" you know, got me through the drudgery of this damned war.' He flushed up, continuing, 'I assure you Alan, I have not passed any of these to anyone, not a soul, so you see – I'm an *enthusiast*, not a spy!'

The General broke into a boorish guffaw on hearing

A striking image of a Chinese man, holding up a tiny bird, feeding it from his mouth

his old associate, so obviously struggling, and so visibly compromised, and all over a subject that the General viewed as utterly trivial.

Bill might have cursed his luck — after managing to keep his obsession hidden all this time, only to be found out now, with the war over — but he needn't have. The General was not in the least bit interested. He just wanted to wish his old pal well. He slapped Bill on the back, thanking him for all he had achieved with the CLC, insisting they both raise their glasses:

'Bloody commendable old chap, putting up with those grubby Chinks all this time, good to see the back of them, eh!'

Bill flinched at the General's remark, recoiled from it in fact, but whilst he knew there was no point in reacting to an entrenched prejudice, he did feel compelled to put up at least a trenchant protest, in reply, 'To be blunt, Alan, these men ended up making a real difference to us out here, they really did, and more to the point, quite frankly, we just couldn't have done what we did without them.'

But the General wasn't listening, just checking the time, which then prompted him to jump up, shake Bill's hand, and depart.

'Must fly old chap, hadn't noticed the time, wife will kill me if I'm late… see you in Blighty!' He strode away to his jeep.

The General then made the journey to collect his wife in record time. He had used the back roads, at speed, to avoid the dock-bound traffic, and now he was back in familiar territory, showing off to her, belting down country lanes for maximum exhilaration.

'Love it around here darling, now the war's over, so once I've grabbed my gear, let's make a short break of it, why not?'

His wife was too busy clutching her hat, chiding him for risking both their lives by driving like a mad thing, 'Slow down!'

It was as he took a particularly sharp bend in the lane, with his tyres screeching, that a large hen appeared from nowhere. The hen had decided it was about to be flattened, but had only mustered a couple of paces before the jeep struck its leg.

Braking to a halt, the General leapt from his jeep to check it out, but not as swiftly as a spritely lad, who had raced to the scene from nearby on hearing the commotion. Now standing there, staring down at the bird, with a younger boy in tow, the lad reacted with alarm at what he saw:

'Oh my God!' the lad exclaimed, horrified by the incident, 'What have you done to my mum's prize bird, why did you do this?'

'It just jumped out at me, stupid thing, nothing I could do about it,' the General retorted, indignantly, but being contradicted by his wife, still in the jeep, now berating him for not listening to her to 'slow down' and 'watch the road'. The lad taunted him, making it perfectly clear, that if he thought his wife was cross, that was nothing compared to his mother's rage when she hears about her hen:

'*Elle va être furieuse, monsieur*!' The boy was Paul, and the youngster, now peeping from behind him, grimacing, was Maxime.

The General was clearly embarrassed, despite his effrontery about the bird's stupidity. He insisted that the boy took him and the injured bird to his mother, so he could 'more than adequately compensate her for her loss', assuming that would be the end of the matter. The boy peered back at him, quizzically, clearly doubting the General's optimism about his mother's measured reaction. Paul gathered up the bird. The two boys, hand-in-hand, then led the General down the path towards the farmhouse door, leaving his wife in the jeep, still cursing her husband's reckless driving, and how their long-awaited 'country jaunt' together, in France, was now in total ruins.

Mme François exploded. She snatched the damaged bird from Paul, who glanced back at the General, with a smug grin. With absolutely no regard for his British army status, the General, now standing there like a condemned criminal, faced Mme François as she launched a string of insults at him, which even shook her son. The hen was, clearly, a vital asset to the family farm. She insisted that the General stayed put, '*Attendez là*!' she bellowed, '*Ne bougez pas*,' she added, wagging her finger. She then disappeared with the bird, safely nestled in her arms.

Paul muttered, looking up, 'Monsieur is in real trouble now.' Everyone, including the General, knew of the inflated importance hens had come to have in rural war-torn France.

Put in his place, perhaps for the first time since he was a low-ranking officer, the General began to chide himself for allowing himself to be scolded, humiliated in public, and of all things, by a woman! In a state of indignation, and in token defiance against being told to 'stay put', he strode outside, exasperated. He turned towards the farmhouse yard where he heard a man's voice mimicking a hen, 'clucking'. It seemed a welcome, random, distraction from the unwanted saga brewing up indoors.

The General's jaw dropped. He had stumbled on Yun, at the very moment he was holding up a fledgling hen, to his mouth, to feed it. He couldn't believe it. The General instantly recognised Yun's profile from the self-same pose, with a bird on his hand, he had just been admiring in a photograph only moments ago, at Bill Hawkings' place. Looking closer, he then also remembered Yun from the depot:

'My God man, I simply don't believe it!' he proclaimed, in astonishment. 'I know who you are "Monsieur Birdman", you're one of Bill's Chinky lads, a CLC, top man according to him; deluded fool.' Then, just as the penny dropped in the General's mind, and with Yun having barely returned the hen to the ground, the General seized Yun by the arm as though arresting him. 'Wait 'til he hears you're nowhere near boarding ship for home, you scallywag!'

Hoping to unsettle his captor, Yun exposed his neck (rather than his wrist), tugged at his tag with his thumb, protesting that the General was 'completely mistaken', for he was a Chinese Worker for the French Army. The General didn't even bother to check the tag, so totally confident that he had just spared Bill Hawkings, by complete chance, the humiliation of having let Yun slip through the net, and successfully abscond, and a high-ranking labourer at that.

'You idiot Chink, where's your wristband?' he scolded, shaking Yun contemptuously. 'I've just caught you as an illegal evader of compulsory repatriation, and now you've added to your crime by confessing to a falsified French ID round your neck,' at which he dragged Yun, by the arm, towards the house. He was hoping to knock Mme François off her pedestal, having exposed a criminal in her charge, but she stole his thunder:

'My prize hen is dead, Monsieur Le Général!' she bellowed, full of menace. '*Ma poule est morte*!' she announced, incensed, her voice betraying an angry wobble, despite her stoutness.

Gathering her composure, in the now stony silence, she stated her resolute intention to trash the General's name with the British Authorities, sue him for all he was worth for the loss of her hen and breaking local laws, unless he compensated her both 'immediately' and 'handsomely'.

Devastated that a mere French farming woman had, yet again, outfoxed him completely, he assured her, repeatedly, and with a raised, agitated tone, that not only would he compensate her 'handsomely' but that he would do so 'right away!' Taken aback, for the briefest of moments, Madame went quiet, enough to gift the General a fleeting prompt to stomp away, down the path, to retrieve some cash from his jeep, as though marching into battle.

In the excitement, Yun's arm has been released from the General's grip. Moments later, Alice had appeared from nowhere, totally obscured behind a bulging basket of clean linen. Hidden though she was, even in her obscurity, Alice had sensed an atmosphere, and a change in Yun. With Yun, Alice, the boys and Mme François, all gathered waiting in the room, the General's reappearance, wielding his wallet, didn't have quite the impact he might have hoped for, or even expected, from the time he had taken charge and exited the room.

Somewhat flummoxed, the General shrugged, then turned to Madame to pay her, but hesitated on overhearing Yun, confiding in the (obscured) Alice, about the trouble he may have just got himself into. The General hadn't noticed Alice there, until then, but realising the two were a couple, he turned towards her.

Though still obscured by the basket, he reiterated that her man was 'indeed in a deep hole'. He could not have sounded more frosty or hostile. It mattered not to him that he was speaking to a suspended basket of linen; he was not expecting a word back in Yun's defence. Then Alice lowered the linen down.

She drew in a deep breath, preparing to address the General, attempt to put him firmly in his place, until their eyes met. They both froze. Now face-to-face, aghast, each instantly recognised the other.

The Deal – 'For Whom the Temple Waits'

The tension was momentarily broken by the sudden 'honking' of the jeep's horn at the end of the path. Alice glanced towards the vehicle, then noticed the General's wife frantically gesticulating towards them.

Mayhem returned as Mme François resumed her rant at the General about her money, and retribution, but then something snapped inside Alice, taking hold of her completely. She took charge, somehow, despite the melee. Alice urged Madame, in no uncertain terms, that she must desist for a moment to allow Alice a meeting, alone, with the General. She might have resisted, but seeing the stern look on Alice's face, one that she had never seen before, she backed down. Oddly, and with such subtle promptness, Alice beckoned Maxime over to introduce him to the General. A little bemused, but seeing his mother's resolve, he dutifully did as he was told, gave a quick smirk up at the General as he shook his hand, then scampered back to Paul.

Then, to everyone's puzzlement, particularly Madame's,

who by now was twitching with confusion, Alice led the General away to Madame's office. Resigned to his fate, nervous as to her purpose, Alice took him by storm:

'I'm so happy, my dear General, to see you again, and delighted you have been able, at long last, to meet our lovely son, Maxime. Isn't he a joy?' she manoeuvred, with the adeptness of a cat. '… you shouldn't have worried about us, *chéri*,' she added, with a cynical grin, 'we have been just fine without you.'

The General may have thought, in the whirlwind in which he was now being tossed around, that Alice was satisfied to have just shocked him about his unexpected fatherhood, if it was true, but she was far from done. To maximise his discomfort, Alice took his hand, then stroked his wedding ring, seductively, with her finger:

'But I cannot help but wonder, my elusive General, what your dear, trusting, wife would say, if she knew…' she murmured, dryly.

The General recoiled, visibly, and with a look of resignation, he released, involuntarily, a gasped splutter at his entrapment. She led him like a lamb to Madame's desk. With the muffled voices from the others in the hallway, now increasing in intensity, Alice, as if by design, conjured up a pen and a sheet of paper and began scrawling upon it. She was drafting a confession for the General to sign. She had clearly thought about this moment, should it ever arrive, since Maxime was born. She was ready and knew exactly what to write. With the General still so poor at French, he knew it would be pointless to even attempt reading it. He signed, angrily, then turned for the door, but not before Alice had clutched his sleeve. She needed him to know what he'd signed and what she now expected from him. She spelled it out: 'Listen to me, my dearest General, we now have a mutual vow.' She maintained her grip, but only barely, 'If you stay silent about my man, I will say no more about our son.' He went to break free, 'But you must first make sure my man can stay here, in France.' He glared back, in scorn. Every drop of his past passion for her drained into the floor. He grunted in disgust. She let go his sleeve.

As they both reappeared, Madame was having apoplexy: '*J'attends depuis des lustres*,' she urged, demanding an explanation as to what on earth the two had been doing whilst she, the injured party, had been left waiting, 'as instructed!' Seeing Yun's puzzlement, Alice took his arm, whispering, as she reassuringly squeezed it, '*ne t'inquiète pas*.' The General was now himself seething at having been rolled over by a second woman, and on the same day.

He thrust into Madame's apron pouch the largest wad of French notes anyone in the room had seen in their lifetimes, insisting that Madame now 'shuts up and stops whining'. The General then pushed past Yun, now completely ignoring him, as off he strutted towards his jeep where the third woman at odds with him was in an even more advanced state of frustration, if that were possible, though she, alone, remained blissfully ignorant of the drama that had just enveloped her husband, compromising him completely. The General meekly soaked up his wife's ongoing tirade, numbed as he was by the bombshell that Alice had just landed at his feet.

As he over-accelerated his jeep, desperate to pull away, Mme François, scuttling towards him, clutching her skirt, blurted out her parting barbed slur; he must now 'Drive properly, as a true French General would do, and not like a

British lunatic breaking the law whenever he chooses'. The grinding jeep tyres finally found their grip. He took off at breakneck speed.

Alice grabbed Yun and calmly broke away from Madame and the two boys, leaving them spouting off about the hen, and the General. She had a distinct twinkle in her eye, one that only resolute protectors of a guarded secret might betray. She would show the General's signed letter to no one, not even Yun. She could only now pray that the truth behind it would never surface.

Later that week, as it happened, Yun received the CLOS clearance notice. He and Alice opened it together. It arrived inside a letter from the General himself. It was on military, headed paper. In it, Yun was offered an unconditional new posting as 'Supervisor of Works', deputising stone engravings and compiling the register, at the dedicated Chinese cemetery at Noyelles-sur-Mer. It was run by The Commonwealth War Graves Commission. Yun's appointment was 'effective immediately'. The two began shaking with disbelief. Alice then pointed to the foot of the letter – Major General Alan Thompson appeared in print and he had signed it personally. Yun may, in any other circumstances, have been baffled at the General's involvement in Alice's successful application for him. Yun had been, after all, on the brink of being arrested by the General, but Yun had long ceased being amazed by any life-changing events that had, randomly, come his way since he began sharing his life with Alice.

In any event, a surge of emotion had well and truly taken charge, and now Yun could not restrain himself. It was a combination of astonishment and joy that melted his guard and loosened his tears.

This life-changing outcome fully sunk in for Yun, he could not hold back disclosing to Alice just how poignant this opportunity at Noyelles would be for him. She knew anyway, but she wanted to listen to his joy: 'I had so wanted to hate that British pig of a General, but I don't now Alice,' he choked. She squeezed his hand, thinking her own thoughts. "This will be the refuge where I can hope to restore my wounds, come to terms with my past demons, salvage what I can from the memories of my homeland, my family, put to rest my hatred for my father's despicable acts.'

'That's some expectation, *chérie*, I hope that unsuspecting cemetery is up to the mark!' she smiled, softly.

All that Alice now wanted for herself and her family, all that she had ever wanted, was to settle in a place where they could enjoy the changing seasons, watch the corrupted land heal and thrive. Yet more than all of this, she needed to forget about the General, the ghastly war, and those terrible lies she had so rigidly kept to about her past.

They smiled at each other, lovingly, both hoping above hope that they had, finally, found their salvation. It would seem they had every chance. Not only had Yun secured a permanent posting, one he could relish, but they could also now leave Mme François; Alice could find meaningful work, and they would find a place of their own.

Overcome with love, Yun grabbed Alice in a fit of emotion, to give her the biggest, most enthusiastic hug of his life, only to feel her resistant palms, assuredly, keeping him at bay:

'*Mon amour*,' she whispered, beset with nerves as the moment engulfed her, 'now is not the time for outbursts, this is the perfect time to use our joy, divert all our energy to plan a family, build the life we have waited for so patiently.'

In the whirlwind, with the General having miraculously gifted them their freedom, they never did notice his postscript:

'P.S. The French Authorities will now pursue your Chinese accomplice for his own criminal act of deception.'

23 MING'S ESCAPE AS YUN

Ming's main concern had been the risk of a placement transfer, now that munitions assembly had ceased. The end to the war had brought many things, but for Ming, it had meant being plunged into uncertainty. For now, in plain sight of his long-established French employers, and fellow workers, all who knew him well, he had to bide his time, lay low, mechanically act out his French contract.

For the moment, the Chinese Workers at the factory had been kept busy stockpiling shells and parts. With every prospect that France should not need to be on a war footing for many years to come, each industrial enterprise needed readjusting, back to peacetime mechanisation, but that would take time and dedication. With no visible change, as yet, at Ming's workplace, he felt calm.

The French had been shrewd, gearing the labourers' contracts to a five-year term from the outset. This showed great foresight and was certainly paying dividends now. With their British counterparts packing their bags in preparation for imminent repatriation, men like Ming still had a two-year stretch to serve under their contracts, so they knew they would be kept busy. This was the ideal bustle of activity, the cloak of distraction Ming needed to deflect all eyes away from him. France now faced an agricultural industry in ruins, its manpower decimated, morale at rock bottom, so once it was determined exactly what would be expected from so many Chinese left behind to serve on French soil, Ming did not want to be around.

So as soon as Ming got the word that the very first British CLCs had been called to their ship, he made his move. The impasse at his work, that transition approaching, the move away from munitions, really helped his cause. With the strict regime at the factory having diminished, for the moment, Ming knew it was time to slip away.

It proved easier than he had feared to smuggle his way onto British transport bound for the docks. They barely glanced at his new wristband, but he had to constantly remind himself it was there and no longer on a necklace fastened around his neck. In any case, he was as Chinese as everyone else, with no recognisable uniform to speak of. Ming just merged into his surroundings. All that he kept in his head was only to speak when he absolutely had to. He knew his dialect might provoke a discussion, unwanted questions, so finding himself at the back of the truck he adopted a mute countenance. Many of his comrades, like umpteen troops out in France, had been traumatised into silence by the war anyway.

As they arrived at Marseille docks, the workers were herded into the longest embarkation queues imaginable. He wasn't daunted by it, but rather relieved. In such numbers, surely the verification procedures would be swiftly actioned. Quick enough, Ming hoped, to prevent anything other than a brief tally of wristband numbers. What he hadn't predicted was the impact a long period of patient waiting would have on his nerves. They were in tatters within an hour, and he was only, by then, halfway towards the entry gate to the ship. Ming began to panic.

For Ming, the painfully laboured procession had given him an excess of time to worry, and to fear for the worst. He had craned, stood on tiptoe, to see up ahead, if anything beyond bracelet-checking was actually taking place. He just couldn't tell, not yet anyway. Yet why was it all taking inordinately long to progress? His mind was racing. If by some cruel twist of fate, thumbprints or some other sundry checks were also being verified, he was sunk.

Others, in the line with Ming, were, by contrast, groaning away to each other to pass the time. Most were nervous about facing another arduous sea voyage, even though this one would mean they were heading home. Others recounted their horrors from their Canadian rail ordeal, recalling how close they had come to murdering the British guards. All that might have just been bravado, boys' talk, but digging up those old, traumatic memories just upped the tension, which was spreading fast.

Ming had explained to Alice and Yun that his plan was to somehow jump ship. He had to do this knowing the British transport route would not include Hong Kong. He knew that all too well, but boarding represented his only realistic chance to head back towards his homeland, and above all, to escape his French contract terms. The further away he could venture from France the better.

Right now, however, in amongst the mob of parting CLCs, his only pressing concern was to successfully board ship, and he was now just a sniff away.

Ming would not have noticed, in his obsession to

constantly check his progress towards the ship, that something odd was taking place among the shuffling queue of men behind him. Unbeknown to him, a small detachment of French military policemen was progressing ever closer to him, moving forward at a far greater pace than he was. Having no reason to look around, nor being tempted to do so for fear of prompting a reaction from behind, Ming was also blissfully unaware of the disturbance the officers were creating as they progressed. They were, forcibly, checking every dog tag, every one of them, seemingly cross-referencing each against a card the police were holding.

Still totally oblivious to anything going on around him, a rush of adrenalin coursed through Ming. Almost sick with nerves, he dropped his kit to the ground to fumble through his things and fiddle with his wristband for the umpteenth time. The front of the line was a mere handful of men away. He stooped to haul his backpack to his waist when, just at that moment, the arm of a uniformed man thrust downwards, alongside his own, and seized Ming's forearm like a vice.

Ming gasped, as the French guard hauled him up to his feet and tugged at his wristband to check the number against his notes. It was Ming they were after. He was arrested on the spot.

As the whistle blew, the officer detachment gathered hungrily around him, pumped up that they had snared their quarry, and in the nick of time. Ming went berserk. It was a culmination of a quagmire of emotions that so welled up in Ming that he was helpless to a crazed eruption. In a fit of rage, he struck the man holding him in the face, with such force that he flopped, limply, to the ground. He wasn't sure if he had killed him. He didn't care if he had. Now free from his grip, Ming made a mad dash for the entrance gate to the ship. It was a futile burst of desperation, but Ming was no longer in control of his senses. With only a few yards to go Ming felt the full force of a muscular pair of arms from behind him, locking, irresistibly, around his waist. His chest struck the ground beneath him.

He knew he was now in desperate trouble, but the agony of the endless wait in the queue, his nerves in tatters from the tension of uncertainty, Ming was now just resigned to his fate. He had, oddly, never fully believed his plan would succeed. The longer the moment of truth had taken to arrive, the more his doubts had racked up. With his final dash 'for the post', he knew in his heart, he was in his death throes. It was his last gasp plunge into the deep abyss.

Escorted, all that miserable way back, past the waiting hordes of Chinese men, Ming now truly felt like a spent animal being herded away for slaughter. He was numb to any sadness. What he felt now was just a colourless sense that everything was utterly pointless.

The calamitous outcome of the maddest enterprise of his life, the seriousness of his plight, all swirled around in Ming's head as he sunk with despair. Sustained upright, only by the shoulders of two guards, he broke down, unnoticed, and wept bitterly.

Ming was beyond reacting to the legal procedures he was next subjected to. All he could feel was a grey desolation. He scarcely cared what fate was about to befall him, guessing it would be a contemptible one-sided charade, a fraud. The Duty Interpreter had only a passing familiarity with Ming's dialect, translating mainly into Mandarin. It hardly mattered. The French Authorities were in no mood for foreign miscreants. Hardened from years of a devastating war on their soil, any chance of even a modicum of leniency fell into the wayside as Ming's charges were read out to him from the irrefutable evidence before The Court.

'Striking an officer, causing grievous bodily harm, engaging in a deception of The State by means of a stolen false ID', were serious enough. Once his wartime antecedent of 'attempted theft at the factory, his place of work' was also read out, Ming's fate was well and truly sealed.

With neither the will nor any real opportunity to recount to the Court the mental anguish he had suffered, as a foreigner, ripped away from his home and his family by both dire circumstance and gross misrepresentation, the court's illicit justice was read out in a dispassionate monotone. Ming was found guilty on all counts.

The Order, with immediate effect, was for deportation to Devil's Island, a French penal colony in French Guiana, for an indeterminate number of years. Ming was taken down.

24 THE AFTERMATH OF WAR

January 1920

With the long Christmas break over, the French Court Clerk had arrived at his office early. There had been a deluge of post now that the 'business of peacetime' had begun to grind into action once more, yet a good deal of administrative 'rust' still needed to flake away.

Amongst the mound of notifications, a single communication stood out from the others. It was from China. It had been stamped with a translated 'Not known at this address', and 'RETURN to SENDER'. It was unusual for any official court notice to be rejected, especially from across the globe. The Clerk opened it, and then cross-referenced his court file. Then he understood, or at least arrived at a conclusion as to what must have happened.

Following due process, Ming's conviction had been notified back to his country of origin, to his 'next of kin'. The Clerk simply assumed the convict's family had moved house on learning the outcome of the legal process. He was not to have known – how could he have done – that not only would Ming's family not have the first clue about Ming's plight, but they had probably moved on, some time ago, in a desperate state of abject poverty.

The Clerk tutted with disdain, as he read the Court's

verdict. He hesitated, for a moment, puzzled as to why on earth a labourer, from China, had travelled all this way, only to conduct himself in such a reckless manner? He then pondered why a Chinese man had been employed in France at all? He was aware of the thousands of French Colonials that had served in The Great War, but he couldn't recall any Chinese. 'He must've been one lonely fellow,' he concluded, then filed the notice and the stamped envelope away. He thought no more of it.

In their new life, Yun and Alice did speak often about Ming, worrying about him and his family, but at least believing Ming must have reached home safely. In moments of doubt, they had prayed that Ming's wife had, somehow, managed to cope without Ming's money and, hoping above hope, that they had indeed been reunited. It helped them to believe that this must have been the case.

In any event, now that they had a child on its way, Yun and Alice had plenty of their own distractions to occupy their attention, more than enough daily life-challenges of their own to address. Maxime was getting increasingly excited about his future sibling, and this prospect dominated the family's time:

'I do hope it's a boy *maman, pour jouer avec moi.*'

Alice reassured him, constantly, that he wouldn't have to wait long to find out. It was due 'anytime now, *mon cheri*, just look how big "he" is already!'

Maxime had missed playing with Paul, since they had left the farm. He so longed for a brother. Alice fought hard to stifle her discomfort on seeing her young son's hair take on the early signs of redness. She didn't want any suspicions aroused, just the assumption that he had inherited his late father's features. She may have wanted no reminders of her failed romantic past, but her uneasiness wasn't born from that. Not at all. She had 'refashioned' her own historic past, and as for the truth, she had used this, with guile, to secure her future.

25 YUN'S VISION

Cemetery at Noyelles-sur-Mer

It had been a long day.

Having worked his way to the end of, yet another, long line of cemetery headstones, Yun propped himself up against a young tree to ease his back. He loved his posting, felt forever grateful, but it was hard.

To his joy, he was startled by Maxime's inimitable pitched yelp from the distance: 'Papa, Papa..!' As Yun turned, he watched Maxime racing down the alley of graves towards him, with Alice waving from beyond. Then it struck him, nearly sending him to his knees with dismay – 'Oh my God!'

All Yun could now see, in the figure of that little boy scampering towards him, with his red curly hair shining in the low evening light, was the face of General Alan Thompson. In that seminal moment, mere seconds though it may have lasted, the shielded truth about Alice's past washed through him like a tsunami.

How stupid he had been, how naïve and trusting. How else could he, Yun, have escaped the law when the General had apprehended him, red-handed? How else could he have gained employment whilst poor Ming had not been offered the same fortuitous protection? That private meeting at the farm, between the General and Alice, the transformation in the General after the meeting had taken place, it all now made complete sense.

Yun did his level best to hide his mental turmoil from Alice. He had barely drawn the strength to stay on his feet as Maxime had launched into his arms. Alice may have read little into Yun's, apparently, crushed demeanour as she eventually caught up with them both, but she was to be left in no doubt whatsoever that night when Yun confronted her.

Dumbfounded how Yun had, somehow, from nowhere, pieced together her carefully concealed past, she now had no choice but to fully confess. What else could she do if she was to salvage any hope of limiting the damage? She would have to come clean, spell out the dark truth, 'warts and all', finally let go of her stubborn resolve and hope that their precious relationship would survive.

Yes, they both knew, their own unlikely love affair had come about through the fractured circumstances of war, and, in much the same way, Alice and the General had found themselves entangled, but far greater fundamentals were at stake here. By concealing this truth from Yun, Alice had surely maintained the most perilous of lies. She was not a widow, and in Yun's eyes, her son, Maxime, was the product of her deceit and not the fatherless son of a brave fallen soldier.

Neither knew how their lives together might now pan out. They both prayed that each would see the past for what it was and that their love would prevail. In their heart of hearts, they had faith that it would. The only unspoken fear they harboured, was how Yun's feelings for Maxime might tarnish over time. As Yun went to kiss him goodnight, as he always did, Yun knew for sure, his affections had already changed.

26 1939
Paris – 3rd Arrondissement

Early Spring 1939

A mature, smart, well-groomed Chinese gentleman, looking impressive for his age, had grown a moustache and a wispy beard of which he was proud. Perhaps, subconsciously, he was emulating those military bullies he had suffered under all those years ago. His way of usurping their air of authority – but without the arrogance – that contemptible colonial hubris, but these were the slowly healing vestiges from his wartime past. It was the cruel mental residue, all that he was left with to suffer inside, that so tortured him. He craved some lasting peace.

He had learned to cope with the flashbacks. These were the sorry lot of so many from the war. He might curse these, but he did not fear them. It was his recurrent nightmare that he utterly dreaded. Over and over, that same haunting episode he had witnessed in the war returned to torment him in his sleep. Helplessly looking on, he would again have to witness the explosion that took his comrades' lives; feel the impact shudder through his body; look down to spy the injured bird struggling in the debris beneath his boots. Then, at that very moment he would stoop to rescue the bird from its fate, he would be shaken back to consciousness by his long-suffering wife:

'Wake up *Cheri*, wake up, you were screaming again, like before…' Her voice, as ever, was soft but insistent.

Yet there were plenty of compensations now that he had managed, somehow, to reach a respectable age despite the appalling attrition from the war years. One thing was for sure; how he loved his beer! The best moment for him, one he savoured every day, was sipping the froth off the top of his special jug, then that first prized gulp. It was 'Tsingtao', which so reminded him of his homeland, the history it had endured. The Tsingtao Brewery had risen from the embers of war, from the spoils of that first, priceless, German defeat. How it tasted the sweeter for it, even though Japan – China's nemesis – had been the true architects of that victory.

Dreaming, for a moment, as he gazed into his drink, lulled by the familiar chattering of the canary from its cage, a young girl's voice rang out from the open door to the kitchen, 'Papa, Maman needs to know what you want to eat. She says you can't just drink beer all day!'

She giggled. He loved her all the more for it. His youngest, his favourite girl, he adored her dainty Asian looks. He prayed she would never lose them.

Then he suddenly screamed out: 'Get down, quick, stay low. Don't they know this is Paris? Idiot pilot. Must be an enemy plane, overhead. There, see, my beer has spilled over!' The canary went silent.

His daughter, alarmed by his outburst, came rushing towards the front window, as though such a moment had never occurred before:

'It's nothing Papa, there is no plane, there's none at all. Just a madman rushing by.'

Her voice subdued him. He peered towards her, settled

down to being unconcerned, as he did after all such previous outbursts. He was done with his latest delusion, yet his daughter remained standing at the window, with her back to him, still gazing curiously towards the sky. Her wonderment was infectious. Her innocence, her naivety, pure gold. He brushed himself down, remained seated, said nothing. His heart melted as the canary piped back into song, then he remembered what he had been asked:

'Tell Maman I'll have a bowl of chicken noodles, not too big a portion. I've lost my appetite.'

Having recovered his decorum, Yun allowed himself to focus entirely on his daughter. He needed no reminder how bewitched he was by her, with her love for simple humour, her soft affections. He mused how much his own mother would surely have doted on her too, had she known her. A rush of melancholy raced through him. Looking at her now, still standing at the window as she was, gazing skyward, she so reminded him of a time, in his very distant past, when a similar glow of light had stolen into the building he was in, exposing the silhouette of a young female, his wife's then seductive outline. There too, the sound of a passing plane, real or not, may suddenly have threatened, yet he would not have cared one jot, so nor should he do so now. His mood settled.

Though he did still suffer the occasional pang of nostalgia, he had long since let go his irrepressible obsession for tending injured birds. So, when his resolve weakened, he would allow himself to reflect on those early memories of home. In China, back then, sparing a tiny bird from its misfortunes was his way of passing on the unconditional kindness his mother had shown him when he was 'wounded', when he was down. Then he snapped to:

'Where's that boy of mine?' Yun moaned. 'About time Li Han played Mahjong with his dad, my favourite "sparrow" game.' He struck the table with his half-empty bottle.

'He's old enough now to sign up!'

'Why don't you ever refer to Maxime that way Papa? His daughter questioned, innocently, 'Is he too old for you now, too grown up these days?'

Yun might have reacted, his feelings ran deeply within him, but he found he could not. He took a final, impetuous, gulp of his Tsingtao beer. Just hearing his stepson's name mentioned sent a shudder through him. Even after all these years, he still could not accept Maxime, not since he had finally learned the full story. With his fine stature and thick red hair, the love of his mother's life, just the image of Maxime in Yun's mind served as a painful reminder of the only truth his wife had ever concealed from him.

Free from all such taunting reflections, his daughter just turned from the window and smiled, lovingly, back at him. Seeing the gentle resignation in her face, Yun knew, in his heart, he should not torment himself so. He should count and savour his blessings. After all, he had prospered in the face of adversity, settled amongst his own kind where he was loved. Better still, he had somehow also integrated into a Parisian way of life, thanks in no small measure to his popular wife; 'French' to everyone. For that alone he should feel blessed.

DEVIL'S ISLAND ('Ile du Diable') French Guiana Early Spring – 1939

Had it not become such an increasing occurrence, of late, the grey, rough-shaven Chinese man might never have bothered to look up, nor garnered any attention. It may have been a squadron of combat planes this time, Dewoitine D 520s perhaps, or something like them, rumbling impressively overhead. He had to offer-up his callused hand to block the sun, but glaring so strongly, it was too bright to properly identify anything for certain. Still, he allowed himself to believe, implausible though it surely was, that he was indeed witnessing a fleet of fighter aircraft passing in some numbers across the open sky and that he had also identified French insignia on each underwing. Perhaps the more discerning of those bothering to look over concluded that this man had, somehow, found cause to remember a similar such spectacle from the recent world war, but as a Chinese man, how likely was that?

The Ganger, at the head of the line of French prisoners, spotted him gawking skyward, bawled out at him to keep working, yet he could not avert his gaze. The air display above him was so real to him that he didn't, for a moment, suspect that the intense heat from the sun, or his state of desolation and exhaustion, might perhaps be entirely to blame for what he was so clearly now witnessing, nor for enabling him to shut out any sound except that which now so captivated him.

Totally convinced, and now overcome, the man spat upwards, growling in broken, accented French: '*Armée de l'air – merde*!'

One could only conclude he had compelling reasons for

harbouring such a contempt for planes, the noise they made, or just an extreme aversion for French grandiosity. But, most likely of all, this poor, wretched fellow had probably, finally, lost his mind. Or had he?

About to face harsh retribution from the Ganger, now pacing menacingly along the line towards him, the man remained oblivious, still fixated towards the sky, until that voice of authority finally struck his hearing like some exploding ordnance from somewhere nearby:

'Get your backside back in gear, slacker, you can look up as hard as you like, but you won't find no heaven. There's no temple waiting, not for the likes of you…!'

Then the ganger followed the man's line of sight, thought he too had spotted some aircraft, some distance away.

Of pure rural Chinese stock, a farm worker all his life, he raised up his mattock once more and struck it, with all his might, into the dry earth, the unforgiving ground he still had to till. How he longed for the smell of home soil, and to be forever buried, at last, within it.

27 THE DREAM

An old Chinese man, now in his nineties, wandered slowly towards his bed. He laid down cautiously. Although he knew he must sleep, he reluctantly closed his eyes. He dreaded being dragged through that same old dream, all over again.

As before, although in ever more detail as each repeat invaded his mind, he became a Chinese worker, in plain issue garments, as a much younger man. He found himself pacing, dutifully, on his own behind a British officer, through a WWI battlefield where it appeared there was a lull in hostilities. He guessed this must again be circa 1917. He concluded that it was.

The eerie silence freed his mind to wander thousands of miles distant to his homeland, away from this profane setting. He felt the ache of nostalgia, yet the grip of resentment proved the greater force. It constricted his longings and purpose. How the hell had he ended up here, yet again? Surely, by now, he might, somehow, have managed to erase the memory of all that had so brutally conspired against him, all that time ago?

The old man tutted in his sleep. This was *his* dream, after all, yet again he had absolutely no control over it. He could intimately relate to the desolate ground now stretching out before him. It was so hauntingly a deep-rooted part of him. Stripped of its soul by some mindless indomitable force, he trudged past the charred tree spires and the flattened remains of what once must have been a verdant landscape. He could so acutely feel, and hear, the crunch and snap of brittle fragments through his boot soles as he paced along. He couldn't truly believe these remnant-shards could ever have been part of any living thing. Pared-back to barrenness, there was nothing meaningful left here to dwell upon, yet his dream held him fast.

Then, from nowhere, traces of his Chinese dialect settled on his dull hearing like a drizzle of charged dust. The old man's face began twitching in his sleep as the stimulation transported across his skin.

He didn't dare slow up as he frantically scoured his surroundings for clues. He scanned everywhere until, finally, the mystery unravelled. There he spotted, in the near distance, way over to one side, three Chinese workers offloading a fresh consignment of gun-shells from a fully laden munitions truck. He cringed; his sweating body tightened like a coiled spring. He had lived through this dream countless times. He knew what was coming. He exhaled a frothing yelp as one of the shells ignited, sending that familiar thunderous 'bawoom' ripping through his dream.

He and his officer hit the deck as the devastating blast lifted all three Chinese workers, and the truck, way up into the air on a fireball.

Spent fire traces then settled everywhere, as did the lingering stench from the acrid smoke. It stung in his nostrils through the cloth he had ripped from his tunic, it made him retch. In his sleep he tugged the bed sheet across his mouth and nose and gasped through it.

With his gaze set downwards, he dragged his heavy limbs forward like a robot, until, out of the blue, he spotted something struggling in the ash beneath his feet. He froze. In his dazed state he stooped down to take a closer look. At that moment a glowing ember floated earthward, chancing to light up two tiny dots. They were the unmistakeable eyes of that same small bird, once more glinting up at him.

The old man sobbed in his sleep as he lowered his cupped hands to gently scoop the bird up to his face to feed it. Had this been an exact repeat performance, it would have ended there, he would have been awakened from his sleep, but the dream endured. With the recent death of his wife there was no one now to shake him to. Wiping the blooded sweat from his brow with his finger, he looked adoringly into the bird's eyes as he preened the worst from its matted face and wings, enough to recover patches of its former softness. Released, at last, to see the event through, now feeling the creature's warmth through his closed palm, his dream could, finally, resolve. With tears now streaming down his face he slid his new companion, like a precious jewel, deep into the sanctuary of his inside tunic pocket.

Then he walked away.

The old man opened his eyes and smiled, for the briefest moment. With his cheeks wet with tears, he sighed as his eyes slowly closed again. He knew, with some relief, as his heart settled, that this would be the last dream of his life.

EPILOGUE
The Legacy

As with many Chinese who remained in France, beyond the end of their WWI contracts, not only did they, historically, sustain their romances there to ultimately build a flourishing community, many also migrated from rural areas to the great Paris metropolis. Where better to settle than in the 3rd Arrondissement, a district already known for its growing immigrant population. It hadn't taken long for the Chinese, and their mixed-race families, to thrive there, make it feel like home.

This is the Chang family, a Chinese worker who married a Polish woman during WWI. They had seven children together. He was recruited by the French and worked in a mine in Burgundy

DEDICATIONS & OUR THANKS

We would like to dedicate this book to three Chinese Workers who came to France during World War One, two of them decided to remain in France after their contract had expired. Both went on to build families with French women.

Emile Hoyongki 何永岐 came from Jinan in Shandong Province.

Emile Hoyongki and his wife. Photo courtesy of Pascale Gang

Louis Yenpaoyong 阎宝荣 came from Shanghai.

We would also like to particularly thank Pascale Gang, the granddaughter of Emile Hoyonki, who has gone to great lengths to grant us access to all the family documents she has in relation to her grandfather, and for the time she so generously gave to share the story of her grandfather with us. Also, many thanks from us to Marie-Claude Yenpaoyong,

Pascale Gang holding a picture of her grandfather.
Photo courtesy Pascale Gang

and Marie Druot, the granddaughters of Louis Yenpaoyong, who also both so kindly shared their memories of their grandfather with us.

Marie-Alice Potencier (top left), top middle; Yen Pao Yong (her husband and the Chinese worker recruited by the French during WWI who stayed in France after the war) and their 6 children. In the centre of the image is the youngest son of the couple, Louis Yen Pao Yong, the father of Marie-Claude Yenpaoyong the woman interviewed by Caroline Chu in her film 'The Boatwomen of the Forgotten Souls'.

Soo Yow was a Chinese worker recruited in Hong Kong by the French during WWI. His matriculation number was '741'. He was in charge of an airfield in northern France during the war.

'Soo Yow' Photo Courtesy Karen Soo

Karen Soo holding the photo of Soo Yow, her grandfather, a Chinese worker recruited in 1916 by the French Army in Hong Kong. He was contracted to work 5 years, 10 hours shifts, and 7 days a week. Although he was recruited as a non-combatant Chinese worker, he was deployed between 1916 and 1918 to keep an airfield in northern France operational where he repaired craters on the runway even as it was being bombed. Soo Yow moved to Liverpool once his contract ended and spent all his life in England.

Photo excerpt from Caroline Chu's documentary film 'In The Frame'.

Our gratitude also goes to Dr. Frances Wood and Dr. Gregory James for their expert proofreading of the complete manuscript. Their specialist expertise, from the British recruitment viewpoint, and their willingness to give up their time to offer counsel, has been invaluable to us.

Moreover, Dr. Frances Wood's support in keeping the historic backbone of our story both authentic and intact was fundamental to our narrative's credibility.

Our grateful thanks also to Li Ma for her tireless assistance in relation to the French recruitment of Chinese Workers and for her inspirational support.

Special thanks to Ming Ai (London) Institute for their guidance and support and similar thanks to Zou Shiquan for the contribution of his art composition.

We are so grateful, once again, to our friend, John de Lucy, for the continued use of his grandfather's archive material – the W. J. Hawkings Collection – and for allowing us to portray his grandfather and create our own story about the part that he played with the CLC in WWI.

John de Lucy holding a picture of his grandfather. Photo excerpt from Caroline Chu's documentary film 'Let There Be Light'. Photo courtesy of John de Lucy

'Very pleased with your references to grandpa and the use of his photographs. Your three characters come across very well and the story is full of surprises.' – John de Lucy

To Jean Vandevelde: For the past three years, your unwavering support sustained me through the entire journey of writing this book. Thank you for your generosity and for making this work possible – Caroline Chu

As this latest book approaches publication, I need to thank my long-suffering family and friends for tolerating my endless periods of absence, either rarely being available, buried in appointments, or simply being mentally 'elsewhere'! The support I have been given has been the lifeblood I needed to see this extended project through to a successful conclusion. I know that Caroline feels the same way from her side, so I can only hope the final verdict is that it was worth all our effort and dedication – Clive Harvey

COMMEMORATION NEWS

It is important that we do not forget that the long-awaited completed CLC monument shown below, an impressive 'huabiao', still remains (to our knowledge), unshipped and stored in a Chinese stone works. This was commissioned and designed to honour the Chinese Labour Corps for installation here in the UK.

Though still awaiting news about this monument from China, two further major projects are currently well underway in this country, for both the St Paul's Cathedral Crypt, and the National Memorial Arboretum, to commemorate the contribution of the CLC to The Allied cause in WWI. The Authors are following the progress of these very closely and expect to announce favourable news as to their funding and planned installation in the near future. For updates, please regularly visit the Authors' respective WebSites:

www.music4art.co.uk www.carolinechu.net

How heartening it might yet be, for those who truly care enough to want to see the record put straight to learn, at long last, that some permanent recognition has at last been secured for passers-by to see.

Characters like Yun, and poor Ming, and even 'their descendants', can then feel their unthinkable sacrifices have at last been recognised.

ABOUT THE AUTHORS

CLIVE HARVEY

For Clive, this novel is the culmination of over a decade of soul-searching meticulous research.

Having stumbled on the unexplained graves of Chinese men in the iconic First World War cemeteries of Northern France, Clive embarked on something of a pilgrimage to get to the truth and to then launch his findings into the public domain. Undeterred by the apparent lack of any significant source material, Clive was eventually able to collate enough data to write his first historic novel.

Yang's War was Clive's inaugural launch pad', translated and published in both China and Japan.

After numerous articles, interviews and appearances on the subject, Clive met Caroline Chu.

Pooling their resources and creative talents, they have now, together, been able to launch *For Whom the Temple Waits* as a ground-breaking historic novel ripe for TV and feature film exposure.

Clive broke away from professional life to dedicate his time and energy to writing, teaching, and music recording. From the days of his flamenco-inspired creations for the BBC, in *Portraits of Picasso* and various record deals thereafter, his unifying platform **music4art** came into being.

Subsequent works, such as *Mouse Trap* and *Little Child*, then placed him in the perfect position to finally engage fully in the creation and joint launch of *For Whom the Temple Waits*.

Clive has a long-standing fascination and empathy for the dispersion of peoples from their homelands. The origins of flamenco, a 1000-year-old refugee migration from India to Andalucia, was the first diaspora to grip Clive as a child. No wonder then, that the supressed story from the First World War of the exodus of some 140000 young Chinese men across the globe was to touch Clive so profoundly.

CAROLINE CHU

Caroline Chu was born in London to a Chinese father and a Canadian mother. She received her education at a bilingual school in Paris and later pursued three years of training at a drama school, where she discovered her passion for directing plays and guiding actors. Caroline holds a Master of Arts in Philosophy, a Master of Arts in Teaching French as a Foreign Language, and a Bachelor of Arts in Chinese. As a certified translator for film and television, she spent several years in post-production, adapting programmes for prominent French networks such as TF1, France 2, France 3, and ARTE.

Compelled by a deep desire to create her own films, she completed a programme in cinema and television production, followed by a filmmaking course at a Paris-based school. In 2011, her debut short film, *The Miraculous Survivor of Saint Sauveur* (*Le Miraculé de Saint-Sauveur*), was selected for the prestigious Palm Springs International Short Film Festival. That same year, it was screened at the American Cinematheque in Hollywood's Egyptian Theatre, and in 2012, it earned an Honourable Mention at the Rochester International Short Film Festival.

This marked a promising beginning for the young director, who has since made her mark in both fiction and documentary filmmaking. In 2018, she relocated to London and obtained a Master's degree in Editing and Post-Production from London South Bank University.

For over a decade, Caroline has explored the history of Chinese workers during the First World War, conducting interviews with descendants and historians while unearthing archival images. Her efforts culminated in two internationally acclaimed documentary films on the subject, which gained recognition on the festival circuit. Caroline is currently completing a new documentary, *In the Frame*, which examines the story of the Chinese workers of the First World War through 'visual archives' that capture raw emotions and societal truths.

This joint project, co-written with author and musician, Clive Harvey, *For Whom the Temple Waits*, weaves together the authentic stories she uncovered during her extensive research in France and England.

Zou Shiquan